PRAISE FOR J.E. KRAFT

I am a little speechless and feeling every human emotion currently. This sequel absolutely didn't disappoint.

— JOJO L.

The Dark Hours was as addictively good as The Survivors.

— BECCA B.

I could do nothing but think about it and try and predict where it would go...which I was incorrect about every time.

— TIFFANY B.

It is well-paced, well written and I really enjoyed it.

— JAE

THE DARK HOURS

THE SURVIVORS SERIES
BOOK 2

J.E. KRAFT

Copyright © 2024 by J.E. Kraft

All rights reserved.

No part of this book may be reproduced in any form or by any electronic or mechanical means, including information storage and retrieval systems, without written permission from the author, except for the use of brief quotations in a book review.

To Liz, for enthusiastically bothering me for a sequel.

CONTENTS

Glossary of Italian	ix
Prologue	1
1. Aftermath	7
2. Concern	10
3. Tangle	15
4. Bitterness	23
5. Existing	31
6. Going	37
7. Strength	43
8. Connection	49
9. Anomaly	56
10. Hiding	63
11. Vulnerable	71
12. Trust	80
13. Wonder	86
14. Witness	92
15. Risk	98
16. Not Alone	106
17. Transmission	114
18. Suffocating	121
19. Concession	126
20. Maternal	131
21. Betrayal	139
22. Belief	147
23. Explanation	154
24. Reasons	163
25. Broken	171
26. Ridiculous	185
27. Choice	193
28. Soothed	200
29. Light-Bearer	207
30. Family	212
31. Community	222
32. Growing	227

33. Bait	232
34. Hijacked	240
35. Direction	246
36. Focus	253
37. Doors	261
38. Impact	269
39. Fire	279
Epilogue	285
Enjoy This Book? Let the World Know!	289
Acknowledgments	291
About the Author	293

GLOSSARY OF ITALIAN

Italian is a creative language with creative swear words. These are roughly translated.

- A fanabla: Go to hell
- Cazzo di merda: Fucking shit
- Coglione: Asshole
- Dio Santo: Oh God
- Figlio di puttana: Son of a bitch
- Madonna Santa: Mother of God
- Ma quanto sei coglione: You're such an asshole
- Merda: Shit
- Porca miseria: Dammit
- Porca troia: Fucking hell
- Testa di cazzo: Dickhead
- Troia: Whore
- Vaffanculo: Go fuck yourself

PROLOGUE
THE INTERIM

The first thing Miriam was aware of was the hot, raw pain in her throat.

The second was that Perry was dead.

She pulled the flannel shirt she'd stolen from his cave—had it been just two nights ago?—tighter around her body, cocooning herself in his earthy smell as she lay numb with disbelief and grief.

It could have been minutes or hours before she finally pulled herself up from the bed to get a drink from the bathroom sink. The eyes that stared back at her in the mirror were red and swollen. Eyes that would never see Perry again.

She gripped the sink as a rasping cry escaped her spent throat. For a moment, her body swayed, but then the sensation passed. Forcing her shuddering breath back into a slow rhythm, she filled the glass and drank.

The water hit her stomach like lava, sloshing around with fiery vengeance until, a minute later, it came back up again.

When the convulsions subsided, she knelt on the cold tile in front of the toilet with her arms wrapped around her stomach and her eyes squeezed shut tightly. This needed to stop. All of this just needed to stop. Everything had betrayed her. Perry had by going that night. The

Therians had by not keeping him safe. Her body betrayed her by living when there was nothing left to live for, and then betrayed her again by keeping this thing alive that was growing inside her.

Her stomach clenched again as if to confirm its commitment to rebellion. She gagged and heaved, tears falling into the toilet water below.

Please God, make it stop.

———

JONATHAN DIDN'T REMEMBER the drive to his house.

He'd found the keys to the Nidhi company BMW on a hook by the door of Adrian's suite. The car had been reluctant to start, but once it turned over, Jonathan's mind seemed to stall. Somehow, he made it even though all he could see was his wife's empty eyes staring out from the surveillance footage. He stopped the car outside the home of a thousand happy memories.

The night was young, but the street was quiet. Warm lights shone from the windows of nearby houses. Jonathan's little yellow two-story sat dark. The front door was shut, but the moment he got out of the car he could smell the blood.

Spent blood.

Moving with the adept stealth of the immortal, he slipped silently past the gate to the fenced back yard. It was a riot of toddlerhood. All manner of balls were strewn about. A sandbox seemed to be eating four or five construction trucks. There was a tricycle next to a plastic fort. A little hand-painted sign declared it to be "Fort Zephyr".

The name of his son brought up the image of a bubbling blond mess of love, and it broke whatever strange detachment he'd been under. Jonathan ran—past the patio area, through the broken back door, and into the house.

He ran room to room, looking for hope in the blood and chaos, calling for his baby. The lower floors offered nothing. A clean-up crew hadn't been dispatched, maybe because the vampires couldn't. Maybe the Therians had saved his son.

The Dark Hours 3

Zeph's room was untouched. Small chairs sat next to a miniature table set with fake food and picture books. Blocks, somehow perpetually escaping their container, dotted the floor along with a menagerie of plastic animals. Jonathan took a deep breath. Under the overwhelming scent of blood (both immortal and human) was the indescribable and sweet smell of his boy.

But the scent wasn't fresh. He knew it wouldn't be. Jonathan refused to think about what that might mean, despite the pain searing his heart.

One place left.

The bedroom door had burst apart where the handle met the jamb. Their dresser was overturned behind it, large planks of wood splintered. It must have been braced against the door. Shattered on the hardwoods were the little figurines Tam had made him, one for each of their seven anniversaries, including the one he was gone for.

Jonathan stood there a moment as the silence told him things he didn't know how to believe.

Then he threaded past it all to the master bath.

She was alone.

Vacant blue eyes stared off into nothingness. Light hair haloed out then turned into a deep, damp umber where it met her blood. It pooled around her, soaking into her faded nightshirt—an oversized t-shirt she'd stolen from him shortly after they were married.

The floor was both slick and sticky, but he managed to sit down next to his wife, her blood soaking into his clothes. He touched her cold skin, gently tracing the laugh lines around her eyes and the bow of her thinnish lips. His fingers brushed down to the gash in her throat and then began to tremble. The burning in his heart was forcing its way up. Pulling her body to him, he clung to her as the pain screamed out.

"Where's my son," Jonathan growled into the intercom at the warehouse gate.

There was no answer for a moment. Then an unfamiliar voice

buzzed back, "Scans indicate your car has been equipped with tracking technology—"

He didn't wait to hear anything else but left the car where it was and stalked around the building until he came to a perimeter door. Rust colored indentations formed where his fists hit the metal, but if it hurt, he didn't feel it. He might never feel anything other than rage again.

Quick footsteps approached on the other side, and his rage centered on the being keeping him from the one thing that still mattered.

"Open the door and tell me where my son is!"

"Jonathan." The muffled voice belonged to Meg. "That team never returned."

The words made no sense. He slammed a fist into the door again.

"Where's my son?"

"We don't know."

"You don't know?" He slammed his body against the door. "You don't know? You bitch!" The rage left suddenly, doused by a wave of despair. His clothes, stiff with his wife's blood, managed to leave smears on the door as he slid to the ground. "I trusted you! I trusted you, and they're gone."

"Perry's gone too." Her voice was small, tired.

He found himself nodding. In an odd way, that made sense.

"Adrian?"

"Alive."

"The bastard," Jonathan said.

He heard a soft breath that, in another life, might have become a chuckle.

"Yes. He is." She paused. "Dawn's coming. Are you safe? Can we bring you inside?"

Jonathan looked down at himself. The sun could burn it all away, all the blood and pain and memory.

"Do you think he's still alive?"

A knife of wind gusted through his stiff clothes while Meg considered her words. He hadn't realized how cold it was.

The Dark Hours

"I think it's possible."

A sob racked him then. Without waiting for his reply, he heard a bolt make a hesitant journey back into the door. He moved, and the door was forced open against the damage he'd done to it. Meg stood over him, two Therians flanking her on either side, but he was too tired to feel threatened. Motioning to the one on her right, she said, "Go. Take care of the vehicle." With a wave of her hand, she dismissed the other.

"All right. Let's get you inside." Despite the worn-out tone in her voice, her arms were strong as she pulled him to his feet.

1

AFTERMATH

Clare's Notes:

I will never have a normal life. Not that I've had one to this point, but I had hope. I miss hope. Hope was nice.

Jonathan's eyes blurred, and he blinked them back into focus as he scoured the screen for any hint about his son. Kitsune, the therian in charge of IT, and David, Clare's human friend, glanced over at him. He straightened in his chair in the control room, but they didn't say anything. They were smart enough to know that, after days of monosyllabic replies, he didn't want to talk. Just as well. He needed to focus.

The vampires made and ruled the dark web. It wasn't safe, it could draw their attention, and he didn't care. The Nidhi coven was down, and who knew how long it would be before they could rebuild enough to find his prowling. He was chancing it with the other covens, but hopefully they were distracted by Nidhi's downfall and not paying attention to someone asking about a missing child on local forums.

When that search turned up nothing, he weeded through police and social services reports looking for...hope.

There was none.

A fiery warmth made him jolt. Clare's hand was on his shoulder. She removed it with a guilty look.

"I'm sorry." She looked from her hand to him. "I forgot."

Since she couldn't see the glow of painful light that clung to her like a living mist, she could forget. It wasn't that which was unbearable though. The compassion in her eyes threatened to undo the tentative hold he had on his grief. Pushing the pain down, he turned back to his screen and cleared his throat.

"It's fine."

He could feel Sune watching. Meg had ordered that "due to his emotional state," he would only be allowed among others during the day. In order to, in her words, "lessen any chance of accidents." That was fair, but the Therians were still on guard around him. Like he could do anything. Despite being provided cloned blood, he was weak from Lachlan taking his life-source back. They could kill him as easily as...as if he were human.

"Jonathan?" Clare was talking to him.

"Hmm?"

"I was saying that I might be able to help."

He tried to smile. She was being kind. But it was a kindness wasted.

Clare waited for him to say something, but when the silence began to stretch out, she just started talking.

"Have you met Aberdeen? Meg assigned her to help me get situated here. Anyway, we were going over what happened the other night, she said I was exceptional at *stretching*. I might be able to teach you, and—"

"No." Sune's voice was quiet but commanding.

However, Jonathan's mind had already made the leap. For the first time in days, hope stirred in his chest.

"Jonathan cannot do that here," Kitsune continued. "Or with you."

Clare opened her mouth, but Sune shook his head and continued. "Here, he risks inciting instincts he's too young to control. With you, he risks your Watcher."

"The Watcher helped me bring him back! They don't just kill vampires for the fun of it. I know I could—"

"No. Jonathan's life is not to be gambled with, and neither is yours."

There was a barb in his words. David made a sniff of disapproval from the other side of Clare. He may have formed an easy rapport with Sune, but he was still fiercely loyal to Clare. There was no telling how much her going to save David from Nidhi had affected Siri's summoning Adrian, affected the whole night, but her friend glared at the Therian to challenge any further comment on the subject.

The silence that descended was tense. While David held Sune's gaze, Jonathan nodded at Clare. He tried to communicate with his eyes what he couldn't with his words, and then said, "It's fine. Thank you...for thinking of it."

2

CONCERN

Clare's Notes:

Stretching can be taught and learned among immortals. Also, apparently some mortals since I can do it. Ask David to try???

Clare tapped her pen on the edge of her notebook while she sat in a vacant seat in the corner of the control room. With a name like "Control Room," why would she want to be anywhere else? Not that it really offered control, but Kitsune was usually patient with her questions, and it was the place she was most likely to get news or updates. Although she was officially banned from online activities— Meg went on a five-minute rant about the kind of problems she could cause with a single wrong click—Sune was usually kind enough to procure a newspaper for her.

News of the explosions at Nidhi Manor was strangely lacking, even without the local vampire presence to squash it. A small blurb in the regional section about a fire in a rural business outside of West End was all that surfaced. Meg took that as an ominous sign and

The Dark Hours

made sure the Therians were prepared for a "vampire free-for-all" in the newly available territory.

Clare twisted the moonstone on her finger. It had been a week since the battle, and Adrian hadn't returned. But he hadn't spontaneously combusted upon leaving either. Sune wasn't as shocked as she was. Apparently, he and the others could smell what was too raw to talk about yet. In as few words as humanly (or otherwise) possible, he let her know Adrian would be fine for a month or so. At least until Perry's blood was out of his system, and the spectacular effects of said blood had worn off.

Meg, red-eyed and worn-looking, was everywhere, ordering labs done on Clare, asking about damage and field reports, keeping everyone busy despite the somber mood. The day after the battle was given to grief and burial, but after that, Therian losses meant that everyone was needed somewhere.

It also meant that David would have to wait to be relocated as part of the Therian survivor program. There was no time or resources to be spared in deciding what to do with a survivor who also had some knowledge of their local Therian base. It was a possible vulnerability they could ill afford.

Not that the delay wasn't also suspiciously convenient.

David had shown quite an aptitude for some of the more incomprehensible internet programs Sune was running. That was all the excuse Meg needed to put him to work. At the moment, he was perched in a chair next to Jonathan, buried deep in code.

Clare glanced over. Jonathan had said little since the night he arrived. Meg ordered a shot of quarterly birth control for Clare the next morning, and that was how she knew he'd be staying at least a little while. Wouldn't do to have random bleeding around a vampire, but leave it to Meg not to trust her to take a pill every day.

Even as Jonathan slowly regained some of his physical strength, a quiet desperation seemed to pour from him. Every day at sunset, he went back to his room. Each morning when he emerged, the blanket of hopelessness was heavier than the day before.

As she watched, he rubbed at his face and clicked various

programs closed at his workstation. Blowing out a breath, Jonathan rose to leave, but as he did, he glanced at her. She gave him a small nod in response.

She couldn't go right away. That would be painfully obvious. Instead, she waited until David got up for dinner and followed.

Dinner was taken in a downstairs cafeteria on the opposite side of the labs and was, not surprisingly, very meat heavy. The Therians liked meat on the raw side, and plenty of it, but they also seemed to enjoy a wide range of food along with it. Despite the cafeteria serving food at all times of the day, Therians seemed to eat at odd intervals. She had a hundred theories why, like: consumption depended on the type of animal they changed to, or it was more about energy transfer for an immortal than metabolism, or maybe they just liked being mysterious and frustrating. Whatever the reason for their fickle eating habits, Clare hadn't been able to familiarize herself with all the faces there.

The narrow room was currently packed with several dozen people, and a savory smell, along with a low din of voices, provided a constant backdrop. There was a wide range of body shapes and sizes, and without being *too* nosy, she'd been able to ascertain that there was some correlation between that and their Therian animal forms. It wasn't an exact science. Meg's human form was small, and she was definitely a wolf, but it did seem that the largest were mostly bears.

Maybe she and David should try and guess who was what. It would be entertaining, but they'd have to do it out of earshot. And she had no idea how far that was. That probably varied creature to creature, too.

From what she'd been able to gather, most Therians lived like they were your average person: marrying, having jobs, and blending into society at large. Those that lived or worked at the warehouse were part of a group actively working toward Therian causes, and that required a ridiculous amount of secrecy and security. Clare could only begin to guess at some of the projects that must be going on, partly because she and David were given a wide berth.

A few were friendly. Others seemed to barely conceal their

hostility and mistrust. Not that she could blame them. Perry wasn't the only one they'd lost, and she clearly was going to keep breaking their rules.

Case in point, Meg had said to leave the vampire alone during the dark hours, but Clare was learning she had a serious defect when it came to following life-persevering rules. She sighed.

David looked up from a plate of rare steak and potatoes.

"You're going to teach him anyway, aren't you?"

"Am I that transparent?"

He shrugged. "You just can't not do a thing, and I doubt taking notes in that notebook is satisfying your ceaseless need for achievement."

A little harsh, but he was right. She was feeling more trapped every day and wanted to be able to *do* something. That's why she'd stayed—to help.

"What about you?"

"What about me?"

"Are you doing okay?" she asked.

"You don't need to worry about me. I'm a big boy, Clare, and I don't need to become one of your projects."

She felt her mouth open, and it seemed like the din of voices hushed around them. David squeezed his eyes shut for a moment.

"That's not what I meant. Everything... It's just a lot, and I don't want to talk about it."

"Right. I understand." It was a lot, but his words still stung. Clare pushed a piece of roasted chicken into a landslide of peas. "I'm going to take Miriam a plate."

"Good luck with that."

She deposited her tray of half-eaten dinner in the trash and plucked the most mellow foods she could find from the food line: a little chicken, some rolls, a bit of mac and cheese. Then she went through a door at the back.

There were rows of rooms for the Therians down a long corridor which ended in another door leading to the labs. Apparently humans, vampires, and transients got the top floor rooms. The feel was entirely different down here, more like a campus dorm. The doors were old hardwood, unlike the industrial metal one to her room that could bolt her in if she pissed Meg off enough. Some were left open, others were shut with notes, and still others were decorated with a variety of homey personalities. The room that had been Perry's, room 9, had a burn mark on the wall by the handle and a yellow stain on the white speckled tile in front of the door. Not intentional decoration, but it felt appropriate to its former occupant nonetheless.

It was quiet beyond the door tonight. No wailing, sniffing, or restless movement. Clare didn't know if that was a good sign or not, but she did know that Miriam wasn't responding to anyone that tried to talk to her.

She knocked. "Hey, lady. It's Clare." Silence. "I brought you dinner."

The sounds of Miriam's misery the days before had twisted her gut, but somehow, the silence was worse. She shifted at the door a moment.

"It's okay to need time and space, but can you let me know you're still alive?"

Footsteps approached, and a small warmth lit in Clare's chest. Miriam was okay, at least physically. But the door didn't open.

"Thank you." Miriam's voice sounded hoarse. "Just leave it at the door, please."

3

TANGLE

Clare's Notes:

Immortals on both sides fear the Watchers. Descriptions of Watcher behavior make it seem like they're farming humans for later consumption. If they pose no threat to living humans, what are they feeding on? Our souls? Do they eat our souls when we die?

There was a tentative knock. Jonathan set down the binder on vampires that Meg had given him—a much better education than his maker had bestowed—and tried not to seem too anxious when he opened the door. Since Clare had mentioned *stretching*, he'd thought of little else. He'd skipped to that part of the binder, but it offered little in the way of instruction, instead talking about its operation being similar in both Therians and vampires.

Clare slipped quietly into the room, the appealing aroma of her A positive blood lingering in the air while Jonathan checked that the hall was empty. The Therians didn't make idle threats, especially not with vampires. They might be forgiving of her, but he had no doubt that they would kick him out.

Or worse.

"Thank you." His whispered words came out in a rush as soon as he shut the door. "Thank you. I've been losing my mind. I don't know where he is, if he's okay. I don't know how to find him, and he's all I have left."

Clare bit her lip. The light that clung to her seemed to highlight every crease and furrow of worry on her face. "Are you going to be okay if it doesn't work? Because it might not."

"I know, but at least it's a shot at something." He didn't say he would be okay. He wouldn't. "So, how do we do this?"

She shook her head, causing the light around her to wreath her like a halo for a moment. "Honestly, I don't know. I can tell you what I did, and what it feels like, but I'm not a vampire. It might be totally different for you." Jonathan nodded, and she continued. "But, to start, let's sit."

There were limited options.

The room was perhaps a clone of any standard dorm room, minus windows and tacky wallpaper. From the entry door, there was an indented closet area, its bar hanging empty, and the door to the washroom. In the middle of the room was a bed with a simple, navy bedspread. A desk and chair sat in the right corner, opposite of the entry door. The back corner contained a pressboard chest of drawers, whose only distinction was a lamp with a rust red shade. He preferred this to the harsh overhead light. Conspicuously missing were any electronics.

Jonathan took the bed and motioned for her to sit in the arm chair at the desk. The corner brightened as she moved to it. Clare lowered herself gracefully but fidgeted once in the chair. She was nervous. He could tell without smelling the slight boost of adrenaline in the air, but was she nervous about being shut in with him or about what they were going to try to do? Taking a deep breath, she looked at him, her dark brown eyes determined.

"I really don't know much about what I can or can't do. The

Therians are curious but haven't had time to work with me on it. What I do know is, I can probably find out if your son—"

"Zeph."

"If Zeph is alive."

Jonathan covered his face with his hands. It was too much, too much hope for the moment. He drew in a breath, the old familiar habit steadying him.

"But," she started, and he tensed in anticipation of what she would say next, "if you want to go find him, it's better if I can teach you how to do it yourself. That way, you don't need me to do...whatever it is you plan on doing."

"And if you can't teach me? If I can't learn?"

"I can still try to find out if he's all right."

Jonathan swallowed back the tornado of his eagerness and despair. Not now. He needed to be calm. "I'm ready then."

"I think you need to change first. I know it made it easier for Perry at any rate."

It made everything harder.

He'd fed before she came. Not that he would ever hurt her, but the...hunger would be distracting. Changing itself wasn't hard though. All Jonathan needed to do was think of the couple of blood bags he'd drained earlier, and his body did the rest.

At least it was quick. Sensations flooded over him. His throat dried. The air of the room was filled with the rusty waft of Clare's blood and the details of her dinner from her gentle intake and release of breath. The threatening musk of Therian was ever present. There were pricks of pain in his jaws as his canines pushed down, and when he opened his eyes, he had to squint momentarily at the harsh light in Clare's corner.

His newly sensitive ears could hear the involuntary uptick in her heartbeat as he looked at her, but she didn't give away the fear in her voice.

"Okay, good." She swallowed. "This is going to sound out there, I know, but I really don't know any other words to explain it. First, what I do is feel the essence of myself apart from my body. They call your body your anchor. You have to be aware of your anchor at all times. If your essence gets separated from your anchor," her last couple words became softer, and she looked down, "you die."

"It's all right, Clare." His voice was as gentle as he could make it with the change, but it still had a rough quality to it. "I know what we're doing is dangerous, and I already know what it feels like to be severed. And you already brought me back from that once."

Jonathan failed to mention the pain he'd experienced when Clare had done that the night of the battle. There'd been no distinction between Clare's deep burning grip and the fiery pain of her Watcher as they ripped him back from the abyss of Lachlan's need. It was like being torn apart by molten metal, but Clare didn't need to know that.

She met his gaze, a faint smile gracing her lips, and nodded. Her heart began to slow.

"Right. Well then, once you can feel the distinction of yourself from your anchor, you *stretch* that essence outside the boundaries of your body. It's hard to explain how things are there..."

She trailed off for a moment. His experience in that place had been confusing flashes of hunger and ripping pain. Sensations and impressions.

Clare continued, "But still, it shouldn't be difficult to find your son. When you hold him in your thoughts, I think you'll be able to find the strand that connects the two of you. Then, you just follow that strand."

It sounded easy enough. Jonathan took a deep breath, preparing to start, but Clare interrupted him.

"Let me go first. I need to make sure my Watcher knows to expect you."

Oh. Good idea. With how little anyone knew of the things, Jonathan wasn't about to presume that they were on friendly terms since their last meeting.

He watched as Clare closed her eyes and relaxed her body. Her fingers splayed then twitched like she was feeling for something. Then, he could feel her near. It wasn't inside himself, like when Lachlan would

The Dark Hours 19

do it. It was like the feeling of walking past a dark alley and *knowing* something was there even if you couldn't see it. His body tensed with the memory of her touch in that place, but she merely waited.

Her presence made it easy. He naturally wanted to move away, but since he wasn't physically close, the only way to do it was to *stretch* away from the radiating heat of her soul. His body began to feel distant, and then its perceptions disappeared. He was an entity of life and energy in a place like none other he knew. Clare was right there next to him. Emotions, sensations, and thoughts moved in and out of the tangle of her being like dancing flicks of fire.

"That's it." Her words were not audible but carried their friendly intent as she thought them into him. "Can you see me?"

"If you can call this seeing. It's more like the idea of seeing, like something Wassily Kandinsky would paint." It brought Kandinsky's *Composition 10* to mind, with its lines of colors and bright almost shapes.

"Sounds about right," she said, and a ribbon of humor flowed through her. Very *Composition 10* indeed. She probably had no idea what he was talking about.

"This is dizzying. How do you find anything here?" He tried to... move? And was momentarily aware of other life—

"Not that way!" Clare's presence was herding him back. "Not yet anyway. I don't know how easily the Therians will perceive you if you move through space. That can be hard to navigate by anyway. I find it easiest through connection."

As she said it, Clare somehow pulled on their connection, and it was a real thing that traversed them. It was a solid strand imprinted with their cautious, companionable interactions. When he caught at the thread, he could feel a medley of Clare, like what he "saw" of her here, but as impressions and understandings.

He could go deeper, he knew intuitively, past the connection. The predator in him knew it could use this to reach in and call to the life, and thus the blood, of a living being.

And there was fire.

Jonathan released the thread, but blazing eyes and a fiery maw were all he could comprehend around him.

"No!" Clare was there between them, but her heat was threatening too, and Jonathan was fleeing back into himself.

He came into his body with a jerk.

"I'm sorry!" She was on her feet but didn't come near. "I don't know what happened. Are you okay?"

He put up a hand to let her know he was okay, or to ward her from coming closer, or both. He shivered, but the change remained. The pounding of her heart assaulted his ears along with the slightly acrid prick of her adrenaline.

"It's fine," he said at last. "It was my fault. I wouldn't..." He looked at her and hoped for understanding. "I don't think I could do anything to you there, but I felt it. Felt the ability," words began to stream from him now, "felt the power that I have—that my kind has. I wouldn't use it against you, and you're burning anyways. I just felt it. As soon as I was aware of it, the Watcher was there." His words dried up on the memory of the glowing burn of those eyes, but then he blinked, and Clare was looking at him.

"It wasn't your fault," she said, a little breathless still. "They told us. I mean, we really don't know what we're dealing with. I'm sorry. I didn't mean to put you in any danger. I was just trying to help—"

"Clare," he cut in, desperate to keep her from quitting. "I'm okay. It's okay. Can we try again?"

"What? No. I don't think it's safe."

"I know what I did wrong, and your Watcher was just," he could still feel those eyes, "being protective of you. Please. Just once more. I need to try again."

She shut her eyes, and he wondered if she was seeing flames. Blowing out a breath, she said, "One more time. More carefully."

Jonathan closed his eyes and let himself feel her presence near him, let it send him pushing away and past his body. The movement of Clare's life was tighter now, and he could recognize anxiety in its tension. What would she see in his?

"When you're ready," she said. "That thread is what you'll want to

The Dark Hours 21

use. To find the one that goes from you to Zeph, try thinking of the feel of him."

The feel of Zephyr? He really was like the wind, full of raging spring storms and sleepy summer kisses. The boy was mischievous and sweet. He felt like joy personified.

And the connection was there.

It was so strong, he wondered how it didn't sweep him away as soon as he got here. Jonathan didn't even have to grab onto it. His heart desired his baby so strongly, he couldn't help but be carried to its source. The bright tangle of life was smaller than Clare's, containing fewer experiences, but it was no less vibrant, even in sleep. And he was asleep, though how Jonathan knew, he couldn't say.

He wrapped his son up in himself and held him. Pain and relief wracked his soul, and for a minute, he was overwhelmed.

"Daddy's so, so sorry, buddy."

There was a spark of pinkish light deep in the sleeping bundle as it absorbed his words.

"And I love you to the moon and back. I love you more than..." He lost all words in the immensity of the emotion, but they weren't needed. He could feel his love, perfectly expressed, flowing into his boy. "I'm coming for you, okay? Daddy's going to find you."

A twinge of fatigue rippled through him, and he felt his grip slipping. Did he have to let go soon?

"I'm coming for you," he said before he lost his hold on his son.

"Clare," he called out toward her being. And she was there, as though she'd been there the entire time. "Help me. I can't hold the stretch. I found him, but I don't know how to get to him."

"It's okay. Come back for now. You found him. He's alive."

The moment he quit struggling, he was slung back into his body with a motion-sick feeling, but he paid it little attention. He was on his feet and across the room by the time Clare opened her eyes. She flinched to find him over her, but Jonathan sank to his knees, resisting the desire to take her fevered hands in his.

"How do I find him?"

She shook her head. "After I found David in that reality, I could kind of feel the connection in this one. All I had to do was reach for it, and the connection was almost like a compass needle drawing me toward him." She placed her hand over his stilled heart, heat spreading out from her touch. "Can you feel him?"

He tried, but Clare's halo was too loud to feel past, especially with the heat flowing out from her touch.

"You're too close."

She pulled her hand back, and a welcome coolness replaced where it had been. He could still feel her though. His senses bucked against whatever she was just like they did against the Therian smell in the building. But even with all that, when he reached out, he could feel the connection with Zeph. It tugged at the deepest part of his soul.

He could find his boy.

He was at the door when Clare's voice stopped him.

"What should I tell them?"

He looked back. Her veins glowed within her harsh light, but her soft eyes searched his. Strange that this should be the one person left that hadn't betrayed his trust.

"If I make it off the property without being stopped, it's because they let me. And they'll know why I'm going."

"What if they don't let you back?"

Stranger still that her concern should hurt.

"They can use all the help they can get. I'm sure it wouldn't be a problem."

It was a lie, and as easy as it came out, it was hard to do. Staying here had come with terms, and Meg would protect her people to an extent that Clare didn't understand. If he left without a word and tried to come back uninvited, Meg would have little choice but to assume he was working with the vampires. His life could easily be forfeited.

To her credit, Clare wasn't easily pacified. "If you get in trouble, tug on our connection."

And endanger her? Not a chance.

"I will."

4

BITTERNESS

Clare's Notes:

The Handbook was right. You can't trust Therians either.

Miriam paced in her room, trying to overcome the smell of dinner enough to force at least some of it down. It wasn't working.

Giving up, she shoved the plate in the mini-fridge and turned back to lay down on the bed again. Raised voices from the cafeteria stopped her. The walls weren't terribly thick, but this was more than the usual amount of Therian after dinner socializing.

Stepping into the hall, she felt exposed. She hadn't been out of their room—his room—in days. A thin red-head was hurrying down the hall, and some vague memory told Miriam that she was kind.

"Hey," Miriam said, reaching out as the woman neared. "What's going on?"

She blinked several times as if Miriam had magically appeared and asked a complex math problem. After a moment, she simply said, "Adrian's back," and continued down the hall.

Miriam's stomach squeezed. Adrian was back. He was the last person she wanted to see, and yet...

Her feet were carrying her through the cafeteria, up the stairs, and to the control room.

There was a crowd of Therians, and though she couldn't see him, his voice carried above the listeners.

"...daytime nests. There are several key vampires still alive." He didn't mention any names, but a low growling from the throng said they could guess who he was implying. "The main danger now is encroaching covens. I encountered more than one scout from the Washington Family Group. They're probably the ones keeping the media dark on the event, but the scouts had no valuable information to tell."

Which meant he'd probably done some seriously nasty shit to them to come to that conclusion.

"The last two nights there's been more activity than I can track. As big as Richmond is, there aren't any areas I would let your families visit at night right now. There's no way to tell where a scout or group will surface. Fulton Hill and the South bank of the river are especially showing signs of hunting." He paused before continuing. "I highly recommend moving operations to a more stable region."

A murmur went through the Therians, and they shifted until Miriam caught a glimpse of Adrian and Meg at their center. He was there in a dark overcoat with wavy black hair tousled over stolen yellow eyes.

And she had never wished anyone dead more.

No, not dead. She wished he'd never been born, that Perry had never known him, never gone to save him, never died. She wished that Adrian had died a hundred thousand different deaths to stop the one that Perry prevented.

Miriam uncurled the fingers digging into the palms of her hands, set her jaw, and moved closer.

Adrian's eyes flicked to hers, and a familiar half smile graced his face.

"How dare you." The words came out before she realized she was speaking. "How dare you come in here with his smile and his eyes."

The yellow in Adrian's eyes receded to a deep brown, but her feet were still taking her closer. The blur of other faces parted as she came in.

"How dare all of you just welcome him back in as if he isn't the cause of all this." She glanced around, her eyes landing on Meg's drawn face. "As if he isn't the reason that Perry's gone!"

Adrian flinched at that, but the pain in his eyes didn't seem to be nearly enough.

"How dare you be alive when he's dead!"

No one followed her back down the stairs to her room. She slammed the door, ran to the bathroom, and let the bitterness come up.

JONATHAN HAD OPENED his door just as Adrian managed to reappear. Adrian would choose that time to come back. The other vampire was speaking with Meg and several Therians in the hall when Meg locked eyes with Jonathan.

It was night, but he was adjusting to Therian presence, and his eyes told her as much. She waved him along with the group, saying that he might as well come too, that this would concern him. But the briefing had nothing to do with his family or where his son might be. Deval and Siri remained unaccounted for. Beyond that, Richmond was now the center of a vampiric turf war.

And he couldn't care less. Only one thing mattered. He'd tried to slip out after Miriam's interruption, but a hand grabbed him as he turned to go. For a blink, everything became bright, and the reek of Therian filled his mind with murder. Closing his eyes, he thought of the sunlight catching in Tam's hair, and the tension drained into sadness.

He opened his eyes on Sune, whose hand was still on Jonathan's arm. There was a knowing look on the Therian's face, but when he spoke, he simply said, "I'll need your help tonight."

"Meg, um, said I should stay in my room at night."

"You're managing." He was. "And it'll be easier for you to work at night."

He wasn't wrong. The presence of the sun was like a constant weight during the light hours, but there had to be some excuse, some way out of this.

"I, uh…"

"I prefer to work at night as well." For Sune, this was shockingly chatty. "And based on Adrian's report, it will be needed."

Jonathan glanced over at Adrian. He and Meg were talking in earnest, low tones as the crowd thinned out of the room.

So was that it? Was he a prisoner here now? Or did he go anyway? What if a surviving nest had Zeph? Would Adrian go get him? How could he trust that? Adrian might lose his child as easily as the Therians did.

While he was thinking, Sune was leading him to the computer banks, and Jonathan found himself staring at police scanner transcripts.

"I've told Meg we need more blood for you," Sune said with that penetrating stare. "You're still weak, and it will take a lot of life to restore you."

"I don't care."

"Carelessness can lead to more loss of life than just yours."

They could have been talking about the battle or about the encroaching covens, but there was only one life Jonathan cared about, and Sune knew it.

Jonathan ran his hands over his face.

The Therian was right. He needed more blood, more strength. Maybe only a couple days more, then he would leave. In the meantime, perhaps Adrian could help him somehow.

Jonathan swiveled around. Clare's human aroma announced her presence. She probably gave him time to get out before leaving his room, but then the group in the hall would have drawn her like a moth to flame.

Jonathan craned his head around the few straggling Therians enough to see her limned form at the edge of the doorway. What could possibly motivate her to stay in this hell hole? He had a child to think about, but Clare? Professional ambition seemed a flimsy reason to live in a den of immortals, despite her constant note-taking. It could be personal safety, given the light she put off, or even her friendship with David. Wisps of blonde obscured her eyes, but she chewed on her bottom lip as she watched Adrian and Meg talk.

Jonathan turned away. It was better not to know. Whatever the reason, Clare was getting herself deep into something that could easily get her killed, and he didn't need any more reasons to grieve.

"Ms. Zetler, are you going to lurk over there all evening or come in and badger us with your impertinent curiosity?" Meg said.

"I didn't want to be rude."

"At least it's inadvertent on your part." Meg sighed. "Humans. You always complicate things."

Clare ignored the comment and addressed Adrian. "So, you're not dead yet." There was a smile in her voice, and despite himself, Jonathan gravitated over to the conversation.

"Neither are you," Adrian said. "Have you thrown yourself at the cause or are you just hanging around waiting for the opportune time to steal my Harley again?"

She flushed crimson and spun a ring around her finger. "I'm sorry about that. If it makes it any better, I didn't know it was yours at the time." The raise of his eyebrow indicated it did not make it better, so Clare continued. "There's not been much for me to do yet. But you... What have you been doing? You've been completely off the radar."

"It's safer that way, even in good times. Right now, the situation is too fucked up to risk much contact," he said. "But, among other things, I've been hunting for Siri. She knows I'm involved with the Therians. She may have made the connection with Jonathan as well."

Jonathan closed his eyes. Siri was better than Lachlan only in that she wasn't systematically delighted by pain, but her ambition was as relentless as her father's. If she had his son, Zeph would live only as long as he was useful. Taking a deep breath, Jonathan tried to distance himself from the consuming void of his pain.

"Couldn't you just *stretch* to find her?" Clare asked.

"Aren't you the little expert now?"

Clare pursed her lips at the insult, but Adrian pushed back his hair from his face and continued.

"Our binding was severed, and I'm not going to reestablish it by *stretching* to that *troia*." He paused, his voice a little softer as he said, "Everything is different now." But then, just as some semblance of human emotion could possibly be attributed to him, Adrian's face hardened. "And I don't have time to waste expounding on it with you. I've risked enough by coming in to try and convince the world's most stubborn old woman to move her operations before the area is so overrun that the place is found by the stench alone."

Clare's jaw jutted, but she said nothing.

"The caves are not a viable option, Adrian," Meg said. "I don't care how big they are. They're too far away for us to be effective."

"Does that even matter now?" Adrian said, his voice raising. "What more do we have to lose?"

The Therians that remained shifted uneasily. Where they stood on the issue was impossible to guess.

"We?" Meg's voice cracked, and she didn't go on.

"Don't you even fucking pretend this isn't my loss too."

There was a ripple in the air, fierce strength on the thinnest chain, as Meg's eyes went yellow. The old human form felt like a paper mask hiding a beast, and before he could even process it, Jonathan's body reacted to the threat. The smell and feel of Therian was so much worse as the change ran through him. Despite her short stature, there was no longer anything diminutive about Meg. She filled the room with a threatening power. The light around Clare had flared bright like a warning, even as she took a step back towards the door. Desperately, he clung to the topside of the world and not the prowling monsters underneath.

The Dark Hours   29

"I have given everything. Everything! I have nothing more to lose," Meg said.

"I have kin in the city." Sune's soft voice was startling. He tilted his head as he looked at Meg. "And you have a great-grandchild on the way. There are still reasons to live."

All the building tension in the room withdrew back into Meg as she drew in a halting breath and collapsed onto a computer chair. Adrian was at her side. She nodded, choked on a word, and then nodded again. She was an old woman once more, lost and grieving, and Jonathan knew that crushing despair.

The room was silent. No one moved until a long minute later when Meg shooed Adrian away.

"I'm fine. You don't need to hover."

Adrian backed up, and she closed her eyes for a moment.

"Perhaps we'll send any unnecessary personnel to set up laboratories and dorms at the caves as a temporary location for the vulnerable, but this is not the time to leave Richmond undefended. The incoming covens are not well protected, and we're positioned here to monitor for any strange activity. This town is ours by day, and we still have some unfinished business here."

Her eyes locked onto Jonathan, their sudden intensity causing his lip to twitch above his fangs. "Isn't that right, Mr. Howards?"

Adrian seemed to truly notice him for the first time. "What's happened?"

A thousand things fought to come out, like Tam was dead and his son was missing, thanks so much asshole for your help. But it wasn't Adrian's fault anymore than it was the Therians', or his. Or was it? Was there any reason in all of it?

"Calla's team didn't come back," Meg said when Jonathan didn't say anything. "We don't know what happened, but it appears his child may still be alive."

"The wife?"

Jonathan could feel his lip curl. That's what she boiled down to for Adrian. "The wife." But Meg just shook her head.

"The official police report states homicide with possible kidnapping."

"Any leads?"

"They have none. Jonathan is their chief suspect," Meg said.

Pounding filled his ears. It was hard to see in the light.

"What?" His own voice was harsh. "Why would they think that? How could you keep this from me? You have me doing what? Looking for leads elsewhere when you know they're searching for me?"

"I didn't think it would help, and you're safe as long as you're here with us." Meg stood, her presence firm. "And what did you expect? Your fingerprints were all over the house and your wife. The Solifugae didn't have to do anything to hide their involvement. You gave them an all too convenient out, as well as putting yourself on their radar for being involved with Nidhi's downfall. You'll have to forgive me for allowing you a moment to grieve before letting you know that all of Richmond is searching for you thanks to your own carelessness."

If all his trembling rage and grief was a person, it roared forward and then was suddenly gone, locked far away. Numbness swept over him like deep waters, and he just nodded.

Meg, steeled for a fight, seemed thrown off balance by his acquiescence.

"Do not quit. This isn't quitting," she said to him. "You just have to learn to fight a different way."

Buried fathoms deep underwater, the words reached him, but they had no meaning.

5

EXISTING

Clare's Notes:

Immortals eat on an infrequent basis. The caloric needs of immortals seem to depend in part on healing/energy usage, which makes sense. The days immediately post battle, the cafeteria was full all the time. Getting a cup of coffee was like running a furry and fanged gauntlet.

Miriam woke with a combination of dry mouth and nausea. She was filled with thirst and the certainty that anything she drank would quickly come back up. But somehow, it was fitting. There should be no joy or comfort when Perry was gone. Rolling up from bed, she wiped the crust from her eyes. Her clothes were the rumpled things she'd been in since...well, at least since yesterday. It would be today too.

Incessant thirst nagged at the heaviness grief made of her body and mind. She sighed and tried to think of something that didn't make her stomach roil when she pictured it. Anything liquid was out. Perhaps a popsicle?

Standing up seemed to take so much effort, but once she was moving, her body managed to remember how to function. Out in the hall, Miriam could smell breakfast. That was unfortunate, but at least the mess hall was mostly empty. Only one person made eye contact with her, and they left soon after. There was a bleachy smell of freshly wiped tables, but her stomach didn't appreciate that either. It seemed as if the smell of everything had tripled. Probably what it was like for Perry when he phased...

"Can I get you something?"

Miriam was startled out of her fugue by a tall twig of a man in a white apron. She wondered vaguely what he turned into. A stork, perhaps.

"Do you have anything like popsicles?"

The stork nodded, eyes somber. "I've got chicken broth too."

God in heaven. He knew. Of course he knew. Everyone was in everyone's business here. It was so much worse than her little Wilmington college town. At least there, you could walk out your door without the neighborhood dog-man being able to smell what you had for lunch and where you were in your cycle.

"Just point me toward the popsicles, and I'll be out of your hair."

She was clutching a box of multi-flavored "juice pops" on her way back to her room when Meg intercepted her.

"They told me you were out and about this morning."

Ten minutes. That's how long it took for word to travel. Miriam drew in a deep, weary breath. The room, her way to lock everyone out, was only thirty feet and forever away. She said nothing.

Meg waited a moment, but then continued. "The situation in Richmond is getting tense. It's no longer safe. We're planning to move our more vulnerable people to Perry's caves in Allegheny."

It really had been like a home. Pleasantly cool, uniquely beautiful. All Perry. They would go and strip that from it.

The cold from the popsicles was seeping into her body. Meg was looking at her.

"I want you to be on the first caravan."

"No." The word came out as all the reasons flashed in her mind.

"Living here is no longer safe."

Miriam spoke from the circle of thoughts that had been part of her sorrow. "You think I plan to stay here? With you people? I. Don't. Belong. Here. Not without Perry. And every time I move, someone is watching me. I can't take this anymore. I can't. I'm going home."

A muscle worked in Meg's jaw.

Oh, that bitch was not thinking about keeping her with them. The daze of her grief transformed into a hot anger. Miriam breathed it in, letting it make her feel alive. Her hands tingled, and her grip tightened on the box, causing it to crumple.

The shorter woman kept her voice measured as she said, "I would feel safer if you were with us."

"Safe! Ha! Being with you is the only reason I wouldn't be safe." Miriam began walking past Meg, to her room.

"I don't need this right now."

"Excuse me?" Miriam whipped around. "I'm sorry that my trivial life is such an inconvenience to your immortal war. I mean your own grandson's death barely put a pause in your step—"

"How dare you!"

"—I can only imagine that my issues must seem like the last thing you need to think about."

A snarl hinted on Meg's lip. "I have lived longer and grieved more than you could ever imagine!"

"Oh, yes. Tell me more about how my life and my suffering mean nothing next to yours."

They were yelling now, pain and bitterness oozing through any outlet it could find.

"You entitled brat," Meg said. "How long did you know him? Not even a year? He was my life for over three hundred years. So, yes. You know nothing of suffering! And you'll have to pardon me for wanting to keep my great-grandchild safe after all of this."

The noise had summoned a few onlookers.

"Mmm-hmm. Now, we're getting somewhere. Forget me, you want

to keep this thing alive," she motioned with the crunched box to her stomach. "But did you ever stop to think that your influence has led to the death of everyone you love?"

This time Meg really did snarl. Miriam tossed the box down.

"That's right. Come on, old woman. I'm not afraid of you or your people. You want to kill me? Then get it over with, but I'm *not* staying here."

Whether it was her hormonally heightened senses or just Meg's strength, Miriam felt the force behind the yellowing of the woman's eyes. She braced her body against the wave of it.

"You have no idea the game you're playing." This was no longer the voice of an elderly woman. It was steel and predatory. "You think I'm going to let you go and endanger the lives of all my people and the life of that baby you're carrying. Vampires need permission to turn someone. We do not."

Miriam felt her heart quicken. This wasn't happening.

But it was.

Perry was dead.

She was pregnant, and he was dead.

And this creature was threatening to make her one of them by force. It might not even be possible. It might be a bluff, but she couldn't risk it. Yet.

"Touch me and you're a dead woman."

Miriam purposely turned her back on Meg. She marched past the battered popsicle box now leaking a sticky red liquid onto the speckled floor and slammed her door.

She didn't lock her door either, didn't want to give Meg the satisfaction of busting in one way or another. Instead, she stripped down and took a shower. Miriam wasn't done grieving, but she needed to be ready, and she needed a plan. Perry would understand.

Her face and hair were dry from a week of crying and lying in bed. She scrubbed the days off of her body, then replaced the grime with a soothing layer of coconut oil, rubbing it into her skin and short hair. The hot water took only the excess off, and she blotted dry with the towel. Perry loved when she did that, said she came out of the shower shining like a goddess.

But Perry wasn't here anymore. And she wasn't about to stay in hell either.

Rummaging through the bag of her things, Miriam pulled out fresh clothes and her journal. She took inventory of the resources she had to work with. Her Smith&Wesson combination blade boot knife was first on the list. She hadn't brought the pistol. That was back at the caves with the rest of her survival gear. Not that a gun did a whole lot of good with what she was up against, but she would take anything that might possibly give her an advantage. And she was pretty sure a headshot would be to her advantage.

The gun went on the list.

When she was done, she flipped to the page where she'd made a primitive map of Perry's caves. After the "incident" when Adrian showed up unannounced the first time, Perry had her memorize the way through a crawl and subsequent tunnels that lead to what he called "the backdoor." It was more like a tight thirty-foot wriggle to a hole that let out on the other side of the mountain. He'd made sure there were at least two switch backs to confuse anyone who might be pursuing by smell. Then he chased her through the route at least once a day until she knew it by heart, in the dark and while followed. Perry would've had a fit if he knew she'd drawn out a map as well. His sense of caution was equal to hers, just in different areas.

Miriam traced the markings on her page. The exercises had worked. She didn't need the map, but she remembered making it, remembered the woman she was sprawled out on Perry's bed while he was out doing who knows what. She'd felt safe there, surrounded by the smell of him, even while she inked the escape route in her journal. Did that woman exist anymore? When did she even start existing? Just a few months with Perry had changed her life beyond recognition, and now she was lost in the maelstrom of his absence.

She drifted into memories. There were snatches of conversation, brief kisses, hot touches. But this time, she brought herself back. If she was going to survive, she needed to be here, in this moment.

Those moments were real and beautiful, but she would have no more beautiful moments to live if she didn't pull herself together. She'd need to start keeping food down, whether the thing growing inside her wanted it or not. If she had to nibble down bits of things all day, that's what she'd do. Eating would give her the strength she needed, but it would also begin to put some of the Therians at ease.

Meg would be the hardest to fool. Giving in to anything the hag said would raise suspicion but denying her altogether would also make things worse. It would be a delicate, surly balancing act, but if Miriam's memories of her teenage years were any indication, she had it in her.

Blowing out a breath of air, she rolled her shoulders, held her head up high, and left the room.

6

GOING

Clare's Notes:

Vampires only consume blood and produce no noticeable waste. Therians must consume "flesh" but can also consume other things. They do, however, use the bathroom. I'm not sure which is superior. ;-)

Adrian stood in the doorway watching a roil of Therian bodies jostling about over containers of steak tartare, sushi, and medium rare burgers. They kept all hours, but meals were rarely skipped. Just recently, the smell here was unbearable, and he avoided the room so full of reminders that he was "other." But now the Therian smell wasn't irritating, and the food actually smelled interesting, even if it didn't smell appealing.

He wanted to burn the room to the ground. Anything rather than think about those changes. *Madonna Santa*, he couldn't even wrap himself in the desperate hate that had fueled him for so long with the way the blood in his veins whispered hope into his being.

Perry's hope.

Perry's blood.

Adrian closed his eyes for a moment and let the dark bring him back to his purpose.

Until that damn glow intruded again

Clare would be easy to find even if she didn't walk around in her own spotlight. She moved differently, taking in everything but more from curiosity than fear. Her glow almost made sense in the way she was alight with life.

The last person he knew like that, he'd watched as the light was snuffed out.

Not this time.

She was sitting facing the other door that led up to the second floor, probably waiting for her friend, when Adrian came up behind her.

"You need to go with them."

Clare looked up from her dripping burger. This close he could trace the eddies of light that moved in the moth-to-flame vampire attractant that she put off. Her pupils dilated. He'd seen it countless times, the pulse of fear in human features. She glanced away.

Cazzo di merda. As much as he hated the response, he hoped it meant she had some sense.

"Clare."

She pulled her eyes back to his. She didn't have the survivors' habit of avoiding eye contact. Not that it was true you shouldn't look a vampire in the eyes. That, along with so many other things, was a myth. It was still surprising that she did it; her bright blue eyes searched his as she fidgeted with the moonstone ring on her finger. He made his eyes glide off the ring, not linger on its history, so he wasn't tempted to rip its taint off of her.

"What about you?" she asked, finally.

"What the fuck does that matter?"

"Are you staying or going?"

There wasn't a world in which what he was doing should have any bearing on the conversation. Before he could say so, her eyes flicked away and a smile stretched across her face.

The Dark Hours 39

David appeared at the cafeteria doorway looking disheveled, not as a point of traumatic indifference after escaping from being held by vampires but perhaps actual indifference. He'd been in the control room half the night, at least, working with Sune on something. And when he'd been absorbed in it, even Adrian's entrance and exits went unnoticed.

"I'm going to help with the move," Adrian said finally.

"So you're staying then," she said.

"There's a lot to be done here."

"None of you people ever say what you mean."

He could practically feel his lip curl. "And what do I mean?"

"The vampires took everything from you." The words came out softly. "You want to make them feel that."

What did she fucking know? Centuries of rage lived inside him, and she acted like she could possibly see any of it.

"Hey." David's lackluster voice broke the moment as he plopped down with a plate of floppy bacon and runny eggs next to her. Clearly, it wasn't his lunch yet.

"David." Adrian's voice was low, controlled. Her friend looked up, sleep clearing from his eyes. He knew Adrian was a vampire. Between that and the hard lines anger was making in Adrian's body, David stiffened. "You're going with the others. Tell Clare to go."

David quirked an eyebrow and his body relaxed slightly. "You're under the mistaken assumption that anyone can make Clare do anything. And besides, I'm not going." Clare's burger slipped from its bun. "Kitsune asked me to stay and assist. The programs he has for hacking are practically sinful and—"

"You can't stay here," Clare said, cutting him off. Right. Now she understood danger. Adrian huffed, and she turned a glare on him before continuing. "It's going to get dangerous. And...and what about James? You haven't been online in forever, and he's got to be worried. And you don't need to... You can go back to your life."

"Go back?" David speared an egg. "I can't just walk back into *You Know It* like none of this ever happened. A few weeks ago, getting an early copy of Zombie Eater Three was the most exciting thing that had happened to me in years. And now...Clare, there are fucking vampires in our city." David's eyes flicked to Adrian, and *Dio Santo,* this was not at all going how he thought it would!

"That's why you have to go."

David shrugged like she'd asked him if there was overtime available, but his lips crushed in a line. She glanced at Adrian then, and oh no. She was going to have to sell those caves to him like he needed to sell them to her.

"Look, I'm the reason you're involved in all this, and if something happens to you, I'd never forgive myself."

David let the unconcerned mask on his face fall away completely. The expression that was left was raw. Adrian could read the hurt and fear, but there was something more too.

"Maybe you could've claimed that when the—" his voice faltered for a moment, and this time his eyes didn't stray to Adrian, "when the vampires took me. Maybe. But from the moment I got here, I've made my own choices. I know what I'm doing."

"I don't understand. It's not like you." Clare wore her concern and frustration in the furrow of her brow and flare of her nostrils. She concealed nothing. David's eyes were kind, but his mask was coming back up.

"I've seen what's happening. I can't kid myself that I'd be safe anywhere right now. Besides, if anything goes down, all the good 'zombie-killing' toys are here." David turned a critical look on Adrian. "And you. Do what you want with your broody attentions, but don't kid yourself into thinking that Clare will back down from anything she wants. Least of all for a man. Or whatever you are."

David went back to eating, like he hadn't just made the most asinine statement ever uttered. Clare tore her horrified eyes from him and looked at Adrian.

"*Madonna Santa!* I don't—"

"That's not what's going on—"

They both started talking at the same time, and then both fell silent. David was very pointedly eating when Clare continued. "No. Just no."

The Dark Hours 41

Adrian couldn't agree more, but David didn't even shrug this time.

She turned to Adrian, "And I don't know when I'm going. They're still working with my blood, and I might need to be here until they move the lab equipment. I'll be wherever they need me to be for right now."

She wouldn't do anyone good if she was dead, and he was about to say so when she pushed back from the table. The movement brought his attention back to the room.

"I'm going to take some lunch to Miriam."

"I think that will be unnecessary," Adrian replied.

Miriam was in the food line getting a bowl of soup. She carried herself with the same confident posture, but there was nothing easy to it. She was tense, and the sight brought back her words.

How dare you be alive when he's dead!

He watched Clare rush over to her, all smiles and relief, while everything in him wished again and again that he had died instead.

For a moment it looked like Miriam would decline when Clare asked if she wanted some company, but then she gave a little nod.

"The smells are too much. I'm going to take it back to my room."

So Clare followed her back down the hall to her room. They sat on Miriam's bed, and Clare watched as the woman took slow sips of broth from her spoon.

"Morning sickness?"

Miriam swallowed and nodded. "I can hardly keep anything down."

"Do you know how far along you are?"

"No." Miriam's voice was curt, not that of an expectant mother wanting to talk about her baby. Clare could feel the frown tugging at her lips, and before she could think better of it, her hand was on Miriam's. "Are you okay?"

She set her bowl down and took several breaths. When she finally spoke, her voice came out in a whisper. "I don't know what to do. I don't know if I can do this. What if it has the trait? What then?" There were tears spilling from her eyes as she spoke. "Will we be hunted for the rest of our lives? I'd rather not have Perry's child than have it, and it be taken from me like he was. I would rather die, and it with me. And Meg won't let me leave. She threatened to turn me, but I won't let that happen. I won't!"

Miriam looked at her, waiting, but Clare was stunned. She managed to squeeze her friend's hand, and said the only right thing that came to mind.

"I'm here for you."

"Help me."

"How?" Sure she'd escaped from here, but that was before there was a full on war happening in the outside world. The Therians weren't going to be so easy to get by now. When Clare left, she knew it was basically a suicide mission. She wasn't planning on being on the run. *If* Miriam managed to get out, they could probably just *stretch* and find her.

"Meg is sending me to the caves. I know a back way out, but if someone was there who could help buy me some time if I need it..."

Miriam had to be desperate because that was crazy. Escaping in the woods would give the Therians way more of an advantage than escaping in the city.

"They'll track you."

Miriam shook her head and gave Clare's hand a squeeze back. "Water."

"Water?"

"It disrupts their senses. I just need to get to the stream and follow it down."

That was the first Clare had heard of it, but she didn't doubt the source. Miriam had been living with Perry, and he'd loved explaining things. Clare almost smiled at the memory. Almost.

"Okay."

Miriam's whole body seemed to soften. "Okay."

7

STRENGTH

Clare's Notes:

How many vampires are there like Adrian and Jonathan in the world? Is there a way we could get a message out and have them join the fight? We could call it the bat signal. ;-)

Of course if they're anything like Adrian, they're a bunch of surly misanthropes who would happily roast hotdogs while the world burns.

Jonathan woke as the sun diminished. He'd worked all night with Sune. Therian man-power was limited. Since they could integrate into human environments in a way that vampires couldn't, not as many Therians worked for their society; however, the technology to compensate for that lack was exquisite. They weren't too far behind Solifugae tech.

At Sune's suggestion, they had David join them as they worked to devise a program that could import data and recordings from the more susceptible areas and flag for suspicious activity. The Therians already had a program scaffolding they used for vampire and human form recon. Jonathan's task was coding for quicker reduction based on movement instead of form. He'd worked until the sun came up, but the program was still far from ready.

Tonight would be a long night, but before that...

Jonathan *stretched*. It took the smallest drop of his mind into that other perception, and he could feel the draw of his son's connection. He propelled himself along the thread, a hot coal of worry and love and *fear* churning his insides. But in a moment, he was there.

Zeph wasn't sleeping this time. Jonathan didn't know what he was doing, but the tangle of his life was agitated. Oh, that boy. When he got wound up, he was a force of nature. Jonathan reached out, laying his hand-self-intention, on his son. Bright fibers of attention and curiosity rose all over the boy, and a single idea filled his whole being.

Daddy?

It speared him with love and grief. His boy hadn't seen him in a year, and at three, he surely didn't remember him, but in this place, there was truth. And somehow, his baby recognized him.

"Yes!" He felt weak with relief...and with the stretch. He wouldn't last much longer. "Yes, baby. I'm here. I'm looking for you, and it might take a little bit, but Daddy will find you."

He pushed the words to his son and felt the response of beautiful, child-like acceptance. Zephyr believed.

Tears were on his lips when he became aware of his body again, and a sobbing laugh spilled out of him. His baby was alive and knew his daddy was coming for him.

And he was, but not tonight. He needed strength. No, no more denial. What he truly needed was blood. There was blood here, and if there wasn't, he would do what needed to be done to get more.

When Tam had been alive, Jonathan could tell himself the boy was better off without him. He'd done everything he could to prepare himself for a life apart. But reaching his son tonight had torn his heart wide open. He couldn't lie to himself any longer. He couldn't live without his baby.

He wouldn't.

This time wouldn't be wasted, though. He'd strengthen himself, and if there was any way of knowing where he was going to find the boy, the Therians were doing it. They were surveilling everything they could and requesting help from tribes in other regions as well. If he was clever, lucky, or both, a program might find them, and he wouldn't have to go in blind.

Of course, if the Solifugae had him...if the survivors of Nidhi had him... That was it, wasn't it? What else could have happened? No local agency had reported finding a boy matching his description. What then? It was unlikely they'd be careless enough to be found, and they'd probably kill the boy... So, it couldn't be, because his son was still alive.

The assault of thoughts just kept swirling until an intercom buzz startled him out of his mind.

"Yes?"

Sune's voice carried over the speaker. "If you're ready, David and I are about to get started."

"Right. I'll be right there, I just need to um...drink real quick."

"Have your fill. More supplies came for you and Adrian tonight, and I'll have them stock your mini fridge while you're working."

They were so very careful around him and blood. Jonathan had no idea what it was like when they first started working with Adrian, but if their caution was any indicator, it had been interesting.

Adrian.

There was an option. Not that the last time he trusted him was a success. Jonathan was alive, but his wife was dead and his son was missing. This whole place had failed them.

No. He couldn't think like that. He had to bury it. There was nothing that could be done. The Therian team had obviously died trying to keep their word. Died on his account. So much death...

No. NO! Bury it. Push it down. It didn't help anything. Focus. For Zeph.

He took his mind to *El Rio Del Luz*, letting deep breaths steady him. His head had only come to the middle of the painting when he saw it in the DC exhibit. It made it seem as though the canopy of the tree stretched over him, and the river lit before him. The torrent in his brain distanced as he considered the delicate palm fronds shining in the morning light of the painting. Jonathan drew back from the pain and raging seesaw of emotions and followed brush stroke after brush stroke until he came to curious detachment. With the numbness in place, he could have his dinner and go to work and actually be of use to Zephyr.

The blood was cold.

He had no way to heat it in the room they'd given him, and he wouldn't ask either. Even a human could smell warm blood. The fragrance of human death would waft through the door and remind the Therians that there was an enemy in their midst. Some of them barely concealed their hate as it was. Adrian had worked with them for a century or more, but he hadn't lived here. The enemy of my enemy is my friend, until he's eating disgusting things under my roof.

They were feeding him though. And the strength flooded down and in. It sank into deep places, places that had previously been buoyed by Lachlan's life. Jonathan drained a second bag of tasteless cloned blood. Those who knew how vampire bodies worked kept that information to themselves, but he could tell he'd been running off of the barest amount needed to function. He had less strength than he did when he was first turned. By a lot. What would happen if he expended it all? Was it even possible to do? Would he actually die if he did? He no longer had a maker who could support his life force if needed, so perhaps?

He took the final bag from his fridge and drank it, letting the cold, empty life replenish what it could.

It was time to work.

ALL THE LITTLE ANTS. All the tasty, bite-y little ants. They scurried to and from their buildings, thinking they were safe in their little colonies. But the spider was watching them, spinning webs for them.

The park by the river was a good place. The night cooled air would set in, and the young ones would come out. They reeked of their drink and slipped off to places where they wouldn't be seen. Oh, but he saw them. Yellow and red with heat. With blood.

They never heard him. Too busy with their own sweaty bodies. He'd kill one first. So easy. Just twist the head, and crack! It was important, though, not to let the other scream. Scared away the other ants, even if it was oh so nice to listen to. He could still let them thrash and cry out beneath his hand. All their power was nothing. They never hurt him, not really.

He drank them slowly. Let them try, hope, and then fall into despair as they drained into him. So good. He chewed sometimes, considering the taste of muscle and bone. It was fun; not as strengthening, but still fun.

One was all he could drink though. His body would swell tight with it until all the bright life became part of his own. The rest of the night, he played.

Take a dead body and prop it up on a park bench. Eventually someone came, and then would come screaming, and the air would thicken with sharp, musky fear. And fear tasted so good. He would be too full to eat again, but he could manage a sip of dessert here and there. Sometimes he just watched, watched them scurry and panic. The colony was under attack. Run about and try to do something to help.

Life had never been so good. He couldn't be sure of that, actually. The spider remembered nothing of his life before waking up in the boiler cellar of some abandoned building, desperate with thirst. Still, he had a sense that this life was new and good.

He felt certain he was never the same sort of thing as these creatures he hunted. And the same sort of creatures as himself... They felt like competition.

He could smell them sometimes, when he went out to hunt, and always the smell made him growl. They should not be where he was. But he skittered away. Always away. The small spider might hunt in the web of a larger one if he was clever and quiet. Too much vibration and the larger spider would eat it. He knew this somehow, knew it was important.

He would grow large and fat, but until then, he would stay in the shadows. And he would eat.

8

CONNECTION

Clare's Notes:

I really know nothing about technology. No wonder they think I'm safe to be in the Control Room. They might as well be speaking Swahili. Or Klingon.

Clare was heading to the control room after breakfast, but the sound of familiar voices arguing stopped her a few doors short. The door marked "office" was closed, and the muffled sounds of Adrian and Meg shouting were easy enough to hear. After glancing to check the hallway for other eavesdroppers, Clare opened her notebook, in case anything "noteworthy" was said.

"... out in the sun when this wears off." That was Meg.

"It's a fucking *change*. It's not going to wear off."

Meg lowered her voice, but Clare could still make out her words. "We can't know that, and—"

"I know that! Don't you think I know my own body. This isn't a boon. I bled out! I'm under Perry's blood now."

"It's. Not. Possible."

"What do you need?" There was a bang from within the room. "Is this what you need?"

Clare's arms prickled as the air around her charged with power. Had she always noticed that?

"This form..." Meg's words trailed off.

"*Figlio di puttana*. Don't fuck with me!" Adrian's voice was now rough and deep. "Your people had to know this was possible."

"Don't be ridiculous! Our forms always follow their maker. This was an old-world myth when I was still young. I never believed—"

The words were cut off with a roar that caused Clare to drop her forgotten notebook. Her heart raced. She snatched her notebook and hurried to the control room. There was no telling if this would spill out of Meg's office.

The control room was quiet. A small cluster of Therians were speaking in techno babble over a bank of consoles. They didn't even look up as she entered. It had taken a couple of days to earn her seat in the corner, but eventually, she was given enough clearance to be ignored. Granted, it probably had less to do with actual trust than the fact that anything other than the most basic com use was beyond her, but she'd take what she could get. So long as she didn't touch stuff, she wasn't a danger. Also, the constant tapping of computer keys was like a lullaby, calming her frayed nerves.

Clare flipped her notebook open to the section she'd allocated for information about Therians and vampires in general. Four pages in, she made a line under the last entry and put a star in the margin:

HYBRIDS EXIST.

SHE STARED at the two words and was still staring at them when Adrian cleared his throat. She jumped and slammed the notebook shut.

"Feeling guilty about something?"

Clare gave her best blank blink. "I was just lost in thought."

The Dark Hours 51

Adrian snorted and looked away. "You're so naive." There was an insulting edge to his words, but before she could protest, he lowered his face to her level in the chair. "Even if the hallway didn't reek from your adrenaline—"

Crap.

"—you're a terrible liar."

He wasn't going to intimidate her, not this time. Rolling her shoulders back, she said, "I lie just fine, thank you."

"To yourself maybe," he tossed back.

"Do you always have to be a colossal bastard?"

"Such language. It's shocking to my virgin ears."

She closed her eyes and pinched the bridge of her nose. Why were they even doing this?

"Can I help you?" Clare asked, giving him a pointed look.

A smile tugged the corner of his mouth, but whatever he was thinking went unsaid. "I'll be with the security detail of the first wave, helping get everyone oriented to the caves. You're going," he said instead.

His jaw was jutted, ready for the fight.

"Okay." The way his mouth drifted open was immensely satisfying. "Preparations are being made now so the convoy can leave in three days. Seven in the morning. Right?"

"...right." He was looking at her like she was a confusing tabloid photo.

She hopped down from the chair so he had to back up for her to pass. Clare recognized a win when she saw it, and she intended to leave while she still had the upper hand.

"See you then."

Her smile was tight as she walked out, but the smile faded altogether as she passed Jonathan's room. She hadn't been able to speak to him in private since she'd shown him how to *stretch*. He'd been working nights with David, the new urgency rescinding past orders to stay in his room after dark. But he hadn't left the compound. It was definitely better that he hadn't. He was safer here, and the Therians could help him.

But...but what? Clare couldn't put her finger on it. He just wasn't well. And of course not. No one who went through what he did could possibly be well, but...

It was silly. She was stuck in this warehouse, and her mind was playing tricks on her. Spending all day observing creatures with impossible "magical" powers was somehow working on her desire to be able to do something more than human too.

Or...

Maybe pulling Jonathan back that night in the woods had linked her to him. Even without being in the realm Kenyon had once referred to as a "liminal place," it was like Jonathan was only ever a thought away. And when she let her attention go to that thought, what she felt was like an iced over lake. The ice went so deep, and at the center was a churning mass. It reminded her of muscle without skin, all raw and bleeding, and there was no help.

She shook the impression away and found she'd wandered to a stop in the long hallway. Clare glanced behind her, hoping the lapse had gone unnoticed.

But of course not.

Adrian was standing against the control room doorway, his head cocked to the side. He was a good hundred feet back, but with his eyesight, he could probably see every furrow in her brow. She rolled her eyes—hopefully he could see that too—and started back toward her room.

Adrian was quiet when he moved, but no amount of quiet completely muffled the swish of clothing or the patter of footfalls on linoleum. She didn't turn around but found herself taking in a deep breath. Vampires often smelled faintly like a meat counter, but all she caught was the scent of woodsy cologne or body wash. He fell into step next to her until they came to her room.

It was weird that he was eye-level standing next to her. He always seemed to loom larger in her memory.

"Well, this is my stop. Thanks for the walk home," she said as she opened the door and started to push inside.

The Dark Hours 53

He put his arm across her doorway, and it was the power that radiated from him that made him seem bigger. Clare backed away.

"What?" His voice was low as he asked.

"Do you have no concept of personal space? You come in with your predator energy and of course I'm going to back up."

"No." A flash of confusion crossed his face, and he waved her words away. "What happened, just then, in the hall?"

That? She was always up in her head, and it was tempting to laugh, except for the force in his eyes. "I spaced out. I'm a writer. It happens."

Adrian's eyes scoured over her, making her feel like she did in the dream where she was giving a speech and suddenly realized she was naked behind the podium. His tone was almost distracted as he said, "The light around you rippled like it did when I *stretched* to you." He looked away as he added, "That night in your house."

At least he'd gained the sense to seem sorry about the hell that night had put her through.

"I thought it kind of moved anyway," she said.

"It does, but not like this. Something happened." He locked eyes with her, as though daring her to deny it.

And it pissed her off. She wasn't lying. Nothing happened. She'd spaced out thinking about Jonathan... Oh.

Oh! It was real. The connection, the feeling. Oh, God. That churning mess must have been Jonathan's core. She'd perceived pain in his frozen tangle when she was teaching him to stretch, but she hadn't reached into it, didn't want to violate his privacy. And this was so much. She could perceive it even now, throbbing with—

"There!" Adrian grabbed her shoulders. "What was that?"

Clare blinked, coming back to reality in front of her. It was strange to be seeing something other than what she'd just been sensing so vividly. Stranger still to see concern on Adrian's face. He pulled her into her room and shut the door before she could respond.

"Are you okay? Did someone try and *stretch* to you?"

She shook his hand off her. "No, it's nothing like that. Well, it is like a *stretch*, but I'm doing it, except I'm not doing it on purpose."

This wasn't coming out right. "I've just been getting these flashes of perception, about Jonathan, and—"

"Jonathan?" Adrian's nose wrinkled.

"Yes. I think that maybe when I pulled his essence back from Lachlan, it connected me to him."

"A binding?"

"I don't know what that is, but I'd say it's more like a bond than a binding. If that makes any sense. I'm not trying to *stretch*, and it doesn't feel like one. I just feel him every now and then."

Adrian's eyes narrowed. "Does it hurt?"

Clare started to say, "no," but before the word could form, she knew it wasn't true. How did she even explain this?

"Kind of. *I* don't hurt, but I feel his. He's not well, Adrian. He's really not."

"Of course he's not." Adrian flung an arm as he spoke. "Does he feel an intrusion?"

"How should I know? I didn't even know I was doing anything? I thought I was just thinking about... Look, I'm worried about him."

"What do you want us to do? Stop monitoring the encroaching covens and get him a therapist? He'll either get over it or he won't."

"Have you no heart?"

It was Adrian's turn to flash a tight smile. "Oh, it's there. It's just dead."

"Yeah, well, Jonathan's isn't, and it's in pain!"

Adrian threw up both hands this time. "We're looking for his son. All this 'feeling' that you're doing doesn't actually help him at all."

"It does because *I* found his son." As soon as she realized what she said, Clare clapped her hand over her mouth. No no no no no. She'd been so caught up in the moment, and from the way his body froze, she knew Adrian wasn't going to let this pass.

"What did you say?"

"I showed him how to *stretch*, just so he'd know if his son was alive." Her voice was quiet.

"Do you have any idea how dangerous that was? You risked his life and yours!" He caught his rising voice and lowered it to a whis-

The Dark Hours 55

pered yell. "And now what's he going to do? The *caglione* is going to go out and try to get his son when the city is infested and he's too weak to even take on a thrip. You're un-fucking-believable. You sit there taking notes and think you understand how any of this actually works. This is why we can't send you to live with the survivors. You're a liability to everyone around you."

"Get out of my room," Clare ground out, swallowing against the constriction in her throat.

"I have to. Have to go while it's still light out and make sure Joanthan's not going to do anything stupid tonight."

Clare groaned. "You're the last thing he needs."

"An expert on that now too, are we?" Adrian said as he stormed out and down the hall.

She hurried after him. Jonathan would be hurt, and she wanted to explain before Adrian did too much damage.

Aberdeen, the red-haired Therian who'd helped her in the lab that night she'd gone to Nidhi, was in the hall. Her eyes rounded as she took in the look on Adrian's face and then Clare behind him. He completely ignored the woman.

"Are you all right," she whispered as Clare passed.

Yep. Magically ruining everything she touched, but she was fine. Clare nodded back at her and kept going.

Adrian was rapping on the door when she caught up with him. He didn't even glance at her, just said, "Oh no. You're not coming in here to do more damage."

Done. She was just done. "Ever stop to think that maybe you're the asshole here?"

And he actually grinned. Not a nasty smirk, but for a moment, there was humor in his eyes. It transformed his whole face.

It was gone in a blink as Jonathan appeared, tired and care-worn, at the door. Adrian didn't wait for an invite—that was the biggest scam in vampire lore—before barging in. Clare took a deep breath, cast Jonathan a look she hoped came across as contrite, and followed in after him.

9

ANOMALY

Clare's Notes:

Vampires can enter a room or residence without permission. The survivors know this, but it bears repeating because Adrian has no sense of boundaries.

Jonathan had actually been sleeping. He'd needed a human amount of it since Lachlan had drawn back the life he'd given at his making. And it was definitely still daylight. He could feel the high sun pushing down what little life he had. But now some asshole was pounding on his door after what couldn't have been more than three hours of sleep.

He opened the door to find Adrian looking for all the world like he was going to kill something. Not that it was a deviation from his normal. As per usual, he barged in without waiting for Jonathan to say anything, and Clare, looking apologetic, followed.

Jonathan sighed as he shut the door. This did not bode well.

"I'm so sorry. I didn't mean to tell him," Clare's words came out in a single breath.

The Dark Hours 57

Jonathan walked over and sat down on the bed. He was too tired for this, too tired to try and think through the consequences here.

"Look at him. I told you he was weak. You should have left it the fuck alone."

"Let her be." Jonathan glared up at Adrian. "She's the only one around here who actually did anything to help me."

"You ungrateful little thrip!" Adrian snapped. "These people lost a team to help you. They're sheltering your weak ass while all hell is breaking loose, and I can guarantee you they're working on finding your son. Give me one fucking reason I shouldn't go to Meg with this right now. Just one."

Jonathan ran his hands over his face, letting his nails drag over the skin as he brought them down. It was all too much.

"You're right," he said finally. "I just needed to know he was still alive. I needed it more than I needed to be alive myself. I knew there could be consequences, and I didn't care." He still didn't care.

"What are you going to do," Adrian asked.

Jonathan looked up at him. Adrian had helped him before.

"Nothing yet. I can't."

Adrian huffed out a breath. "At least you have that much sense."

He didn't actually. If not for Sune, he would've been long gone. "But I'm planning on going. Soon. I can find him now. If you—"

Adrian cut him off. "Is he hurt?"

Jonathan gave a slow shake of his head. He'd felt no physical pain from Zeph.

"I leave in a few days with the convoy. Don't do anything stupid until I get back."

A bubble of emotion surfaced through his numbness.

"How long?"

"It shouldn't be more than two days. If something changes, let Clare know."

Jonathan knew he was tired, but Adrian's last statement made no sense. How would he let her know? Wasn't she going with the convoy? She must have seen the confusion on his face because she stepped closer and answered.

"I'm going, but I've been able to...sense you, I guess."

Alarm evaporated the fog in his mind. "Sense me? Like a binding?"

Clare's hands were up in a placating gesture at both him and Adrian. "I don't know what that is. But I don't think so. It doesn't happen all the time."

It wouldn't have to. Admittedly, he didn't know much about it, but he'd been bound to Lachlan for giving him life. And in a way, Clare had given him life too.

Adrian was studying him like he was trying to follow a line in a Jackson Pollock painting.

"You haven't felt it then?"

Jonathan looked at Clare and reached out his senses for a binding, but the sun, reigning high somewhere outside, was like a vise on his abilities. Still, he'd be able to feel it if he were tethered to her hot light.

Wouldn't he?

"No."

"No intrusions?" Adrian asked.

Jonathan shuddered; the sickening feeling of Lachlan in his soul was too near a memory. "No, nothing like that."

Adrian turned to Clare. "Do it again."

The shake of her head was small but forceful.

"I didn't know I was doing anything."

"It's okay." Jonathan gave her what he hoped was a smile. "I'm curious."

And it was actually true. The numbness had receded a little. Somehow, he was convinced that she'd never hurt him, at least on purpose. That safety allowed for a sort of release from the cycle his mind had been trapped in, if only for a moment, and he wasn't going to squander it.

Clare pursed her lips and studied him. Finally, she blew the air out of her cheeks. Jonathan tensed, ready to feel a push into his soul, but there was nothing. Clare's eyes seemed to unfocus, and then the

The Dark Hours 59

light around her rippled like a small pebble had been dropped into a pond. It was beautiful.

With a few rapid blinks, Clare was back, her halo returned to its normal clinging around her. And she was smiling.

"You really were curious. You didn't just say that to make me feel better."

If it had been Adrian, Jonathan would have felt threatened to be known without his permission. But he hadn't felt Clare in him. She didn't have any hold over him, except for concern maybe. Whatever she was doing, it was something different.

"It's not a binding." Jonathan looked at Adrian. "She wasn't reaching into me."

"Well, she's fucking doing something."

"I'm still in the room, thanks," she shot back. "And all I'm doing is thinking about him, directly. Then, it's like I sense him for a moment. I'm not trying, not like a *stretch* where I have to push. It's just there."

Adrian began to pace, the air of anger shifting to a sort of impatience. "Have you experienced this with anyone else?"

"No."

"Have you tried to do it with anyone else?"

Clare raised her eyebrow. "I told you: I didn't know I was doing anything."

Adrian's wearied look of being surrounded by idiots was replaced with an expression of suppressed excitement. "We should experiment. See if it's more than just Glitch. God, Perry would be getting off on this."

"So let me get this straight." Clare's eyes narrowed, and Jonathan was glad not to be on the receiving end of that look. "You rip me to shreds, insult Jonathan, and now *you* want to get to play with whatever this ability is to satisfy *your* curiosity."

"*Madonna Santa*! You're impossible."

Clare came toe to toe with Adrian, but he didn't back down. Years of dealing with Meg might have hardened him, but for a human, Clare was pretty impressive...save for the reality that Adrian could break her in half with a single movement. What the hell was she doing?

"You haven't begun to see impossible. I haven't gotten this far in life by staying in the nice little box everybody put me in."

Adrian sneered down at her. "Maybe not, but I happen to know your weakness." Her weakness? She was human. Everything about her was weak, but Adrian continued. "You're dying to know about it even more than I am."

Red crept up over Clare's cheeks, and she turned away. "You're not getting a thing from me until you apologize. To both of us."

Fat chance...except that Adrian's hands balled. He was invested in this. Vampires didn't blush or flush with anger, but Jonathan was certain color crept up Adrian's neck as he glared at Clare's back. And it gave him an idea.

"Quid pro quo," Jonathan said.

Adrian's brow furrowed, but Clare turned on her heels, triumph written all over her face. She knew what he meant, and this was going to be so much more satisfying than an apology.

"Yes! You want something from me? I get something in return. Tell me what's going on with you. Are you..." Here the triumph faltered. This was personal, and Clare seemed to second guess herself for a breath. But then she continued on, a little quieter than before, "Are you part Therian now?"

The grin that spread over Adrian's face was predatory. "Curious are we?" The way he loomed over her had Jonathan on his feet and Clare backing up. "Is this what you wanted?"

His voice had taken on a growling quality, but it was day. Vampires couldn't change during the day. Jonathan had noticed that Adrian's smell was different when he first came back, but that could've been the effects of drinking Therian blood.

This was not.

Jonathan had taken a single step in their direction when Adrian whirled around. Yellow eyes nearly glowed against the black of his hair and clothes. There was no other physical change, but the atmosphere in the room felt like the air before a storm lands.

"Did you think I'd hurt her?"

Jonathan hadn't thought. It'd been instinct. Adrian looked at him a moment longer, and then raked his hands through his hair.

"*Porca Troia!* I don't fucking know what's going on with me. I haven't fed, haven't needed to after—" His eyes slid shut. "He was so fucking alive. There's no way to know what's permanent and what's a blood boon until his life is used up."

There was silence, and then Clare said, "I'm sorry. I shouldn't have asked."

The charge in the room lessened, and Adrian opened dark, inscrutable eyes. "No, you shouldn't have, but now you owe me."

A flame of guilt lit in Jonathan's gut, but Clare only frowned and nodded. He watched the light around her. It clung to her with barely perceptible currents. There was no ripple. Perhaps, it was being pulled back from the brink by her that forged such a strong connection.

After a few minutes, Clare sighed. "Nothing. I could try and stretch to you, but that's not what I'm experiencing with Jonathan. It's just there, like the flick of a switch."

Adrian's mouth drifted open, but then he blinked and snapped it shut. He realized something. The look wasn't lost on Clare either.

"What?" she asked.

"Nothing." His eyes flicked to Jonathan.

Right. Because he was the untrustworthy prick here, but suddenly, he was too tired to be bothered anymore. It was all too much. The blanket of numbness fell back down on him, and the pressure behind his eyes begged for sleep.

"Look, if you're satisfied neither Clare nor I am a danger at this moment, I'd like to get back to sleep. The sun is killing me today."

Confusion flashed across Clare's features. That woman was an endless fountain of questions, and half the time he didn't have an answer for her anyway.

"Would the rock of the caves help that?" She directed the question at Adrian. "It's got to be better than cinder block and sheetrock."

At least she was kind about it.

Adrian turned his eyes up like he was beseeching whatever power may heed a vampire's prayer. "You're insatiable. You know that?"

A smile touched Clare's lips. "I am, but this question wasn't for me."

"Well, it doesn't fucking matter because, one: The convoy is leaving during the day. Two: Meg hasn't offered the invite. And three: Jonathan isn't leaving the city without his son."

It was all true, but it was also just another power play from Adrian. He'd purposely avoided answering Clare's question.

"No. It wouldn't help, but thank you for trying," Jonathan said.

They both turned toward him, Adrian in irritation. Jonathan shrugged. It was true that he didn't know much, but Lachlan had been insatiable too. The sadist didn't hold to any Solifugae beliefs. He was convinced the vampiric sun aversion was produced by residual solar radiation and an organism's natural protective mechanism to things that could kill it. Jonathan had been subject to some testing of that theory since newborns were apparently more transparent in their "reporting" during research.

A memory of pain stabbed through unbidden. He could remember with perfect clarity if he wanted, but he let it drift away like it had all been a dream, a very bad dream.

"Well," Clare said, her expression tight. "Let me know if there's *something* that would help."

"I think you've done enough, Clare." The bite in Adrian's words was unmistakable.

"Don't you ever get tired of being the world's biggest asshole?" Jonathan asked as he lay down on his bed. He was done. "You're fine, Clare. Thank you."

He closed his eyes, and they actually managed to leave without any more bickering.

10

HIDING

Clare's Notes:

Do all light-bearers have a Watcher? If not, that might explain why I can do things that the immortals are surprised by.

The deep numb had its limits. In his dreams, there was screaming. Sometimes he was flayed alive, skin peeled back with monsters feasting on his organs. Sometimes it wasn't him the monsters were eating, but a baby from Tam's belly. There was always blood.

He woke with the smell of it in his nose, and hunger and disgust curling his insides until the numb could crush it down again. By the time he'd eaten, the horrors were firmly locked outside the museum he walked in his mind.

This night, Jonathan actually felt a little stronger. It was like all the blood he'd been pouring into himself finally quit draining out and a small bit of life remained clinging to the edges of him. It was a start.

The control room was quiet when he entered. Sune and David were already at their stations working on separate parts of the program. David didn't look up, but Sune offered a nod. Jonathan returned the silent greeting as he sat down at a console.

As usual, David was broody and Sune thoughtful. Both could be intense, but the feel in the room was usually amiable. Under different circumstances, he might've actually enjoyed working there. Unlike at Nidhi, where there'd been a threat behind every job, mistrust in every relationship.

A couple of hours and a few interruptions from Meg & Co. later, Jonathan was in need of a break. His brain could only take so much before it rebelled and all the words and numbers congealed into one thick lump.

He rubbed his eyes and switched to the cache where the background surveillance program dumped files. Said files were sorted by probability of importance from low to high. Dayshift would have already sifted through the high hits, but there was always a mountain of lower probability hits that were never so much as glanced at.

Nidhi would've had at least three people on a task like this at all times. The mind was much better suited to recognize a pattern than a computer program, but the Therians didn't have the manpower to waste. Instead, they relied on computing that Jonathan didn't trust, especially as the new parameters hadn't been fully inputted yet.

He let his brain uncoil as he flicked through the surveillance stills. Fifteen minutes or so of looking at people walk around at night, and he'd be bored enough to get back to real work.

Click, click, click. Click.

And then there she was.

Against the backdrop of some Italianate architecture cast in a too-blue street light, Siri's long raven hair was caught by a gust of wind. Her face was only a blur in the still, a quick glance she cast toward the camera she knew was watching. Even so, the rise of her cheeks and slope of her nose were just enough that the facial recognition pinged her as a possibility from its list of high-profile vamps. A long-nailed finger was pressed against her lips as if to silence him through

The Dark Hours 65

the screen. Everything about it was perfectly staged. She was positioned in such a way to be noticed by facial recognition software but not with a positive ID.

It was obviously a trap, and he was going to take the bait.

Nightmare images surfaced in his mind as he opened and watched the graceful figure come to life. Lowering her hand, she pulled something out of her pocket. The resolution on the camera wasn't great, but he could see as she shot it away that it'd been a rubber band. Then, she clapped her hands twice, and a little boy came trotting into the scene.

The blood in him froze.

Fluffy baby hair floated on the breeze. Jonathan knew exactly what those silken strands would feel like, smell like. How heavy Zeph must have grown since he last held him. An ache opened deep and raw as Jonathan watched, transfixed at those toddling movements, until his baby was scooped up in Siri's arms and carried out of the frame.

Jonathan forced himself out of the motionless, alert posture his body had stiffened in and stretched in his chair. He had to stay calm, couldn't alert the others. It was obvious what that hell spawn wanted, and with his son in her arms, he'd give her anything. He desperately skimmed through any nearby surveillance footage, but the pair seemed to vanish into thin air.

He'd been able to hide the truth from Siri and Lachlan when he found out about Adrian, but this... Seeing his son with that monster was gutting him. If he didn't leave the room now there was no way Sune wouldn't sense his distress. Hell, even the human might be able to tell.

"I um...need a break. Everything's just blurring together."

Jonathan didn't wait to see if they responded before he was out the door and heading down the hall. He forced himself to keep his pace steady all the way to his room. Grabbing the blanket off his bed, he rushed to the bathroom, and shoved the blanket against the opening at the bottom of the door. He leaned his head against its cool surface.

Siri had his baby. And she wanted him to *stretch* to her. That had to be what she meant with the rubber band, but he didn't even know if he could find her that way.

The Therians hadn't been able to protect the boy and then hadn't been able to find him. They would take care of their own first and foremost. He wouldn't find help from them.

Adrian was powerful. He could find Siri if he was willing to *stretch* to her. But freedom was Adrian's god, and he wasn't going to sin against it to help Jonathan. If Adrian did deign to find her, he would probably go in first to kill her, and Jonathan's baby could end up as collateral damage. Just like Tam had been. And Siri was ruthless when it came to getting what she wanted. She wouldn't hesitate to hurt Zeph.

But she had no way of knowing if he'd gotten her message. He had time. He could wait for Adrian to get back from the caves. Maybe there was a chance that working together—

Right. Because Adrian played so well with others.

Who was he kidding? In a hundred years, he wouldn't have the strength to take on Siri. What difference did a few days make? Jonathan wanted to slam his fist into the floor or wall, to break something. Anything. But healing an injury would be a drain on what precious little life he had.

It was pointless. His whole life had been pointless. Worse than pointless. If he'd never lived, Tam would still be alive. But there wouldn't be a Zephyr...

Oh God, what if she was hurting him now?

Jonathan *stretched* out to his child and was surprised to find the small mass of life stilled in sleep. It was the middle of the night, but somehow he expected his son to be a mirror of the torment he was feeling. Being there quieted some of the anguish. The *stretch* was getting easier to hold, too. He drew his son's life to his own, relishing the feel of his baby.

Then she was there.

And he wasn't stretching anymore. He was gripped, held in place. Fear ripped through him.

The Dark Hours 67

"I've been waiting for you." The voice seeped like ink into his being, velvet and black.

He released his hold on his son. Whatever was about to happen, he didn't want Zephyr to feel it.

"It's remarkable that you survived when Lachlan's other spawn died that night. I'm fairly certain he didn't intend to leave you alive."

Jonathan could feel Siri probing, trying to stretch into him.

"So, how, I wonder, did you survive?"

The enormous weight of her power pressed on him, but he thrashed against it anyway. She was stronger, but she did *not* own his soul.

A line of amusement rose in the hardness of her being. "Really? I'm in the room with your son. Shall I hurt him to make you see reason?"

The words cut the fight out of his will. There was utter truth coming from her. She'd hurt Zeph, and it would cost her nothing.

At his surrender, he was crushed by her essence pushing into him.

"Yes. This is how I like it." There was a considering pause. "Oh, you needn't be repulsed. That's not what I meant. But if I wanted, I could make you feel things..."

Far away, his body responded, and the pleasure was revolting.

"Please...please stop." He flung the words at her being.

The feeling evaporated.

"It's good to understand one another. Now you understand what I can do to you and that I can hurt your son should I sense you lying to me. So, tell me: How did you survive?"

He wasn't afraid anymore. Fear was for those who had a choice.

"Clare and her Watcher pulled me back."

Surprise streaked through Siri. Whatever she'd thought had happened, that wasn't it. She clearly hadn't even known it was within the realm of possibility, and he took the moment of her confusion to try and focus on that fact alone.

There was only one way to hide something from a deep *stretch*. Intense focus was needed on something to drown out all else that he

68   J.E. KRAFT

knew. It needed to expand until there was nothing else. There was no hiding Clare's involvement now. So, he let her fill his mind. His friendship with Clare was a beautiful accident. Nothing more.

"I helped her escape."

"Why?" It came out like a hiss.

"I was afraid for my family."

It was true, but Siri was no idiot, and Jonathan could feel her readying.

"So interesting that you'd say that when I'd promised your family to you. That and Adrian's position. So interesting that Therians also raided the house your family was at the night they attacked us."

He could feel her anger as the claws of her purpose drove into him, testing his soul.

"You must be very clever that Lachlan didn't sense treachery in you. He would have loved tearing secrets from you."

The words, sent into his depths, brought up with them memories of Lachlan with "research subjects" and the terror of being at his whims.

"Oh, I see," Siri said. "He went too far. Your fear of him, even in death, nearly overruns you. That fear might drown out quieter emotions or ambitions. What a brave, clever bunny to stand up against him. But you weren't standing alone, were you? You brought the big bad wolves, and they came for my Adrian!" Spikes of fury rose from Siri's life and speared him in her hate. "I should kill your son now, slowly and painfully."

"NO!" The words resonated in every fiber of his soul.

"I'm not unreasonable." There was a purring quality to her words. It lay gently overtop of a deadly intensity. "I don't want much in return for your son, only blood for blood. At first, I was after Therian blood, but I've recently heard a very interesting rumor from one of the vampires that survived the attack. Tell me: Have you seen Adrian?"

A thrill of alarm went through him, and Siri was in his soul. She must not have been sure of the answer herself because the sudden knowledge that Adrian was alive caused lines of elation and fury to rise and mingle in her.

In a moment, the disturbance quieted, and she was composed. She had what she'd come for: Jonathan's betrayal. Without even trying, the numbness enveloped him again. He waited, like a mouse limp in the jaws of the cat waits, either to be played with or discarded.

Strands in Siri's being rose and submerged as she picked through what to ask next.

"How is this possible? I felt the thread to his anchor break, and I've searched for him. He's gone."

Keep it simple. Give her the truth, nothing more. "Therian blood."

"But he was dead! Quit toying with me. I can feel you trying to hide things. Do I have to show you how serious I am."

Jonathan could feel her fury directing toward his son. God forgive him. What they might do with this information.

"It changed him. They changed him. I don't know. He goes out in the sun. I don't know what he eats. He said he hasn't fed yet."

Everything in her froze. If she didn't have his son, he could probably have gotten away from her then. Something deep and desperate was screaming inside her, and he knew that feeling. Ironic really, that she was probably to blame for that feeling in both of them.

Finally, slowly, she spoke again. "He hasn't fed yet. It might not be permanent." She turned her attention back to him. "Does he trust you?"

It was almost laughable. "Adrian doesn't trust anyone."

"I need you to bring him to me."

That *was* laughable. "I'm not free to come and go," Jonathan said, and he held onto the thought, letting his feelings of imprisonment with the Therians rise to drown out any nuance in the truth. But Siri grabbed the thought and made her own conclusions.

"You're all with them. You, the light-bearer, Adrian. You're all with the Therians."

A bright jealousy rose in her, and her grip on him tightened. Somewhere distant, pain rose in his body.

"I don't care if you're free to come and go or not. I don't care if it kills you. You *will* find a way to bring him to me. But to show you how generous I am, I'll give you a little time before I start taking my anger out on your son's soft flesh."

A location was imprinted deep in his psyche, and then he was hurled toward his anchor.

His body twitched as he returned to it, still tingling with phantom pain. With the feel of Siri still in him, he buried his face in the blanket on the bathroom floor and screamed and screamed.

11

VULNERABLE

Clare's Notes:

I'm aware that I don't know a lot factually about Miriam, but I feel like I know her. And I know she's not going to let anyone dictate her future. Can I be her when I grow up?

The convoy left as soon as the late autumn sun crested the distant horizon. Miriam had been up long before, unable to sleep despite already preparing however she could. Her survival gear was in the caves, but food would be a concern. This time of year there should be plenty of wild plants she could forage to help supplement her supplies, but she'd been grabbing as many protein bars a day as didn't seem suspicious. Whether or not she could keep them down had yet to be determined.

The city went by in window flashes reflecting the too bright morning mixed with the stale heated air of the truck. It seemed like a lifetime ago that she'd hiked up to stay with Perry for the weekend.

She'd been due back on a Sunday night weeks ago. How long had it taken people to miss her? She'd withdrawn more and more from friends and activities since she'd met Perry. How do you maintain a close relationship and hide the fact that you have a werewolf boyfriend?

She hadn't had enough time to figure it out.

After months of odd behavior, she finally had to admit to her parents she was seeing someone because theirs was a relationship she wasn't willing to sacrifice. Not that the meeting went well, even with them thinking he was human. They were right to be concerned about the changes in how she'd been acting, and right to blame him for it.

No wonder she'd seized the chance to hang out with Clare. She'd been starving herself of relationships without realizing it. Even now, with Clare sitting beside her in the backseat, it felt good to have a friend.

In the car, Aberdeen sat shotgun. The freckle-faced woman looked like she'd been born and raised in the West Virginia mountains, but with Therians, there really was no way to know. She'd acted friendly enough, but Miriam was not feeling especially trusting of Meg's tribe at the moment.

Adrian drove with sunglasses and a fierce smile on his face. Must feel good to still be alive. She couldn't even look at him.

Their truck was leading the convoy. Two black SUVs followed. Her jeep had been deemed too risky to take. But that was fine. If they thought they could keep her just by taking away her wheels, they'd grossly underestimated the situation. She had burned too many bridges. Miriam wasn't going to continue to let her parents think she was missing or dead. She wasn't going to let Meg run her life. And she sure as hell wasn't going to take any of this laying down.

"So, how's the pregnancy going?" Aberdeen asked, turning in her seat.

Really? This strange woman was going to ask her that?

She continued on as if Miriam hadn't just ignored her. "I hear that B vitamins and ginger really help with morning sickness. Not that I

The Dark Hours

tried them. It was a long time ago that I was changed, and we didn't have access to those things back then. My children grew old and died a long time ago..." Her hand rested on her stomach as if phantom remembering. "I'm so sorry. I'm sure this is the last thing you wanted to talk about, and I can't imagine how hard this must be for you."

And this was why she stayed in her room. People had no idea what to say and said whatever came to mind to make themselves feel better in the situation. Clare reached over and squeezed Miriam's hand.

"It's fine," Miriam said, but she turned away, watching the buildings give way to houses.

Adrian clicked on the analogue radio, and soft violins filled the silence.

LEAVES WERE CHANGING color up on the mountain, and the air hung with the scent of petrichor and pine. Until two weeks ago, the smell had been home.

Around her, Therians hefted packs and prepared for the hike. The drivers would go back in the morning and wait for the next wave that needed to be ferried. Barring any unforeseen circumstances, she'd make her move right after they left for the city.

"Hey." Clare stood next to her zipping up an athletic jacket and shouldering a gym bag and a ridiculously red briefcase. It was so out of place that Miriam couldn't help but smile.

"Don't rough it much, do you?"

"Guilty as charged." Clare smiled back. "I am kind of excited about these caves though. I visited Mammoth Caves when I was little, and it was magical."

These caves used to hold all the magic in the world, and Miriam wasn't ready to go back. Not that it mattered. She would do what she had to.

The Therians began following Adrian up toward the caves, but Clare was staring at her, brow furrowed.

"What?" Miriam asked.

She shook her head as if to clear it.

"I just—" She bit her lip, and then said, "It's...nothing. You've got enough on your mind without listening to me babble."

There was more there, and Clare was the only person she knew who had her back in all this mess. The woman needed something, even if it was only to talk, so Miriam would give what she could. "I officially give you permission to babble. Who knows, maybe it'll take my mind off of things."

Clare gave her a searching look. "I wish we'd been friends before all this. I bet you're amazing at a party."

Miriam laughed. "I have no idea where you get that from. I'll take the mountains over a party any day."

"That's exactly what I mean." And Clare gave an easy laugh. "I bet you could repel unwanted interactions with a single look, and I would introduce you to all the people who are actually worth talking to."

"Oh, you mean like David? He's perfectly asocial too."

They both chuckled.

"I guess I like people who aren't pretentious."

"No, girl. You like people who are complicated. That way you can spend all your questions trying to figure them out."

"Wow." Clare stopped and looked at her. "Wow. That's actually really insightful."

She let out a little "huh," and then they continued in silence for a few minutes, a thoughtful look on Clare's face. Their pace wasn't bad, but they were no match for the immortals, and soon they were far behind the group. It would be so easy to slip away now, but she'd be noticed sooner rather than later if she did. And she'd be without her gear.

"Ready for some more insight? You're still not telling me what's on your mind."

"I think you missed your calling," Clare said as she huffed from the walk up the slope. "You'd make an amazing therapist."

"Oh, I didn't miss it. I minored in psych. Wanted to run a wilderness survival program for at risk youth during the summers."

The Dark Hours 75

Sudden tears pricked at her eyes. She'd planned to do that since high school, and now she didn't even know how she was going to get through tomorrow, let alone have a future.

"That sounds perfect for you."

"Right?" Miriam wiped at the tears that were so easy to form now. "But you're still stalling."

"Okay. Fine," she said, smile fading. "I don't know if it's because I managed to *stretch* and humans aren't supposed to be able to do that. It could be a light-bearer thing or that immortals are kinda contagious. I don't know, but something's happening to me. I'm starting to see things, or sense them. I'm not sure which." Clare shook her head. "Oh God. It sounds like I'm crazy, but when we got out of the truck, and I looked at you... I don't even know how to describe it. I was seeing you, but for a moment, it was like there was more. At first it was only with Jonathan, so I thought it was because I tried to pull him back, but now, I think it's growing. It scares me, and sometimes I wish I could take it all back."

That was a feeling Miriam knew. Being with Perry had been amazing, but now he was gone. Half the time she was furious and wished they'd never met. The other half of the time, she missed him so much she thought it might kill her. But all that was overshadowed by something growing in her, and it was terrifying.

"Yeah. Me too," Miriam said softly. "And the Therians? Do they have any ideas about what's going on with you?"

"It's been so chaotic getting ready to leave I haven't told them. Just Adrian and Jonathan."

The sound of Adrian's name made her stomach turn. She'd probably forgive him someday for being the reason Perry got himself killed, but it wasn't today.

"I'm sure those two were bundles of help."

Clare shrugged. "They did what they could think of, but they're both dealing with other stuff."

"Look," Miriam said. "I'm aware that I'm more than jaded right now, but you need to be careful about them."

"I appreciate the concern, I really do, but what would they do?

They can't eat me. I'm poisonous. If they try to harm me, my Watcher can attack them. They're hurt, but they aren't trying to hurt anyone on purpose."

"I find your distribution of faith disturbing," Miriam said with a deep voice.

"Did you just quote that old space movie at me? I didn't know you were a sci-fi nerd, but I think it's 'I find your lack of faith disturbing.'"

"I like my way better." And for a moment, they were just two girls enjoying each other's company. Clare was right, it would've been nice to be friends before all this. But now everything was bound up together with life and death and blood. "Just be careful—of all of them, okay?"

THE CAVES WERE about the same temperature as the air outside had been, but it was strange to hear them echoing with other voices. To her surprise, Adrian had kept the others out of the main living area. He hadn't said anything to her other than, "Let me know when it's okay for them to use the kitchen."

She wandered to the bedroom and let the smell of Perry take her back. She was crying then, but it wasn't the fiery, stabbing pain she'd been experiencing since he died. Perry had been more than she thought could exist in a man. He was playful but brilliant, fierce but gentle. He lived like a fire burned, lighting everything until nothing was left, not even him.

Eventually, a rising feeling of nausea reminded her that there were things to do. Miriam grabbed some crackers from the kitchen and nibbled on them as she gathered her things from around the room. Her pack had been under the bed, and even though she knew she was coming to stay with Perry, it had all the necessities: a tarp, line, ferro rod, hatchet, MREs, and her pistol, to name a few. She wouldn't be caught unaware in the mountains. Of course, that's how she ended up shooting Perry in the first place. And the gun had worked. It'd bought her time.

She just didn't run afterwards.

The Dark Hours 77

She released the magazine, added another .380 to replace the one she used on Perry, and then stowed it in a side pocket in the pack. As much as she would like to have it on her hip, carrying in the caves would attract undue attention. When everything was packed, she went to the kitchen and grabbed what small staples could be crammed in her bag. The hike down would be easier if she didn't have to forage on top of everything else.

"He kept a stash of jerky in the bin on top of the fridge."

Miriam jolted and whipped around. Adrian was lying on the couch, only his head visible against the armrest.

"Ugly, I swear to God if you try and stop me—"

Adrian was on his feet so quickly it was dizzying, but he didn't come any closer. His face contorted in pain.

"The last thing he said to me," the words came out quiet and harsh, "was to protect you and his baby."

His baby. The last thought he'd had was of her and their—

"And I'll spend eternity at Siri's feet before I see any harm come to either of you."

She raised her chin and drew herself up as straight as she could. "I am *not* staying here."

"Why the fuck not? Have you got a safer place to hide? I know this place. It's protected and defensible."

Because she wasn't going to live her life in subordination to some other people, with her perpetually being "them" and not "us." She could think of a hundred tiny instances she'd experienced of being "othered" while living in the South, and she was the same species as that group.

Clearly, if she was getting out of here, though, Adrian would have to be convinced that she was staying. She took a deep breath and leaned against a cabinet.

"I didn't know that was the last thing he said. The only thing they told me was that Lachlan killed him, and then you killed Lachlan."

Adrian nodded, his eyes far off, and despite every nightmare she'd had, she didn't want to know what he was remembering.

"I was dying, and I was okay with that," he said, and then his eyes focused back on her. "I never wanted this!"

It was so much easier to hate him, to blame him for everything, than to have to admit that Perry willingly gave his life. Oh God, and she was crying again. She would rather not be vulnerable around Adrian, but her hormones were overruling her.

"I know," she said with a shaky breath. "You should have seen him when Jonathan came and said Lachlan had you. I didn't ask him to stay, but no one could've stopped him anyway."

"Fucking idiot," Adrian said.

"You got that right," she said with a sniff. "I may stay mad at him forever."

"He'd deserve it. But still, I'm not going to let anything happen to you. I'm not stupid. I know you're not staying. You're too much like Perry to be confined. But you're smart; you have to see the sense in staying until all this blows over in Richmond. Meg's in the relocating business. We can find a place that's safe."

"Meg," she spit out the word like it was something bitter in her mouth, "threatened to turn me."

She shouldn't have said it. Anger got the best of her in the moment, but the shock on Adrian's face was satisfying and emboldening.

"Are you going to keep me safe from that bitch too?"

Adrian let loose with a string of Italian and kicked at a pile of binders that was on the ground by the couch.

"Has everyone lost their fucking minds?!" He raked his hands over his head before fixing her with an intense look. "Meg isn't coming up here, not yet with the shitshow happening in Richmond. And there's at least one more convoy coming up. *I* will talk to her. If it's not safe—I can't believe I'm fucking saying this—but if *she's* not safe, I'll get you out before she comes. Just stay here in the meantime...please."

In all their interactions, Adrian always had a motive, something under the surface that she didn't trust. But this felt real. She'd at least consider it.

The Dark Hours 79

"Okay."

He held her gaze a moment longer, and she could feel him testing the sincerity of her words too. Finally, he nodded and stalked out.

12

TRUST

Clare's Notes:

I might be able to deal with the dirt, but the lack of light and being surrounded by rock is suffocating me!

Like a long-used coat, the caves still smelled of Perry. This place had been sacrosanct, and all of that was gone now. The imperative of safety and a feeling of dwindling time didn't allow Adrian the luxury of grieving like Miriam. People's lives depended on his actions.

They would need to overhaul Perry's main living area. The bathroom and kitchen were of particular importance since there was already plumbing there but it wasn't fit for this amount of use. But not tonight. He would give Miriam at least one more night in there, with the smell of him.

So he mapped out the more well-known areas of the branching cave system. They were roomy, but not for a whole tribe, and there was no telling how long they would need to bunker. Temporary spots were

The Dark Hours   81

claimed and more long-term lodging planned. Tools were carted in and fissures marked for enlarging. Grief and rage were channeled into physical movement. His body was giving expression, but his mind had no thought other than the practical needs of the moment. And it was a relief.

Until evening.

Work stopped and they picked an open area a little ways down from Perry's living room to set up cots and folding tables. Adrian had nothing to do with the food prep but was not surprised to see a large pot of meaty chili appear with various fixings. Therians filled their bowls and chatted.

Neither chatting nor eating appealed to him in the slightest. Now that the work for the day was done, however, there was one other thing he'd been wanting to explore.

He was waiting when Clare joined the line for food. It was actually surprising that she didn't have her notebook with her. Not that it stopped her questions. Aberdeen seemed a willing victim though. Adrian focused on their voices as they meandered through half a dozen subjects while eating.

At some point, his mind must have wandered. He was aware of the smells of the cave and the sounds of voices rising and falling like a stream. Then Aberdeen was looking at him and speaking.

"I think he's waiting for you to finish."

Adrian watched Clare follow her friend's gaze to find him across the room. He didn't look away when she met his eyes. She sighed and turned back to her new friend.

"Do you trust him?"

Madonna Santa. She had no idea how absurd her question was and clearly didn't know how well sound traveled in here. He listened with more interest.

"Adrian? Of course." Aberdeen likely knew he could hear them, but she wasn't looking at him. "He's risked his life for years for us. It was hard for some when he was still a vampire. The smell brings on our instincts, but that's gone now."

Adrian swallowed. *When he was still a vampire.* He'd hated being that, but now he didn't know what he fucking was or where he belonged.

"What is he, if not a vampire?"

This was not a conversation he wanted anyone to have. Adrian pushed off the wall, to say what, he wasn't sure. Aberdeen shrugged and took a bite of food.

"He's not exactly the talkative type, and there's still a lot of grief there. It would be insensitive to ask."

That should be oh so very obvious, but Clare just nodded.

"Not everyone seems to like him."

Figlio di puttana! Was she trying to goad him on purpose? He'd had enough! And yet he didn't move. A part of him wanted to hear Aberdeen's response. That part needed to be fucking murdered. What did it matter what anyone thought of him? But he still listened.

"You can trust someone without liking them. When you live a long time, you learn to appreciate many types of people, whether or not they're your flavor of being. Those who don't like him can at least appreciate him."

That was...surprisingly true of immortal relationships, those that had built trust anyway. Adrian watched Clare take in the response. Her lips pursed slightly. She didn't trust him, would be a fool if she did, but then the expression softened to a playful smile.

"So you're saying that if he wants to whisk me off into the deep, dark cave, it's totally cool."

Aberdeen laughed. "I'm pretty sure that handbook says something about affiliating with immortals at your own risk."

Clare laughed with her. "I'm sooo good at following the handbook." Then she got up to take her bowl to a large plastic bin. She'd taken two steps when the light around her gave a slight ripple, and she paused.

That. That right there was what he had to figure out. She was moving again; the light stilled when Adrian came up beside her.

"Mind if I whisk you into the deep dark?"

"Of course you were listening," she said with a roll of her eyes.

So, she didn't know.

The Dark Hours 83

"Immortal ears are sensitive, caves are echo-y, and I was bored."

Clare huffed. "You really have no sense of boundaries, do you?"

He smiled. "I'm acutely aware of them. I just choose to ignore them."

"Yeah, that's not better," Clare said and took a step back, the space between them a reminder that their short history hadn't been pleasant. "So, what do you want?"

"To test a theory about what you've been experiencing." While this could be for Clare's benefit, there was a deep thirst for understanding that hadn't been a part of Adrian until Perry's blood had become his own. It made him feel as if Perry was still with him, and there was no telling how long the effect would linger. "It does require going deep into the caves."

"Of course it does, and I bet we need to be alone too."

He took a breath of frustration. "Yes, but—"

"Fine. Just lead the way," she said.

"Really?"

"Yes, really. It won't even be the craziest thing I've done this month."

"Very true. This, for instance, won't involve motorcycle theft and breaking and entering a stronghold of the Solifugae." He turned as soon as her face began to redden and lead the way down the corridor. His baby had been recovered from Nidhi that night, but there were several scratches and one small dent, and she would probably die of natural causes before he was done making her feel guilty about it.

There were motion activated lights for only the first few minutes. When those stopped, he handed her a small, but ridiculously bright, flashlight. The cave walls sparkled under its beam. It would have been a handicap...before, but Therian eyes adjusted better to a variety of light.

"I'm going to change, partially, to help me navigate." Adrian turned away. He still wasn't used to this. It was not like letting the vampire in him rise. It was like loosening the leash, ever so slightly, on something that was always ready to burst free of him. It rippled under his skin, begging, but he held it back even as his eyes and nose felt liberated by its touch.

This was seeing and smelling as it was meant to be, and the beast in him whispered that living, as it was meant to be, would feel as freeing. He had only to release his hold.

Clearly, this beast didn't know him well.

Adrian began sniffing as he walked. The distinction of smells were as vibrant and easy to discern as the color spectrum. He paused at forks and crevices, smelling for the passage of Perry and water. Once, he glanced back at Clare. Whatever she saw, her eyes widened, and he turned away quickly.

The way went from wide open to a tight shuffle and back again. Each time it narrowed, he could smell the tangy scent of fear rising in Clare. She hadn't mentioned being claustrophobic, not that he'd expected her to admit to any weakness. It was a trait they shared in common, and he understood her in that way.

By the time they'd reached the crawl, her heart was thrumming at a speed very unnecessary to the amount of walking they'd done. But she'd kept following. Not that she had much of a choice. It was unlikely she could find the way back, but she hadn't even tried to turn around.

Until he pointed to the hole in the rock and said, "It's just down here."

Her heartbeat spiked, and he knew she wasn't going through there if she had any choice at all. So, grabbing a small pen light from his pocket, Adrian got down in the stale cave dust and army crawled the short distance to the other side. He brushed the tan sediment from his clothes as he stood and called to her.

"It's a little squeeze, but it's short."

Her laugh was flat and muted as it came back through the rock.

"Not a chance. Look, I know we don't know each other well, but I don't do great with confinement, and there's no way I'm doing that."

"It's just two feet of crawling."

"Listen, Mr. Broody Vampire Man, I don't care what's on the other side of this boulder, how important it is to your cause, or to me personally: I. Am. Not. Going."

That was about how he expected the exchange to go. He relished imagining the look on her face as she realized she couldn't find her way back and that his immortal body could well outlast hers in a standoff.

Silence. Then the light patter of pacing footsteps.

"Come on back," she called at the rock.

"No."

"This isn't funny. I'm serious about not going in there."

He was winning this one. "That's fine. I won't make you, but I'm not circling back through that way. Good luck finding your way to the base. The route's a little twisty."

There was a decided grunt of exasperation, and her footsteps diminished. Adrian could feel the grin stretching his lips as the footsteps came back. The bright beam of her light shone through the hole and then away again. If he had to guess, purely based on her fear response, he'd say she would do that two more times before attempting the crawl. But he knew he had her. She'd be logical when it came down to it.

It was three more times, but once she got on her knees, she didn't back away. Adrian crouched to help her if needed. The smell of her adrenaline was wafting from the small space, but she didn't pause. The sound of her hurried scrambling preceded her slight tumble into the massive cavern.

"See. Just a few feet." Adrian stood, hand proffered, meeting her death glare with a smug feeling of triumph.

13

WONDER

Clare's Notes:

Someone has to know more about light-bearers, but it's clearly not Adrian or the Therians. My abilities seem to surprise them. Am I different even in this?

Clare brushed the dirt from her palms onto her pants and took Adrian's hand. "For the record, I hate this, and I hate you."

"I'm fairly certain that's not much of a change of situation."

There was a smile hinting on his mouth. He was absolutely impossible.

"Give me one of your words."

"What?" At least the smile was gone.

"I feel like I've earned one of those Italian words you're so fond of."

His brow furrowed in mock seriousness. "For a situation like this, you may be looking for *a fanabla* or perhaps *testa di cazzo*."

"Say it again, slower."

He complied.

"And those mean?"

"Well, *a fanabla* means 'go to Naples,' but we mean it like 'go to hell.' If you'd been to Naples, you'd understand." He chuckled. "The other is a more vulgar way to call someone a 'dickhead.'"

"Those are exactly what I'm looking for. Can I combine them? *A fanabla testa di cazzo!*"

He laughed, and it echoed throughout the chamber. "Your accent needs a lot of work, but I think what's important is that you're trying."

"*A fanabla*, Adrian."

"Your contextual use is excellent."

Clare favored him with a glare. "All right testicle head—"

"Not even close to how that translates."

"—what have you dragged me down here for?" The openness of the space was so much better, and it was almost as if there was a breeze. There wasn't—she didn't think so anyway—but the air wasn't as dense. And there was a lake! Without waiting for her guide, Clare scooped up her flashlight and walked out into the vast cavern.

Even her soft steps cast echoes about. When she reached the edge of the water, she dipped her hand into it and brought the liquid up to her nose. It smelled of minerals, but was otherwise fresh.

"Do you think there are fish in there?" she asked softly. Even whispers carried here.

"It never even occurred to me to wonder." He came to stand next to her, looking over the water. "Perry called this place the amphitheater."

"It suits it."

"He thought so." Adrian looked at her then, eyes golden but not threatening. They roved over her like a person might look at a painting. "It amplifies our experience of the ethereal realm."

"That's the *stretching* place, right? The liminal space?"

He nodded. "There's more danger here. That reality becomes so much more...intrusive." Adrian reached out a hand. She tensed a little for his touch, but instead of touching her, his fingers curled the air in front of her. "The effect it has on your light is stunning."

It was strange to feel bashful about something she'd never even seen. "So, you thought that it might heighten whatever I've been experiencing as well?"

"Yes. Maybe give some clarity to it."

It was her turn to smile. That's why she'd assumed that name. She loved clarity.

"What do I do?"

He shrugged. "Whatever you've been doing."

Whatever the hell that was.

"It may help to sit and let your hands rest on the rock," he said.

Adrian sat, and she followed his lead. The moment her flesh touched the rock, there was a tingle under her palms. It was like a hum without the noise.

"So...that's weird."

"You can feel it then." It was more of a statement, but Clare nodded anyway. Adrian looked at her expectantly. At her hesitation, he added, "I have a suggestion. I'm not sure, but it may be something like when an immortal phases. If so, try letting your cognition go and your deep self rise."

Let her cognition go? Ha. Her mind never shut off, and the thought that whatever was happening could be an immortal trait was definitely discomforting. Still, her inner journalist squirmed with questions, and if this place could answer a few of those, she may as well try.

First step, let her deep self rise. Deep self? Like her inner journalist? There really was no telling with immortal things.

Clare had done an intro to meditation on some app or another. Sitting for minutes and doing nothing was not her idea of a good time, but she tried to remember it now. She looked out over the lake and breathed deeply, feeling the strange sort of humming in the rock. The hum seemed louder, if that was even possible for something that didn't actually make a noise. Clare let the sensation fill her, and then, like she had several times before, she directed her thoughts to Jonathan.

And her world exploded.

Sensations and colors assaulted her senses. Currents of white

The Dark Hours 89

flowed in eddies over the lake. She could also feel Jonathan, awake and burying anguish. Turning to Adrian, she was surprised to see him shrouded in a purple cloud of...energy? She reached out then, like he'd done earlier, to run her hand through it, and her own hand was covered by a golden, fiery glow.

Clare's gasp echoed off the water.

"What does this mean?"

Adrian shook his head. "It means there's something more to light-bearers than we thought."

She waved her hand in front of her face and watched bits of golden color eddy off to join the current that circled in the lake. "Is this what I always look like to you?"

"No. Usually, it's more like sunshine hugging you. This is like fire." He smiled. "It doesn't draw on my instincts like it used to, but it still feels a little dangerous."

That was just the sort of statement that made her inner journalist scream for more, but then again, everything about this created a black hole of curiosity.

"This is like *stretching* but with visuals instead of perceptions. Well, that, and without having to *stretch*."

Adrian blinked. "I hadn't thought of that before, but that's exactly what it's like."

"You don't have to look so surprised. I *am* a writer. It's my job to put things into words." Clare looked around. There was no way she could actually put this kind of beauty into words. Then she remembered something. "Oh! This is a thin place!"

"What?" Based on the look on Adrian's face, this wasn't something he was familiar with, but Clare went on.

"Kenyon, he talked about it when driving me and Jonathan to the warehouse. He said something about there being places in Ireland where the barrier between our world and the spirit world was thin and even humans could see the other side. This has to be what he was talking about. This is a thin place!"

Then there was a look of recognition, but Adrian stopped short of hitting his head with his palm.

"Fuck me. I'm old enough that I should know better than to dismiss the myths of other cultures. I'm surprised Perry didn't make the connection, but he was always more focused on the science side of things." Adrian paused then, lost in thought. "I'll have to tell Meg when I get back to Richmond. She might know if we can utilize it."

"So...now what?"

His eyes snapped back to hers. "Now that I've established that we're dealing with a trait like immortals have, though it seems to operate a little differently than Therian or vampire, we see what we can find out about your kind."

Her kind, like she was some sort of creature. Like him. Her mind revolted against the idea, her stomach clenched, and then the cave popped back into its original state. No more colors or currents. Just Clare, looking at her hands in the dim light, wondering about her "kind."

Adrian's voice was surprisingly gentle when he spoke. "What do you know about your mother?"

The word echoed around her. She remembered the dark-haired woman with gentle eyes and strong arms. Her mom had been quiet but playful at the same time and had hair that smelled like flowers. They'd built tent forts and had dance parties. They'd cuddled to movies and ate cookies.

And then it was over.

Her mom was gone, and her father trudged the family on as best he knew how.

"She grew up in New York, met my dad at NYU, and taught dancing until my brother and I were born. We were in a crash when I was eight. She didn't make it."

So many times she'd said those words: *We were in a crash. She didn't make it.* Curious new friends would ask about her mom. The occasional boyfriend would inquire. It was always shrug it off and say, "We were in a crash. She didn't make it."

Every beautiful thing twisted down to those two sentences.

People would invariably be horrified and offer their condolences, and she would say, "It's okay. It was a long time ago." As if that really changed it, but she'd do anything so they would please move on. Talk about anything else so she could at least pretend to forget. In the end, it'd been easier to just sweep that whole life under the rug and start a new one. A life in which she was successful, and no one ever got close enough that she had to say those words.

The silence in the cave was tangible, and Adrian let it stretch out as he held her in his gaze.

Finally she shook her head and said, "I don't really know anymore. She didn't have any close family. She didn't know her dad, and her mom died the year I was born. So I never met my maternal grandmother."

It had never seemed strange before, but as she said it, the oddity of it struck her. She knew nothing about her mother's family. Clare spent so much time running from her past, she'd never even stopped to think about it instead.

"I have to get back to town."

"Absolutely not." Adrian's voice rose, and the echo emphasized his point.

"I need to talk to my dad."

"That place is a death trap for you," Adrian hissed, trying to keep his voice from the torrent of echos.

"Only at night."

"Are you even thinking? It's not necessary. Meg has resources to pull information on your mother that even your father probably doesn't know. Give me her maiden name, and I'll be back in a couple of days with more information than you know what to do with."

That was going to feel like an eternity while she was stuck in this hell hole.

"Eliana Mayer was her maiden name," Clare said. "Is this experiment over with? Can we go now?"

Adrian nodded, and she followed him back across the cavern to the cave wall. When they came to the crack she'd crawled through, she said, "Wait. I thought you said you weren't circling back through this cavern."

"I lied."

14

WITNESS

Clare's Notes:

I wonder how many survivalists, wilderness trekkers, and hermits were actually Therians. Henry Thoreau, famous poet and loner...and shape-shifter! He definitely had the facial hair for it.

Jonathan needed to focus. David and Sune had the bulk of their parts of the program written and were working out the bugs now. It'd come together quickly. While Jonathan was trying to hold up his end and act normal, Sune could see something was off. That much was obvious. The Therian had asked, twice, how his work was going. Coming from Sune, that was almost an intervention. Each time he asked, Jonathan had to press harder against the door that held everything. He'd shrug and let them assume his issue was concern that they hadn't found his son rather than that Siri had...

It took everything to try and focus on his work. If he thought about anything else, it all crumbled. And he had to hold it together.

The Dark Hours 93

He couldn't even think about why, just that he had to hold it together and do the work.

Like he had when he lived with the vampires.

He knew how to do it, had known even before Adrian told him. And nothing changed really. He was still an outsider, still vulnerable to death, still just a tool. So, coding it was, while another part of his mind wandered down the vast rooms of the Richmond Museum of Art. He'd spent literal hours looking at Monet's *Poppy Field*. Every brush stroke was imprinted beautifully in his memory. And the antiquities area was striking. How had so many things survived so long?

His fingers continued on in their work. His mind, blissfully divided now. Part of him was coding. Part of him was screaming, but that part was locked deep down. And all the while, he was pondering the majesty of a Monet.

———

"YOU CAN COME WITH ME. I plan to leave as soon as the drivers head out."

Miriam would prefer to go alone. Clare wasn't exactly survival savvy, and she'd get farther if someone was covering for her. But if the woman wanted out, Miriam wasn't going to leave her behind.

Clare shook her head. "Being here occasionally makes me want to hold my breath until I lose consciousness. But I'll stay. One: It might give you time to get farther, and two: As much as I hate to admit it, and I really do, Adrian's right. He can probably dig up more info than I could get out of my dad. We don't exactly talk about Mom."

After the Therians had finished with the morning cooking and cleared the kitchen area, Clare had brought Miriam breakfast. Grits were surprisingly something she could hold down. The two of them had used the opportunity to fill each other in on the day before.

Listening to Clare talk about her loss didn't make Miriam's any less, but it was comforting to feel like she wasn't alone in it. That Clare was struggling with the idea of her mom being something other than human was also, in a way, something Miriam could relate to.

Clare took a deep breath. "You could stay here. Adrian said he'd let you know if Meg was a threat."

"Then I'd just be at his mercy instead of hers. Everything they're doing 'for me' has nothing to do with me. Nothing. It's all about the pregnancy. If I keep it, and they know, this will always be my life." Miriam glanced around at the rock walls that once felt so much like home. "No. I have to figure things out for myself."

The compassion in Clare's expression was a balm to her soul. Clare didn't have any other motive. She actually was just worried about her—not her pregnancy, not a cause, just her.

Miriam smiled. "Hey girl, don't worry. I literally went to school for this. I'm amazing at wilderness survival, and some time in the woods is all I need to clear my mind and figure out what I'm doing."

She was only half joking. But even as she said it, certainty appeared in all of the overwhelming question marks. She would escape to the woods, get far from here, and things would look different.

A plan began to form, a next step that would lead to another. The future was still too much to think about, but for the moment, she could manage thinking about today.

The volume of chatter trickling in from the next cavern rose slightly, and the two of them went out to meet it. The drivers were saying their farewells before going. Adrian noted her and Clare's entrance and came over to them.

He studied them before saying, "If the next convoy's not for a week, I'll come back before then."

"Don't worry." Miriam still wanted to call him Ugly, but his crazy ass had actually been trying to rise above himself. "I won't do anything stupid. Of course, I can't speak for Clare."

The way his head whipped over and his eyes narrowed was hilarious...for a moment. But as Clare denied any plans for wrongdoing, Miriam had to wonder at his protectiveness. She could think of only two reasons, and she didn't like either one. They'd taken Clare's

The Dark Hours 95

blood and told her, back when Richmond was still safe, that she could return to her family. So, either he saw her as a tool that he was going to keep for his own uses, or he felt some sort of attraction for her.

"All right, Ugly, I think it's time to go."

Adrian looked up from their conversation to see the rest of the drivers had left. He nodded. And Clare watched him go. Uh-uh. This was getting addressed. Miriam pulled her back into her bedroom.

"You can*not* be serious," she said in a forced whisper.

"What?"

"You're attracted to him."

"Adrian? Oh, absolutely not."

"So, you weren't just flirting with him?"

"God, no," Clare said. "I most certainly was not."

"Tell me again why you're staying in this cave you hate so much or why you were staying in that warehouse where you felt trapped?"

"I'm here because Richmond is crawling with vampires!" Clare's own whispers were getting heated. "And I was at the warehouse because I want to write something that could save lives. The more information I can get, the better. And besides, Adrian's an asshole."

Miriam might have smiled to hear Clare finally use some profanity, but using it now only furthered her suspicions. The reasons seemed logical, but the lady doth protest too much.

"All right. Listen, I'm not going to tell you how to live your life—"

"I'm not interested in him! Why does everyone seem to think that?"

Miriam held up a hand and continued, "—but just remember where all of this got me, okay?"

Clare looked like she wanted to say more, but she just nodded.

"Good. Time's wasting. I need you to take my bag down the central corridor to the fourth branch on the left. It's not a squeeze, but they shouldn't be working there yet. Leave it about a hundred feet in. Once I'm gone, buy me as much time as you can. I'm sure the whole playing on sympathy bit can earn me one more day and night holed up in Perry's room before they need to start work on it."

Meg was going to be so pissed, and her fire would likely fall on Clare. Miriam took a deep breath and tried one more time.

"Are you sure you don't want to come? I can modify my plan. Who knows what Meg'll do when all this gets out."

"We both know I'm not sleeping out there with the spiders and snakes. I'll stay here and deal with the werewolves."

Clare smiled then pulled her in for a tight hug. An unspoken knowledge hung in the air. Clare's companionship had been instant and excessively loyal for the short amount of time they'd known each other. And if things went according to plan, Miriam might never talk to her again.

When Miriam's best friend Marcus had committed suicide in high school, her mother had told her that grief was a sign that love was present. She said that when grief turns to anger, you create change to make the loss matter. Those words had propelled her forward. Her plans to open a survival camp, her entire future had been shaped by that loss. Now those plans were gone, and there was no change to make these new losses matter.

The tears started small, but Clare held her tighter and soon everything was pouring out: the loss of certainty. Dreams. Love. All of it came out in great heaving sobs and in gasps and wails that rebounded in the cave around her. But Clare's tear-streaked face had given sacred witness to it, and it too had been held. Sharing her private pain hadn't been part of the plan, but there'd been more healing in it than her weeks of isolated mourning.

Time had a strange quality in grief. It could have been ten minutes or an hour when they finally got up from where she'd sank to the floor. Without a word, Clare grabbed the bag and disappeared.

Miriam headed to the kitchen to rummage through the food supplies, her hunger roaring for the first time in weeks. She eyed a piece of leftover cornbread. Well, her stomach wasn't turning at the thought of it.

Several pieces and no nausea later, Miriam was back in the bedroom squeezing through a small opening behind Perry's dresser. Clare would move the dresser back into place when she came "to

The Dark Hours 97

bring her lunch." The squeeze was tight for about twenty feet. How Perry managed it was unimaginable, but finally, the way opened and joined a sort of corridor. Her green bag was waiting for her, fat and heavy with supplies.

And with it—freedom.

15

RISK

Clare's Notes:

Did ancient Therians and vampires compete for the same food sources? Humans and animals. Maybe that's the reason they're hardwired to hate each other.

Though she was sure no one knew she'd left, Miriam's heart pounded as she hurried down the wooded slope. Even with a trekking pole, it was tricky. The stream was only about two miles down, but two mountain miles were very different than two city miles.

The first time Perry had brought her here, explaining how water would disrupt their ability to track her physically or otherwise, she'd thought she finally understood the risk she was taking in loving him.

But she'd mistakenly thought the risk only affected her.

Now, here she was fleeing to the ocean, wondering if her family thought she was dead. They'd all be crushed, but it was probably the worst on her daddy. He'd always been protective of his baby girl. But

The Dark Hours   99

how could she let any of them know she was okay without endangering them?

Then there was the matter of the pregnancy that was never supposed to happen. One of the few things Perry had been very open about was their need for protection. And she'd trusted a thin sheet of latex against supernatural sperm.

God, she'd been so stupid.

All the red flags had been there brazenly shouting at her to turn back, and yet, she now found herself on the slope of a mountain, pregnant and alone. And furious.

He had no right. Perry was ancient. He *knew* the risks, and yet he did this. If he'd really loved her, he'd have let Adrian Z.I.P. her.

Adrian.

That fucker. He'd had more sense than both of them and more compassion. But here she was trekking down a mountain with only the thinnest scrap of a plan and still ignoring that asshole's advice. Was it really advice when it involved giving up your whole life? If she was going to do that, it would be on her terms.

And then she was at the stream. Her body was hot with the effort, and the cold water that sank into her boots and pants added to the backdrop of relief. She'd have to make a fire to dry them out later, but she made it this far. Now it was just a matter of putting one foot in front of the other until she found a good spot to stop for the night. She knew what she was looking for too. The stream would widen as it flowed down, and eventually there'd be a sand bank that rose up and split the water around it.

Eventually.

It was well before evening when exhaustion set in. She was used to hiking hard terrain. It should've been hours before she was this tired. Just another reminder that even her body was conspiring against her. It was another exhausting hour of working her way downhill before she found a sand bank that rose enough for her to build a Dakota fire pit. She sat on the sandy bank, wet to the waist from several falls on the slick rocks, and chewed on some jerky.

The thing in her belly apparently felt like cooperating today, and all the food stayed down. Another day of this was ahead, if she made good time. If she didn't...

Miriam shook her head. She couldn't go there. Even the thought of getting through the night was overwhelming right now. It was enough to get through the next thing. And with a chilly fall evening ahead of her, the next thing was a fire hole.

WITHOUT CLOCKS, the passage of time was marked by food, and after dinner, Clare had been exhausted. As well as covered in cave dust. The stuff had worked its way into places even she wasn't aware existed. Every inch of skin, hell, every pore was inhabited. Standing under the shower, she could see the tool marks in the stone and couldn't imagine how many years it'd taken Perry to open these caves. One day of working at it, and she'd had enough.

That night, she fell into bed, and despite her concern for Miriam, sleep came quickly.

Breakfast was ham, eggs, and biscuits. Clare got two plates and carried them back to Miriam's bedroom. With all the work she'd done, downing two plates would be easy.

The kitchen connected directly to the bedroom, but the "doorway" was more of an angled hallway. Clare was already in the room before she saw Aberdeen standing at the dresser.

Her abrupt stop swished the food on the plate.

"What have you done?"

Clare stammered, but before anything coherent could come out, Aberdeen continued, "Where is she?"

"I don't know."

"Why would you do this?" The question was soft, almost pleading. "Anything could happen to her or the baby out there. She's not safe."

Clare knew this answer. "She didn't want to stay here, and Meg wouldn't let her leave."

"Miriam's planning on hiding from her," Aberdeen said, a look of revelation on her face. "But Meg would never allow that. You have to know she'll do everything to find her."

"To find her grandbaby," Clare said. "Not Miriam."

Aberdeen's eyes narrowed then widened. "You're not suggesting...? No. Miriam wouldn't. She loved Perry."

"I don't know what she's going to do, but she's going to be free to make her own choice."

Aberdeen snarled, eyes turning a deep amber, and Clare dropped the dishes. It'd been easy to forget that under that sweet exterior was a beast, and for a moment, her body froze. But Aberdeen didn't continue to phase. Egg yolk oozed at Clare's feet while those animal eyes stared.

Then Clare realized: Aberdeen was *stretching*. Finally, she drew in a sharp breath.

"Water."

Clare smiled. It worked.

"We'll have to search—form search parties and—"

"Stop it! Can't you just let her be? Let her grieve and process."

"You don't understand what this baby means to us. It's a rare gift," Aberdeen said, and there was pleading in her words.

"And I think Miriam will see that but not through you forcing it on her. What she needed was to be supported, not frightened and bullied."

"You can't understand." Aberdeen shook her head, a wounded look in her eyes. "We never should've trusted you."

Clare sat down on the bed while Aberdeen left to spread the news of her betrayal. Shouts and exclamations erupted through the caves. She couldn't focus on that or the pain of Aberdeen's reprobation.

Instead, she reached out, *stretching* to see if she could find Miriam herself. The connection was there and with surprising strength, but it seemed to lead to a sort of static. In the crackling fog, she could almost discern the movement of Miriam's life but couldn't touch her through it. Couldn't warn her. Hopefully, enough time had passed that Miriam was lost to them.

Jonathan was up early.

Adrian and the convoy had come back the day before but had been tied up discussing logistics with Meg. So, Jonathan brought to mind the looming *A Sunday Afternoon on the Island of La Grande Jatte* with its hundreds of thousands of dots to peruse and went to the control room. Adrian would likely come there when he was free anyway.

The dayshift had recently gone, and Sune and David must have just come from dinner. The smell of chicken and gravy still hung on them. Jonathan hadn't been situated long when a beep signaled someone in the drive. He couldn't see the screen from where he was sitting, but Sune cocked his head and pressed the button that opened the gate.

The young man who walked into the control room several minutes later had purple spiked hair, painted nails, and something almost feminine about him.

"Uncle!" His boisterous voice filled the room as he spread his arms wide.

Sune nodded in reply, eyes crinkling. "David. Jonathan. This is Akito."

"I see they have you working with all kinds of riffraff these days," Akito said. His nose wrinkled as he took in Jonathan. "What's wrong with that one?"

Jonathan could have asked the same question. He took a deep breath to try for a better scent.

"Hey pal. Respect the privacy," Akito said, giving Jonathan a look.

"A lot has happened," was all Sune replied.

"Yeah, I figured when you sent me a message saying, 'leave Richmond,' but bringing in fresh meat and bloodsuckers at the same time must mean we're completely desperate," he said. "So, I'm here. Where can I help?"

"That would be the opposite of leaving," Sune said.

"I get it. I'm young, but I think if you're enlisting humans and

The Dark Hours 103

more vampires, you can use all the help you can get. Look, I brought my shit and everything. I'm prepared to stay a while and get us through whatever's happening."

He didn't just look young, he was newly turned too. How new was hard to say. Akito wasn't threatened by a vampire in the room, but Sune clearly didn't think it was safe for him to be in the city.

"The situation is bad. All Therians should leave," Sune said.

"If you're staying, I'm staying."

Sune's voice took on more firmness. "Meg is planning to relocate *all* our operations."

"Holy fuck. Seriously?" Akito spun the chair Clare liked to use and straddled it backwards. "We're abandoning the city?"

"We are talking with the other tribal leaders. Meg is trying to contain this situation before going, but the long-term plan is to leave."

Akito's face fell. "I started over here. There's people here I care about."

"All the more reason to leave." Jonathan hadn't meant to say it out loud, but he continued, "Take them with you, and go."

"Oh, ho. That's rich, bloodsucker. I'm not taking advice from you."

"Jonathan just lost his human wife in this."

Jonathan wasn't sure if Sune said it to convince his nephew or come to his own defense, but Akito had the decency to look horrified.

"Shit. I'm so sorry, man. Shit! But I didn't even know vamps could remember their families."

Jonathan was trying not to, trying only to exist in the present moment.

"He's like Adrian," Kitsune said.

He was nothing like Adrian, but Akito nodded. "Okay. I get why he's here then, but you're letting a human help too. And I don't want to start over again. Is there a chance Meg might decide to stay, or you? You've given her enough."

Sune didn't answer, and Jonathan couldn't read his tight expression.

David spoke for the first time. "Can he work code? We could actually use another hand in the fire."

"I don't, but I can learn."

There was a flash of color in Sune's eyes, and he stood. "Come. Speak with me."

David arched a brow at their exit. "Ten dollars says the nephew stays," he said.

"You know they can still hear you," Jonathan said dryly.

"Ten dollars says the nephew stays," David said, raising his voice more.

Jonathan chuckled. David's "I don't care" attitude landed on the enjoyable side of the spectrum. He briefly wondered if this was how Adrian had been before hundreds of years had pushed the trait to the completely intolerable side.

"If I had money, I might take that bet."

"And I'd be ten dollars richer. Under all the duty and seriousness, Sune's a marshmallow. And his nephew clearly has him wrapped around his finger."

"Clearly." Jonathan was unable to match David's sarcastic abilities but was willing to try.

"Scoff all you want, but when Sune comes back, silently put out with his nephew in tow, you'll have to acknowledge my superior abilities."

"And what do I get if I win?"

"Taking the bet, then?"

"Fine. Yes, if you win, I'll acknowledge that you're evolutionarily advanced. What do I get if I win?"

David clicked his tongue. "How about the award for best vampire I know?"

"Who else do you know? Adrian? That's hardly a compliment. How about you admit I'm the better coder?"

"You wound me, but I'll win the bet, so deal."

Jonathan and David fell into a zone where anything but the job at hand didn't exist. However, the longer the time stretched, the more cheerful David's keystrokes seemed, until over an hour later when

The Dark Hours 105

Sune trudged back in. He thrust himself into his chair and started typing furiously. He didn't look when Akito came into the room and pulled up a chair between his uncle and David.

"So, I just open the program and look through the hits?"

Sune grunted and nodded while David pushed back from his console and turned his whole body toward Jonathan in expectation.

"My liege. You've bested me with your superior abilities," Jonathan said with a mock bow.

Both Therians looked up, but David simply nodded in acceptance and turned back to his screen.

A few minutes later, the silence was broken. "Oh, that's cool. It lets you know why each shot was flagged."

If it was possible to scowl without scowling, Sune was doing it. He grunted again in response. David glanced sidelong at Jonathan but kept working, and Jonathan smiled, surprised at how normal this all felt.

He couldn't even hear the part of him that was still screaming.

16

NOT ALONE

Clare's Notes:

I should never have children.

Miriam had only been able to sleep a few hours until the fire went out. It was cold, her clothes were only marginally drier, and she was hungrier than she could ever remember being. Chewing down some jerky was neither filling nor particularly enjoyable, but her stomach quit making noises. Doing her best to cover her camp, she packed up and headed out.

This was stupid, traveling by stream in the dark. She stayed near the bank where there were less slick rocks and more sand, but it was still treacherous. A large, yellow moon had risen, casting pale shadows and offering some light, but she was still out of her mind to do this.

"What was I supposed to do?" she ground out at the moon. "You left me. I can't live that life without you... I can't do this alone."

Then, she felt it, a small thump on the inside of her body. It was too early to feel movement. Wasn't it? But then it happened again. For

The Dark Hours 107

a light touch, it carried so much force. She dropped her trekking pole, and let her hands go around her lower belly where the mystery was.

"Not alone, huh," she said softly. "Hey there." A rush of protectiveness welled up from deep within her and along with it, more of those damned tears. But she hadn't let herself have these ones yet. These were for the life inside her because, in the quiet, she finally knew: "I want you. I want you so bad. But I'm afraid for you. How are we going to do this without your daddy? How am I supposed to keep you safe if you're like him? It would be amazing if you were like him. He was the best man: strong, wild, and funny. And so kind. Baby, if you grew to be kind like him..."

Miriam looked up at the moon again. "I miss you so much, and I'm so mad at you, but somehow you're gonna have to help us with this."

She picked up her trekking pole and continued down the water, her mind catching up to her heart.

"I was going to take us out to sea for a little bit, but I think we're going to your grandparents, instead. I got some things to sort out, and your Poppop is the best at sorting things. That's what he does. Spends all his time in dusty rooms sorting through old letters and making sense of things. Used to send me to sleep with that deep voice reading some old scrap that I didn't even understand. But I knew he was there, and I knew he understood it."

As she made her way down the slope, Miriam continued to talk. Her heart, which had seemed crushed beyond repair, was full of so many things: purpose, anger, readiness, love. She'd grieved and would still grieve, but the future was morphing in front of her. Her old plans and old life were gone. There was only one thing she was sure of now, and she was sure of it with all her being.

She was keeping this baby.

SHE'D HIKED countless miles across wilderness territory. Her body was fit, but by the time the sky began to lighten, Miriam was sore everywhere. There were small waterfalls to avoid, and walking in the shallow stream took constant balance and vigilance. Even with a trekking pole and the moon providing light, she fell again and again.

Miriam was tired, she was hungry, but she was off the damn mountain. There were several streams near Perry's den. He'd chosen this one for a possible escape route because it led straight into a small town. She could still remember the sound of his voice, the look in his eyes as he said, "Should anything happen, follow that stream all the way down."

Survival was about being prepared and ready because things would go wrong. You had to have a backup for everything. Should you lose your ferro rod, you also had matches tucked in with the MRE's. The back of your hatchet was also a hammer. Should that get lost, you at least had a knife and pommel.

She and Perry had made this contingency plan, not counting on it happening, but because in survival that's what you did. But in none of their imaginings was she pregnant and running from an entire tribe of Therians. She'd been taught that nature will always surprise you. This was not a surprise.

It was a razing of everything.

Miriam lowered herself down on a large rock that parted the water and grabbed a protein bar from her pack. The sun was cresting the horizon with a riot of color. As she ate, a small smile came to her face.

"What do you think of the name Phoenix? You're gonna rise from these ashes and be fierce and free."

It was true, though she didn't know how she knew. The knowledge was just there, as much a fact as the water her feet were resting in.

"I bet your grandma Meg will hate it. It's not a very wolf name. But there's no guarantee you'll be Therian." Miriam sighed and looked down at her stomach. A small bulge was present.

There shouldn't be, not yet, not this early.

A tear found its way down her cheek. She didn't even know how to plan for this kind of survival. Miriam blew out a breath and swiped the tear away.

The Dark Hours 109

"Don't mind me. I've still got a lot to sort out." There was a slight fluttering motion inside her, and she chuckled. "All right. You ready then? We've still got a few miles."

"How could you let her go?" Meg's eyes were yellow, and her face was contorted in rage. Adrian stood behind her, fury lighting his own features but betrayal darkening his eyes.

When the Therians couldn't find Miriam, they sent someone to hike down and call Richmond. By the feel of it, it was probably around midnight when Meg and Company made it back up. Meanwhile the Therians had her on "house arrest," as if she could go anywhere anyway. But Clare was not backing down from this fight.

"This isn't your choice. Either of you!"

"And it wasn't yours," Meg growled. "Do you know the kind of danger she could be in?"

"I have an idea." Clare held their gaze. She'd been captured by vampires and wasn't ignorant of the stakes. "If Miriam hadn't felt trapped and forced maybe she wouldn't have thought running was the only option. I can't imagine how much this baby must mean to you, but her life matters too! And when you devalued that, how was she supposed to trust you at all? She can trust herself, and now you'll have to do the same."

It was like there was a sizzle in the air, and in an instant, Meg had Clare's neck in an iron grip. A toothy, wicked face was inches from her own.

"I don't need your lecture," Meg growled. "Tell me where she went."

Clare's heart was racing, every warning bell her body and mind had was blaring, but she took a breath against the hot fingers around her throat.

"She didn't tell me, and if you think she would, you're grossly underestimating her." The pressure around her neck increased. "Stop. You're hurting me."

"Compared to the life she carries, your life means nothing to me."

Clare was finding it harder to breathe. "That's...exactly why...your grandson...showed her...how to...hide from you."

With a snarl of frustration, Meg flung her onto the rough rock floor. Clare lay there gasping, knees aching, arms scraped and bleeding. When she looked up, she saw a crowd of eyes. So many different expressions: anger, sadness, hostility. Adrian's face was a surprised blank. The room was filled with tension that could break in any direction, but Aberdeen moved first.

"I'm angry too, but this is not how I fight," she said, splintering from the group and kneeling by Clare.

Aberdeen kept her hand held out until Clare reached back. Gently, she grabbed her arms and looked over the scrapes.

"Meg was never human, doesn't know human pain." Aberdeen didn't look back at Meg. "I'm sorry. I don't even know if we have any first aid here."

"I'll be fine. They're not deep." Her neck hurt more than anything. Aberdeen helped her up, and her knees protested loudly, competing for priority.

"I'm going to take her to Perry's room until a decision is made on what to do with her," Aberdeen announced. Despite the words, it came out like a threat to those gathered. She stayed by Clare's side as she shuffled gingerly back to the kitchen to clean the debris from her cuts.

"Seems a shame," Clare winced as Aberdeen dabbed a wet rag at a scrape on her forearm, "to be letting my blood go down the drain." It was a sad attempt at humor to break the tension, but the other woman didn't bite. So Clare gave up any pretense and let herself sit with the tight feeling. "Thank you. I have no idea what that cost you, but thank you."

"It would've cost me more to do nothing." Aberdeen wrung the blood from the rag, wet it again, and went to the other arm. "You really don't understand, and you can't. You're human. But Meg has wrapped herself in this world so much she can't see the one you live in. That doesn't excuse either of you." The Therian drew in a weary breath. "I don't agree with you, and your actions have complicated everything, but that doesn't justify the way you were treated. You can't handle someone like property because they have something you want. Your life is different than ours, but it's not less than."

Somewhere Clare had read that "us" and "them" was one of the first concepts to develop in children. The fear of strangers was supposed to keep them safe at an early age. It looked like humans weren't the only ones afflicted with drawbacks to that concept.

"Either way," Aberdeen continued, "as much as I disagree with it, I thought what you did was loyal and brave, and I can respect that."

"Yes well, it seems idiotic bravery is something I have in abundance."

Aberdeen smiled at that.

"Something you and Perry had in common." They looked up at the voice to see Adrian leaning in the shadows of the doorway, and Clare felt her stomach clench. Whether it was anger or anxiety, she had no idea. He pushed off and came into the room.

"Are you okay?" As Aberdeen had, he reached for her arm but didn't take it. And Clare drew away.

"You won't be if you touch me."

He tensed and dropped his hand. And then Clare realized how that must have sounded.

"I didn't mean it like that. I mean, my blood. It'll hurt you."

"Oh." Adrian swiped at his face. "Well, I don't think it will. Not anymore." He held out his hand again.

Clare looked to Aberdeen for some sort of confirmation or assurance, but the woman just shrugged. Guess that went under things you didn't ask a newly Therian-vampire hybrid.

She held her hand to him, and he took it. His grasp was warm, and he didn't draw back from her. Must be okay. Then, a tremor went through him, and Aberdeen gasped. Clare snapped her attention up to his face. His eyes. They were black, and she hadn't seen them like that since...that night. But they were encircled with Therian gold. He glanced up at them, then back down.

"I can see her veins better this way. Other arm."

Clare brought up the other hand, and he turned it over looking at the still bleeding arm. He swiped a drop with his thumb. Definitely didn't hurt him then, but it felt exposing and strangely intimate. She had to fight the urge not to pull her arms back to herself.

"It's not deep, but the one on the left is going to be a bleeder. Nicked a small vein." He looked up at Aberdeen. "You'll want to get a strip of cloth about a hands-width for a makeshift bandage. The pressure and absorption will help."

And with a nod, she was gone, leaving Clare alone and bleeding with a vampirish...thing. He rinsed the rag Aberdeen had been using and held it to Clare's arm. She hissed a little at the sting.

"That's very rude," Adrian said matter-of-factly.

"What?"

"Hissing at an immortal. You can't imagine the things that translates to."

"Are you...joking with me right now?" Clare looked at him, but his face gave nothing away.

"Just educating you. I know how much you love fact gathering."

"I see," she said with a smile. "So, it doesn't hurt anymore?"

"No. There's a strange sort of tingle to it, but that's it."

She probably shouldn't ask. She knew that, but she couldn't stop herself. "Is it hard, seeing blood? Does it make you...want it?"

His eyes flicked up for the first time. "Are you afraid of me?"

The question surprised her. Not because he asked it, but because the answer had changed. "I'm not, actually. Just curious. I was afraid with Meg just now, but more afraid of pain than for my life. If I thought she'd really hurt me, I could've called my Watcher."

Adrian's mouth dropped, then curled into a smile. "*Madonna Santa*, my track record with underestimating people is getting worse. Remind me not to piss you off anymore."

The compliment made her feel inordinately pleased and, oddly enough, powerful. Everyone respected Adrian's prowess, and though she was still figuring out her place in this world, his respect of her ability made her more confident in it. "Are we calling a truce then?"

The Dark Hours 113

"Oh, I wouldn't go that far. Fighting may be as near a form of affection as I'm capable of."

Clare laughed. "Well then you must love me." Her brain processed the words as soon they left her mouth. No! That was not what she meant! Oh hell. And Adrian's stiffened posture only confirmed how he must've taken it.

"You should hold pressure on that," he said, and he let go of the rag.

She placed her hand on it as a feeling of déjà vu hit. That was what he'd said that night in her room when the blood had soaked through her bandage. Clare's brain was trying to reconcile the idea of these two instances, two different versions of Adrian. She looked down at the rag, pink with blood, and when she looked up, he'd done exactly what he did that first time.

He'd disappeared.

17

TRANSMISSION

Clare's Notes:

Okay. So Watchers are only on one side of the liminal space. Humans are only on the other. Vampires and Therians can travel both and affect both. I can travel both and can act like a conduit for my Watcher. Light-bearers are not immortal, but I'm definitely more than human.

So what am I?

Jonathan was being crushed. Pain radiated through his body, and he couldn't move.

"I don't care that he's not there," Siri seethed into his mind. "You find a way, and you bring him to me. He could be feeding at this moment! How can I better communicate this? Shall I do this to your son perhaps?"

Then Siri was surrounding him. Her essence pushing in and lighting every surface with slices of pain.

The Dark Hours

This could *not* happen to Zeph. There was no other way to prove to her that he was telling the truth. So, Jonathan did the only thing he could think of: He lowered his defenses, and let her further in.

She flooded him, her soul violating his own. The only defense he had was the numbness that blanketed him as he gave up what she wanted. He brought up the memory of Adrian coming, of being unable to see him, of his sudden departure. She wouldn't be able to see it, but she should be able to track all the emotions attached to each person and follow the implications. Adrian and Meg were gone. Even if he'd wanted to trust them to get him out of this, they weren't here to help him or his son now.

She'd won. She held the trump card because he would do anything to keep her from harming his baby.

Anything.

The pain stopped as she sifted through his mind. She was deep enough inside him that he could feel her pleasure at his acquiescence and the knowledge that he was hiding nothing. But that was short-lived. It came because she thought it meant she'd get what she wanted, but Jonathan was truly trapped here with no way to communicate with Adrian. Except Clare—

It was too late to hide the aha moment or try and make his mind blank. Siri's own being flared with malicious interest. "Tell me," was all she said.

She had a special place in her soul for despising Clare. There was no way this could be glossed over.

"Sometimes Clare can sense what I'm feeling."

"The light-bearer has some sort of bond to you!" There was more venom in her words than it was possible to communicate audibly. A jealous hatred of Clare radiated off of Siri. "How is that even possible?"

"I don't know. No one knows."

But Siri was clawing at the idea. There was no more information to be had from Jonathan, but she was forming her plan.

"Someone knows, but no matter. Use that. Get her to send him to you."

"I'm not even sure it'll work. My distress hasn't gotten to her so far."

An ominous calm was growing in Siri's being. "I think I know a way."

And suddenly he knew what she intended. "No! Please, no. Hurt me more. Don't hurt him. Don't hurt my baby. I'll do anything. You know I will."

"Just be sure to lead Adrian where I showed you. I know you could find my nest, but I'm well guarded here." She let the truth of that seep into him. "If you show up here, I will peel your son's skin from his body strip by strip while you watch."

"Yes. Okay. And I'll contact Clare. I can reach her. You don't have to do anything else."

But she'd somehow brought Zeph's sleeping life into the space with him.

"I'm begging you. Please!"

He reached for his son's life. She gripped his soul tightly, but he pushed with everything he was. Then she was gone. Relief filled him, and he drew his son's life into his own. He folded himself around his boy.

Then, pain radiated from his small being in large spikes.

She had crushed a finger and flooded both father and son with agony and terror.

***

CLARE GASPED AWAKE. Something was wrong. Very wrong. Her movement triggered the low nighttime lights in Perry's room.

Aberdeen had been resting in a chair next to her but was instantly alert.

"What's wrong?"

What *was* wrong? Clare tried to shake the sleep from her mind and orient herself in the damp, duskiness of the cave. There was nothing here, but it felt like her heart was breaking.

No, not hers.

The Dark Hours 117

Jonathan's.

And she was there. His life was like a vortex of pain. There was no separating out strands, no nuance of being, just a whipping ice storm of torment. And she couldn't endure it.

There were tears on her cheeks when she was once again aware of her body in the cave. She was on her feet before Aberdeen got out the first word of protest. Her bruised knees felt even worse than they had when she went to sleep, but she'd had worse and still managed to escape a vampire compound. The Therian was much quicker than her on a good day though, and Aberdeen blocked the doorway to the kitchen before Clare got there.

"You need to stay here while tempers are high and they're figuring things out. Just tell me what's going on."

Maybe it was because she was still groggy, but Clare didn't think about what she did next. She grabbed Aberdeen's hand and *stretched* Jonathan's pain to her.

Aberdeen jerked her hand back, eyes wide.

"I need to talk to Adrian."

Clare pushed past her, despite feeling a sudden drain on her already depleted energy. Aberdeen, her mouth open in a stunned "O," didn't resist this time.

"What was that," the Therian managed to get out.

It hadn't been planned or thought of. Clare had acted on some instinct and done something she didn't even know was possible to do. But she didn't have the mental space to deal with it now.

Motion activated lights flicked on in the kitchen area as she walked through. Aberdeen trotted up next to her.

"At least wait for me. I took up for you. You can't let them think I'm not up to the task of keeping you out of trouble."

"I don't think anyone's up to that task." Adrian sat up from the couch in the living room as the lights flicked on around him.

Funny, she'd never thought the sight of him would fill her with such relief. The play of expression on his face went from humored to concerned, and he was on his feet before she got to him.

"What?"

She grabbed his hand. It was harder this time. It took a strength she wasn't familiar with using, and the instincts that had guided her action the last time stumbled over her conscious intention. Clare couldn't manage it for more than a few breaths, but Adrian didn't jerk away when the pain hit.

"Jonathan?"

She nodded.

"Come on."

Adrian didn't release her hand but led the way through the central cave that the Therians had been operating in and down to the bunks. They'd picked an off-shoot that was long and somewhat narrow. The sound of trickling water reverberated up from somewhere. It was perfect for a dormitory. The low lights were on, and though a few were actually sleeping, Meg and a handful of others were engaged in heated, whispered conversation. It abruptly stopped when Adrian came in with Clare and Aberdeen following.

Meg's nostrils flared. So, she was still on her crap list. Oh well. It was totally worth it. Meg's eyes traveled down to the hand Adrian was holding. It was like a spotlight was shining hot on that hand alone. They both dropped their grip.

"Shove the debate, Meg. There's a problem," Adrian said. To Aberdeen, "Make sure they give us a moment." And he walked past everyone and further down the corridor.

Clare snorted as she weaved after him. What a power move. He didn't wait for a response because he wasn't going to argue or talk about it. He was going to do exactly what he wanted. And he *knew* Meg was going to follow. Clare wasn't sure if it was impressive or manipulative assholery. But Meg's footsteps stalked up from behind them.

"What the hell is going on!" Meg brushed past Clare and faced Adrian.

"There's a problem with Jonathan." Adrian turned to Clare. "Show her."

She blinked and took a deep breath as Meg brought the full force

The Dark Hours

of her murderous glare on Clare. Okay then. Her turn. She took Meg's hand.

She was getting better. Finding the part of her that could walk in the liminal space was beginning to feel like reaching out for a friend rather than dragging a corpse up from the bottom of a lake. But even without that, Clare could sense Jonathan. The moment she reached out at all, his pain was as loud as if he were screaming. The problem was transmitting that sense, and this time no amount of fumbling worked to push it to Meg. It reminded her of middle school gym class: two push-ups in and her arms refused to give one more. Whatever she'd used before was spent.

And Meg was shifting her weight impatiently.

"I'm sorry. It's not working." Clare dropped Meg's hand but looked at Adrian. "You'll have to do it."

"Do what," Meg asked as Adrian huffed.

"I'm not even sure what you're fucking doing."

How could he not know? It wasn't like she was pulling a rabbit out of a hat. They were the ones who knew about *stretching*. She was just *stretching* Jonathan's pain to them. Or maybe she was connecting them to him... She honestly didn't know what the hell she was doing either. And they were both looking at her.

Clare bit her thumb, then said, "It feels like grabbing his pain and touching it to you."

Meg's eyebrow arched, and she and Adrian seemed to engage in a silent conversation that involved a multitude of pointed looks.

In the end, Meg shook her head. "This doesn't prove anything. I can just *stretch* to him and feel it myself."

"She didn't *need* to."

"She's only connected to Jonathan."

"I'm right here," Clare said. "And actually, it seems to be getting stronger. I caught a sense of Miriam the other day."

As soon as she said it, she knew that was the wrong thing to say. Meg's head snapped to her, eyes narrow. She didn't look at Adrian but snapped her fingers in the air and said, "That thin place. We're going. Now."

Adrian, who'd seemed in charge of this interaction moments before, only nodded and turned to lead the way.

"Don't I get a say in this?"

"No," Meg said, and Clare could feel pressure building. Meg was ready, should she refuse.

Absolutely ridiculous. Trapped between two immortals and being marched down a dark cave tunnel.

"You people are all a little extra dramatic, you know that?"

Meg didn't answer, but up ahead, Clare was sure she heard a low, masculine chuckle.

18

SUFFOCATING

Clare's Notes:

So there's clearly the physical world and another world layered on top of it. If this is another dimension, and it's populated with Watchers, are there still more dimensions populated with other things??

The trek back to the amphitheater was every bit as suffocating as she remembered but worse this time as she was groggy and still sore. Her knees protested especially when she bent down for the crawl through. By the time they stood at the lake edge, Clare was no longer curious. She was tired, annoyed, and worried. All this felt like a pointless game.

Meg's eyes went yellow, and she cast an appreciative glance about the space. Her eyes stopped on Clare.

"Ms. Zetler, when Adrian first asked me to intervene to keep you from the vampires, I told him you weren't worth the trouble. Since then, you have personally been the catalyst for more pain than I could've imagined."

Harsh but not unwarranted.

"I want nothing more than to dump you back in the middle of Richmond and be done with you. And I'm quite certain the invading vampires would repay you more than adequately for my pain."

Clare's gasp echoed off the water. She hadn't been sure what to expect from Meg, but it wasn't this. She glanced toward Adrian. He gave a slight shake of his head as Meg continued.

"And I would celebrate your loss." The slow, soft words caused Clare to flush with hot anger, but Meg continued. "Others, however, think this rash and have suggested everything from relocation to continued partnership." She practically spat out the last word, and it caught and bounced off the cave's surface. "*If* you want to continue with us, you'll do what I say, or I *will* personally take you to the most infested place in Richmond and drop you there at twilight. I don't have the time or energy to deal with your ill-conceived notions of heroism while trying to save both the city and my grandchild!"

Clare could feel her body shaking with rage, and a not small part of her was surprised she didn't feel scared or helpless under the threat. Oh, Meg could try...but unlike Adrian, Clare knew how to pick her battles. She hadn't made it where she did in her career without the ability to grit through to a fake smile and give a "yes, sir" when needed. It was different when the authority in question could kill you, and Clare wouldn't forget the threat. But within all that vitriol and bluster, Meg was giving her a choice. She didn't need to poke the proverbial bear, not yet at least, because Clare knew what she wanted.

Maybe it was part professional curiosity or because she'd finally started actually living. And who other than immortals knew what the hell to do with what was happening to her or how to dig up information on her mom? What there wasn't, was a part that wanted to go back to how things were before all this. Or a part that wanted to be brutally murdered by vampires. Those were both missing.

So, she unclenched her fists and met the intensity of Meg's stare. Forcing a calm into her voice that she didn't feel, Clare asked, "What do you want me to do?"

"Use this place and find Miriam."

The Dark Hours   123

Of course. That said, Meg didn't say Clare had to tell her where she was, and as a writer, she could be very clever with words. "Then what?"

"One step at a time. First, can you find her?"

She could handle that and decide at each step if that particular request was doable. If nothing else it bought her time, but she didn't know if Jonathan had time. Just the memory of his pain made her stomach clench.

"I'll try, but what about Jonathan?"

"At least we know where he is," Meg said. "When we're done, I can send someone back to check on him."

It wasn't ideal, but it was a start, and a little more give from Meg than she was expecting in these circumstances.

"Okay."

Clare sat down on the rocky floor, letting the hum of the place come up through her fingers. She glanced up, and both Meg and Adrian stared back down with their changed eyes.

"Umm. Do you mind? I mean, at least sit down. I feel like a freak on display here."

Meg breathed out like an animal one second from charging but complied. Adrian's expression was more schooled, and she wasn't sure if it was humor or annoyance behind his look.

It suddenly occurred to her that she could be sure. Especially in this place. She could *stretch* to him and know exactly what was going on inside that unfathomable gaze. It was tempting, but only for a moment. Her inner journalist had standards and violating people's emotions was a clear infraction of those standards.

All right then, time to do this.

Clare closed her eyes and let herself fall into the place that the humming cave resonated with. Even with her eyes closed, she felt the expansion of herself and her senses. And she *stretched*.

The push beyond her body happened like a drop of water joining a stream. It was like being filled with the cavern. Empty and old, it carried the memory, the echo, of water pouring out of crevasses into passageways.

Without intention, she flowed with it lower, and lower still, random points of life shone like stars in the darkness. She coursed deeper until she spilled into a cavern still alive with blistering water and growing crystals. In the heat and crushing pressure were hungry eyes in twisted forms that were a darker shade than black.

Clare had time to register that these must be the dark Watchers, and then the one nearest reached out, its lips curling up over pointed teeth in a too wide mouth.

"The spirit is in the wind, in the breath." Its words reverberated through her soul as it reached into the center of her being with fingers like death, and far away, she felt her body exhale.

There was no struggle. No pain. Everything in her had been taken in that single breath. There wasn't even curiosity when a sudden screaming fire appeared. Her Watcher. Its rage was deep and primal like the cave itself. And the dark Watchers shuddered. They circled around her, their claws sinking in with the desperation of the starving around a feast.

Then her Watcher was in the circle, and flame cut through the pitch-black thing holding her essence. A tight and painful gasp drew into her lungs from far away, and sensation rushed back in. Pain and terror. Every claw seemed to be drawing life from her. She was going to die here in the dark nothing.

There was a tug on her soul, and it felt like she was being ripped apart. But as her Watcher fought and a few more dark claws released their hold, the tug became a pull, like a familiar hand reaching to her. And she grabbed back. Another set of talons released its grip, and with an agonizing wrench she was catapulted back toward her anchor.

She slammed into her body and rose up, wheezing and coughing, from Adrian's lap. How did she get there? Meg was crouching in front of her, one hand gripping her hand, like she intended to pull her somewhere. There was a flash of guilt in the old woman's eyes, but it disappeared as Clare's breath calmed to a pant.

Adrian shuffled his body behind her and asked, "Are you okay?"

Sure. Almost being eaten was becoming a regular pastime for her.

The Dark Hours 125

But she didn't even have the breath to be able to make light, so she just nodded.

"We should've known there'd be Watchers in a place like this," he said to Meg.

Meg ignored him. "I'm going to *stretch* to you. Just rest."

Before she could even protest, Clare could feel Meg's touch on her soul, but it was gentle, like a doctor probing a wound. And then Meg hissed and withdrew from her Watcher's fire.

Clare's eyes were beginning to shut. She was safe, surrounded. Adrian, Meg, and her Watcher. Adrian's arms tightened around her, though she didn't remember leaning back into him. But it was fine. Clare could feel hot strength all around. It was like being held and carried as a child. The currents of energy that flowed around the cave bathed her.

The voices of Adrian and Meg murmured far away. And, from somewhere, there was singing.

19

CONCESSION

Clare's Notes:

Stretching for me is different than it is for them in some ways. I can share...push...what I experience. I can only assume this is because I'm a light-bearer.

Meg was gone, and time passed slowly. Adrian's mind kept going over what had happened.

He'd sat when Clare requested it and watched as she closed her eyes to *stretch* for Miriam. Even without the erratic spiking of her light, he had sensed the finality of her exhale. Then her body slumped over, and he didn't remember moving, just holding her body and *stretching* for her. There was a moment when he was sure it was going to be the same as the last time he reached for Perry, but then, her body drew in a single breath.

And he found her shining, but surrounded by feasting Watchers. Her Watcher was there as well, not feasting, but raining fury like a vengeful god. It could easily kill him in the melee, but not entering into the fray wasn't something he considered. He rushed to Clare.

Grabbing her was like grabbing onto sunlight. It was intense and bright but without pain now. Everything in him was ablaze with "Not This Time!" And he pulled.

The Watchers didn't relinquish their prize easily, but he held and the fiery one fought until he was tugging Clare back to her anchor. She'd coughed and sputtered before slipping from consciousness.

Adrian pulled her into his lap and held her as her breathing and heart rate evened. The hard cold of the cave floor was the last thing she needed now. The light around Clare had dimmed, and there was no telling how long it would be until she woke.

At points Adrian seemed to drift but not in sleep. It was more like he lost track of himself but didn't realize until he was back. He could tell it was still night though. He hadn't lost the ability to sense the sun though it was no longer a threat to him. And it may just have been a trick of having nothing else to stare at, but he was certain Clare's glow was strengthening.

The slight uptick of her heartbeat was the first signal she was waking. At first, he thought she must be having a nightmare, because it was too soon to wake from such a draining. But then, she smacked her mouth and grimaced. She pushed as though to get up, but that landed her hands against his torso and his leg respectively.

Her eyes flew open, and he released his hold as she skittered away from him. It wasn't fear but embarrassment that filled her features as she looked away from him, red cheeked. At least there was that. He was so sick of seeing fucking fear.

"Where's Meg," she asked, as she looked anywhere but two feet in front of her where he sat.

"We didn't know how long you'd sleep. She left to send someone to check on Jonathan." He left out the bit about how they were making plans to drag her on his coat through the hole to get her out.

"How long have I been out?" She stretched then rubbed at her arms.

"Only a couple of hours. Not long considering you had Watchers trying to sever your anchor and feed en masse on your life-force. I thought you'd sleep much longer." He'd tried to say it in a humorous way, but that wasn't his strong suit, and it didn't land. A shudder ran over her.

"I'm not looking forward to trying that again."

"What the fuck do you mean? You're *not* trying that again."

Madonna Santa! The feeling of desperation as he tugged at her essence was still in his arms and fingers. Did she have no idea how close she'd been to dying? But he could see the tilt of indignation in her chin and knew even before she started talking.

"Look, the only one who decides what I will and will not do is me. It's not you. It's not Meg. It's me."

"Oh, so when you almost get yourself fucking killed *again*, we're all supposed to let you go ahead and do it because you're too ignorant not too?"

That barb was aimed at the right spot, and it hit Clare with enough force that she was on her feet and yelling.

"Maybe it wouldn't have happened in the first place if Meg had been more forthcoming with what she knew, because she sure as hell knew there'd be Watchers."

Adrian was on his feet in the assault of echos. She had no idea what Meg knew or how much she risked in trusting Clare. He could feel his gums pricking with his anger as he advanced into her space.

"You don't know anything," he whispered.

Clare didn't back up. "And you don't scare me anymore. You're nothing more than a bully."

She couldn't even fathom what he was.

"I'm so much more."

Clare breathed a laugh even as Adrian's face came mere inches from her own. Her eyes bore into his as she said, "All you are is bravado and insecurity wrapped in a facade of power."

Adrian curled his lip over sharp fangs, but before he could say another thing, a voice said, "She's right."

They both whipped around to see Meg standing at the far wall. *Merda!* Who knew how long she'd been there.

"About both of us. I knew Watchers were attracted to thin places. But between knowing she had a Watcher of her own and my desire to locate Miriam, I judged the risk to be less than it was. I was wrong." She advanced to them, the air around her seeming to bristle despite what could vaguely be construed as an apology. "Of all the lives that depend on me, I can't value yours the least, Ms. Zetler, and then expect your trust or cooperation."

She turned to Adrian. "And you've always liked to flirt with danger." Adrian scoffed, but she continued, "Go ahead and laugh. It won't be so funny when we lose you to her Watcher because you can't control your temper and she doesn't know what she's capable of."

He reached for a retort, but too much of Meg's statement felt true.

"And do *you* know?" Clare asked, the question laced with almost as much curiosity as with accusation.

"I've started looking into things, but we'll discuss that later. Now, if we're *all* ready to be adults... Clare, are you able to use the boost of the cave without being sucked into its flow?"

Absa-fucking-lutely not!

But Meg raised her hand as Adrian opened his mouth to protest.

Clare took a breath but then smiled. "Is there a way you can 'hold' onto me while I try?"

"*Stretching* and *soothing* are skills that we learn to aid in survival," Adrian said, his frustration oozing through the words. "They don't usually involve playing Red Rover in the spirit realm."

"But I felt you grab me last time and pull me back."

"You quit breathing. Your body went limp. That doesn't mean it'll work in a controlled setting and—"

Clare stopped him with a hand on his arm. Heat didn't prickle up it like it had the first time she touched him, but its effect was the same. It derailed him completely, and he hated it.

"Thank you," she said, eyes softer now. "I don't know what would've happened to me if you hadn't done whatever it was you did." He wrinkled his nose at her, but she kept talking. "Look, if I'm being honest, I would really like to know that Miriam's okay. I think I know how to counteract what happened last time I tried, but I want to err on the safe side. I'm not being reckless. To try again is me being brave."

Meg gave Clare a look that Adrian had seen before; she was appraising this human. And then the look turned to approval, and he knew that somehow he'd lost the fight. Clare was a disadvantage both as a human female and light-bearer. Meg didn't view her as an equal, she may just barely view her life as having worth, but she was definitely going to keep Clare around a little while longer.

This was insane, but he couldn't leave and not know if Clare just up and died while on some fool's errand for this stupid, old woman!

Adrian stalked toward the lake kicking every rock he came to into the water and venting with all the profane Italian words in his arsenal.

"Before we try again," Meg said as though neither Adrian nor his tantrum existed. "You'll need to do something about your Watcher."

20

MATERNAL

Clare's Notes:

Can Watchers lie?

The moment she let herself dip into the liminal space, Clare could sense her Watcher. Its fire was a conflagration. She hadn't felt fear of it since they'd met, but she'd just had a reminder that when this thing was done with her, it might eat her. No one really knew much about Watchers. And hers was *mad*.

"This place is not safe for you."

Okay. So, how does one convince the biggest kid on the block to let them pass? Maybe this would be the time it stopped playing nice.

"I know. I—"

"These people are not safe for you."

It's...her?...anger lashed the words, but Clare could feel a desire for her own life underlying them. It wasn't a desire to take it or siphon off her energies. It was a desire for her to grow old and happy. And Clare was completely unprepared. Her mind stuttered as she was thrown off balance by the unexpected affection.

"Why?"

In the physical, she would've had to clarify her question, but part of the beauty of this place was that words carried the nuance of the person's intention. It would be amazing if she could interview people here.

The conflagration flickered down to a low roar that was still much more intimidating than usual.

"Little one, I will offer you all I can, but I do not want this life or this death for you. I tried to shield you from it, but it found you anyway. And you chose it wholeheartedly. I must continue to accept this."

Her words were a soft caress in Clare's being, and the Watcher's fire returned to its normal lava-y burn.

Even apart from her body, Clare could feel her throat constrict. Love was in those words, and it flowed from them and around her like a warm blanket. To feel seen and not alone made her want to curl up and stay in this moment.

"Thank you." Outside this space it would have been totally inadequate to convey how deep that went.

"Your wandering friend is safe."

The words jarred Clare from her cozy bubble.

"You know? I could've just asked you this whole time?"

"Water is no barrier to us, and neither are bodies. We know what is in a soul. I know what hides in your heart."

There was an implication there that Clare refused to acknowledge. She was not about to talk to strange fiery creatures about her love life. A band of humor rose in her Watcher, and its flame rippled. Was she...laughing?

"If you wish to see her yourself, I will help you stretch rightly. She's out of water now."

All this time the Therians had been refusing to work with her on *stretching*, and she could've had a private tutor. The Watcher's fire rippled again.

"In a way."

It was answering Clare's thoughts without her pushing them out.

Stretching didn't translate thoughts like that, at least not any way she'd done it. Could her Watcher just hear hers?

"They are like a net of language over a mountain of emotion, subconscious, and instinct."

Okay. Mental note. Her Watcher didn't wait for any questions though.

"Be on guard. This place can catch you in its pools and flows as it caught the dark ones. To use it, you must set your intention before stretching and hold it firmly the entire time. There is power here, but you cannot let it overtake you."

As if to illustrate, her Watcher strummed the connection between her and Miriam. Again, it was like the cave rushed in. But Clare gripped the connection, and the force that had seemed to be expanding into her funneled into the connection.

She was there with Miriam so strongly. Morning was beginning to break, Clare couldn't see it, but she could feel the change of atmosphere on Miriam's skin as she sat awake in the predawn. If Clare had wanted, she probably could have felt the turning of the earth. She could certainly feel coursing anxiety but also a firmness that wrapped protectively around a strong pinprick of life within Miriam.

Clare reached out, softly saying "hello" with her presence.

MIRIAM SAT in the musty motel room, lit only by the bathroom light. The stale tea bag made a drink that was doing about as much against the nausea as her boots had done against the water, but at least it was warm. She sat staring out the window at the small, dark town and the graying sky.

And then, she wasn't alone.

The feeling of presence made her skin prickle. Before she could turn to look around her, the feeling became familiar. It was Clare. Perry had *stretched* to her a few times, sending warm, sometimes sensual, feelings as his way of telling her not to be gone too long. It was different this time. This was much louder. And expectant.

"Hi, Clare," she whispered into the still morning.

"Are you okay?"

She didn't hear Clare's words but felt them. It was more than words too. It was concern, and happiness at finding her, and...something else.

"I'm fine. Good, actually. I figured some things out."

She rested her hand over her small bump and didn't bother to try and hold back the tears. In the aftermath of her friend Marcus' death, she'd been to therapy. She'd been taught about grieving, about letting the pain flow through you, and she'd learned to choose those tears. Now she was going to have to learn to embrace her sudden inability not to choose her tears. Miriam was going to try and hide from the Therians, but even she knew fighting pregnancy tears was a losing battle. Besides, these were happy tears. Somehow, happiness was still available to her in the midst of everything else. It felt strange and beautiful.

Then she was feeling Clare's own bubble of happiness, and Miriam laughed. Stupid, weird, immortal shit. She kind of loved it. It was raw, and new, and magical.

She sighed into the paper cup of her tea. That was why she was in this mess in the first place. But she wouldn't take it back. She knew that now.

"I can feel the nuance of you so strongly. This is wild. How are you even doing this?" Miriam asked.

"Pretty sure I'm *stretching*, but I'm in that place deep in the caves that Adrian took me to before. It provides a boost to whatever it is that I can do." There was a pause, and then Clare added. "Are you coming back?"

Miriam could feel pressure behind this question. It was the something else she'd sensed earlier, but now she understood. It wasn't just Clare's question. It was Meg's.

"Is that hag forcing you to do this? Knew I'd hit water the moment I felt her ping me?"

"She did ask me, yes, but I was worried too. I haven't decided what to tell her other than you're safe."

"Well, let me make that real simple for you. You tell her, if I come back, it's on my terms. I will end my life before I let her control it, and I know you can feel that I mean it. That bitch will *not* turn me. She doesn't own me or my child. If I feel anyone other than you *stretch* to me so much as once, I'll go live afloat on the ocean. And if she comes looking for me, I can promise she'll regret it."

There was stillness for a moment, but Clare hadn't left. And then, almost with hesitation...

"Your baby is beautiful."

Of course she'd be able to sense it. Miriam hadn't even thought of that, and she felt a pang of jealousy that someone should get to touch her baby before she did. More than that, though, she wanted to know.

"What can you see?"

"It's strong and bright inside you."

Miriam smiled. Strong and bright, just like its daddy.

"That works with the name I'm thinking about: Phoenix. I'm going to wait until I know if it's a boy or a girl for the middle name." The warmth of the moment faded as more unknowns surfaced in her mind. "Can you tell if it's Therian...or twins?"

Then, more than before, she felt Clare. It was like the other woman was pressing in on her. Miriam didn't have time to protest before the feeling lifted.

"I can't tell if it's Therian, but I only sense one life."

It was worth a shot. She looked down at the slight bulge and sighed.

"Don't tell Meg. But, I'm scared. The pregnancy seems to be progressing quicker than normal. I thought that might make sense if it was twins or...if Therian pregnancies gestate faster. If it's Therian, I don't want it to have its daddy's life." What she didn't say, didn't need to say, was she didn't want it to have Perry's death. Miriam had paused on the thought, but now she continued. "I'm on my way to talk to my parents. I just need some perspective."

Clare was close again, but it was more like being wrapped in a blanket of care than being intruded upon.

"Okay. Be safe."

"You too. And Clare, you hit me up again sometime. It's nice not feeling alone."

"I will."

The sudden absence of her presence was a palpable void. Miriam set down her tea and mostly dry boots. There was no telling how Meg would react. It would be better if she was on the road, and besides, truckers left early.

WHEN CLARE OPENED HER EYES, Meg was lit by the two lanterns they'd brought and pacing around the lake edge. The clean, spicy smell mingling with the dust behind her, let Clare know Adrian was sitting very close by. She shifted and wiped the dirt from her hands.

Meg whirled at the sound.

"There you are! You have no idea how to stick with a plan do you? You ask for us to help hold you, then disregard that, and leave us with only your breathing to inform us of your safety. Based on its presence, we could only assume your Watcher was helping, but that would make our involvement difficult, now wouldn't it? We couldn't freely enter and follow you. I haven't had this much trouble with rule following since—"

"Me." Adrian stood and offered her a hand up.

"Yes, and we see how that turned out," Meg said.

Adrian's face was neutral, but he said, "I think you should take her concern as a compliment."

"It's Miriam I'm worried about. Clare has been a thorn in my side since the beginning. Speaking of, can I assume by how long you were gone that it worked?"

"She's safe, doing better."

Clare paused. How does one basically deliver the message "go to hell" to a Therian and have it received well? Probably impossible

The Dark Hours 137

considering Meg's eyes were already narrowing. May as well try bad news first.

"But she said that she would rather die than be turned or have you control her, and that if she felt anyone else *stretch* to her, she'd go live afloat in the ocean." The building of Meg's anger was like a static charge, and Clare plunged on before the older woman could begin the inevitable tirade. "She's keeping the baby."

The tension drained, both from the room and from Meg's face. The raw relief was too deep to be instantly covered, and Meg put a hand over her eyes while she took in a long breath. In a moment, she had her composure again.

"Can you tell me where she is? She needs protection whether she wants it or not."

Ha. That rang so very sincerely.

Well, it did a little actually. God, she hated the games these people played. There was no telling what they really planned on doing, but she knew she wanted to stay with them, so an outright refusal was probably not her best tactic.

"I could probably lead you in the right direction, but why does she need protection? I told you she was safe. Are you planning on ruining any chance you have of her deciding to come back? I think she just needs a little time. She's been through so much. Give her a moment."

Meg's hands curled into tight fists, and her nostrils flared, but it was Adrian who spoke.

"Meg, I fucking get it. With his last breath, Perry asked me to protect Miriam and the pup. It *kills* me to know what's going on in Richmond and to have no idea where she is. But your intuition built this tribe and made it powerful. When you met her, what was your assessment of Miriam?"

Meg curled a lip at him, but he continued.

"She's strong and smart." Meg huffed but didn't interrupt further. "If she's planning on keeping the baby, she's not going to endanger her life."

And then, right when Clare thought he might be, oh coming to her rescue or something with his little speech, he glared at her. "Will you be able to keep tabs on Miriam outside of this place?"

"It's much easier here, but I'm pretty sure—"

"Then we can go before you get yourself killed. How many times does this make in the past month?"

Clare ignored him and started walking toward the way back, but her muttered, "*Testa di cazzo,*" echoed more than she intended. A suppressed snort from Meg reached her in return.

21

BETRAYAL

Clare's Notes:

Vampires forget their human life, but Therians can lay out on the beach during the summer. This one is close, but I'm gonna go with Therians are superior here.

It was harder now to silence the internal screaming, to forget that anything but the present moment existed. But his son's life depended on it, depended on his ability to bury his love, worry, fear... betrayal.

As he drank a breakfast of O positive, Jonathan could feel strength returning. He wasn't strong before Lachlan took his life back, and he didn't have half the strength that he had at that time, but it was gaining again. Even so, he didn't dare try to *stretch*. Physical strength was different from mental, and he already felt like he was cracking. If Siri hurt his son again...

No.

He turned his memory to walks through his galleries. He passed by Munch. Those were the feelings he was putting to rest. *Impressions of a Sunrise*, now that was an experience. So much left understated with the blues and greens of morning fog hiding the docks and boats. His favorite part was the contrasting orange of the obscured, almost baleful sun.

Jonathan was considering the waves of the painting as he walked into the control room. Only Akito was there, sitting backwards on a rolling chair and clicking through images with a bored expression. He didn't turn to look at him.

"Someone's here for you, bloodsucker."

The slight ire that no-one seemed to be able to use his actual name distracted him from the words for a moment. When their meaning hit him, Jonathan didn't let himself sink into surprise or hope.

"Adrian? Clare?"

"Nah. Aberdeen. Said Clare sent her though." Akito glanced sidelong at him. "Said you were in pain."

"Yes." Jonathan kept true concern locked away from himself outside the museum, or he might get sucked into that endless vortex of pain. He put on a mask of worry, even as he focused on the outlines of ships in the painting in his mind. "I know we're doing everything possible, but I can't help worrying about my son."

Akito turned to face him fully. "Why didn't you talk about it to anyone?"

Jonathan shrugged. "What good would it do? Everyone's doing whatever can be done. Adrian said when he got back he would help me, and I know he can't come any sooner than they send him. Mine isn't the only problem here."

The teeth in Akito's smile were too many and too pointy. "I may not be old or experienced, but I'm very familiar with hiding important shit from those around you, and you're doing it. I've asked around. I know why they're trusting you, but I don't."

Before Jonathan could respond, Akito's pitch and demeanor changed.

The Dark Hours

"Uncle! You took so long at dinner I was beginning to wonder if you'd eaten yourself into a coma."

Sune walked in and David trailed behind him. Both of them looked at him as they came in, but it was Sune who spoke.

"You're wanted in the conference room."

As was the Therian's way, he conveyed little else in his manner, but his eyes lingered on Jonathan's a moment before he went to his console. Jonathan felt a prickle at his gum line, but he shushed his body. Nothing to worry about. It was only his pain; they were just concerned...friends? The word made his chest tighten, so he brushed it from his thoughts as he walked to the conference room.

Two doors down from Meg's office, the conference room wasn't large. Nothing like the room at Nidhi. A long table, seated with ten or so chairs on each side, dominated the room which was otherwise bare.

Nidhi, nightmarish as it was, had been teeming with art and flourishes of wealth. Meg's realm was more utilitarian. Her office held a woven coat of arms with a wolf on its hind legs and was dotted with celtic bric-a-brac. But in the areas of operation he'd been in, there wasn't so much as a potted plant.

He felt a sudden pang. What had become of the art in that other council room? Had it been saved or burned? Those were priceless pieces of history, pieces of beauty.

"Jonathan?"

He startled. Aberdeen had been sitting there the whole time. He knew that, and yet somehow missed it at the same moment. He'd been looking at the room. Tam used to tease him about having a photographic memory only when he actually paid attention to something, which she said was rare.

She was rare.

He blinked the memories away.

"I'm sorry. I was lost in thought."

Aberdeen reminded him of a backwoods country girl that found herself trying to blend into a city environment. Slight southern drawl, clothes that didn't take into account current styles, and she seemed kinder than those around her while also more naive. He chose the seat across from her. Near but not so close that she should be inclined to feel threatened by his presence.

Her eyes roved over him, searching. "Clare shared your pain with me. What happened?"

He didn't even know that was possible, but then again, maybe it wasn't. Maybe it was just Clare. She seemed to be doing the unexpected on all fronts.

And that was dangerous. His dangerous friend.

The word sat better there. Even though her very touch was painful, he couldn't seem to think of her and be threatened. His instincts, his logic, yelled at him to be wary, but she seemed the only trustworthy person in all this mess. Which was exactly why she couldn't know. Any of it.

Dangerous friend.

"I'm sorry," Jonathan chanced to reach outside his museum, past the numb, and let the brokenness out. "I didn't mean for my pain to touch her. I'm just afraid for my son, and there's nothing I can do."

He dropped his head in his hands and sobbed. No acting was needed, no augmenting his grief. He'd been suppressing so tightly, that it streamed out with the slightest permission. Everything lost meaning in the overwhelming crush. When Aberdeen's light touch met his elbow, he recoiled with an unintended hiss.

She froze, hand still raised, eyes instantly yellow. Never safe to touch a hurting animal, but he turned his palms out to face her.

"Sorry. I didn't mean to. I forgot myself for a moment."

She gave a single nod. "I wasn't here when Adrian first arrived, but they said it took a while before he mastered his instincts. *I* should've known better." Her eyes remained yellow though. "Clare wanted me to check and see if you were okay. I don't even know what to tell her."

He gave her a wane smile, salty wetness in its cracks. "I'm not okay, but Adrian said he would help when he got back. Until then, they're doing everything they can here to help find my baby."

The Dark Hours   143

Aberdeen's lip twitched, but there was no way to know if what she was holding back was sympathy or suspicion. It didn't really matter. He'd dropped Adrian's name. It only made sense that if the Therian's were concerned about a vampire for any reason, they'd send him back.

The sound of Akito's shout snapped him from his thoughts. Both he and Aberdeen were up and heading toward the control room. There they found Akito on his feet, both hands running through his purple hair, and looking over David's console. Kitsune was on a CB radio relaying a message to the teams in the field. Whether it was to go to the area or avoid it, Jonathan didn't catch on, but he couldn't take his eyes from the image on the console.

Shining green eyes were caught in the security camera. There were no fangs visible, but there was blood on its mouth and staining its clothes.

Vampire.

The creature moved backwards as David reversed the footage. It scooped up a woman's body, neck grotesquely chewed open and hanging to the side from under the light in the parking lot and backed into the wooded perimeter. Then the footage started forward again.

With fluid movements and careful consideration, it placed the woman down. The Solifugue propped her up, adjusting her position until her torso stayed upright against a pylon. It looked so pleased as it scurried back into the woods.

Akito's body shivered. That was the only warning Jonathan had before he was being thrown to the floor. Teeth and red fur filled his vision, and searing pain ripped into him as claws raked open his shoulder. Time slowed with perfect clarity, and a part of himself opened up with it.

Instincts took over. Flipping his inexperienced enemy was easy. Youth among Therians was decidedly less violent than the one he'd experienced among a vampire horde. Jonathan let the momentum carry him on top of the snarling beast. Claws cut at his arms as he worked to hold them down, the smell of his own stagnant blood saturating the air around them. He avoided the neck. Snapping teeth were too close, but he buried his fangs in the crook of an elbow and ripped. The enraging flavor of dead blood filled his mouth as a howl of fury erupted from his foe.

And then Jonathan's body was once again airborne.

He crashed into the doorway, back snapping against the frame. His legs went numb. Jonathan rushed life to the area, but that kind of damage would take a moment to heal. He didn't have a moment. He could hear the sounds of scuffling and growling, but it didn't descend on him as his vertebrae knit together with painful scraping and popping.

"Oh my God!" It was David. Jonathan could hear his heart racing with furious percussive timing.

"It's fine. Just don't move," Aberdeen's voice was close and rough. "Sune has Akito, and Jonathan can heal."

"Oh my God oh mygodohmygod!"

Spine now straightened, his nerves could reconnect. The life he'd been hoarding licked into the area, and as soon as he could feel his feet, Jonathan was on them. David was pale, glimmering with the heat tracks of his blood. The smell of his adrenaline was sharp and appealing. Aberdeen stood, arms at the ready, looking at Jonathan, and waiting for him to decide what he was going to do. He looked past her.

Sune had phased only slightly. His claws were out and his body seemed to barely contain a human form. He restrained a lithe beast in tatters of clothing that were bespeckled with blood. Murderous intent flashed in the beast's cunning eyes. Jonathan's hands tingled to rip the thing apart. Rip them all apart.

Everything was betrayal. No one and nowhere was safe.

From somewhere deep, the echoes of his own betrayal were still there.

He wasn't innocent either.

Instincts began to subside. Perhaps dying this way would make atonement. If Siri reached out and found him dead, she'd have no reason to hurt his son. Or maybe she'd take out her thwarted fury on

The Dark Hours

the boy when she had no other link to Adrian. That was just as likely, maybe more so considering the pattern of pain Jonathan brought to everyone he loved. He was worse than useless.

He was cursed.

Jonathan spat blood and fur from his mouth, drawing a snarl from the vulpine creature that he no longer cared to look at. It would kill him or not, but he wouldn't fight back anymore. It had been a careless waste of what little life he had.

Instead, he simply walked away down the hall. If he'd wanted, he could've listened to the whispers that followed him from the control room, but what did it matter? Footsteps were coming up the stairs, no doubt drawn by the noise of the scuffle, but he slipped into his room before he could see their owner look at him with mistrust.

There was no lock from the inside, so Jonathan wedged his chair under the door handle. They'd bust it down if they wanted to kill him, but it would discourage any unnecessary interactions. He'd already healed the gouges on his shoulder, but the use of life had left him drained. Weak. Still, he didn't feel like sleeping with the stench of Therian blood all over him.

Turning the light on in the bathroom revealed a savage, blood smeared face staring at him from the mirror. He and the creature on the console were clearly of the same family. No wonder Akito had attacked. Jonathan stared, unable to look away from the disaster that he was. Finally, he just closed his eyes. He should go back out and let the Kumiho finish the job, but he didn't even have the strength of will to do that.

He got in the shower with his clothes on, letting the water wash over all of it. It felt like he should be deliriously weeping with the futility of everything, but he didn't have it in him to do that either. Peeling off his clothes, he ran soap over his body like an afterthought. If not for the smell of blood that lingered on him, he could almost believe he didn't have a body.

He washed again.

When he got out of the shower, a voice was talking in his room. Kenyon's Irish lilt was coming through the intercom asking if he was all right, asking if he needed anything. Jonathan simply walked to his bed and got in. They probably had cameras in the room anyway. He needed blood, needed to replenish the life that he'd expended, but fuck that.

He was only going to wake up to the same nightmare again.

22

BELIEF

Clare's Notes:

What would it take for humans to accept that immortals exist? Video can be faked. Everyone knows that. Any immortal that turned themselves over to science would literally be studied to death. Clearly, they're not going to do that. But there has to be something better than The Survivors' Handbook. Something.

It was Sunday morning, and Miriam knew where to find her folks. She'd hitched her way into town the night before, but she wasn't about to go visit them looking like...

Well, like their pregnant, unwed daughter who'd been held against her will and escaped by fleeing through the woods for days. Especially not after she'd been gone for— how long had it been now? She'd lost track of time.

It would have been better to do this at home, she knew that. But she also wanted privacy. This was a conversation where she needed to be free to say whatever she needed to without fear of consequences, and she didn't trust the Therians not to have bugged her parents' place.

No. Better to crouch in the woods surrounding the building until they pulled in for church. She'd go up to their car, get in, and have them drive while she talked.

Let's be honest, her dad would be in no position to drive. Mom would have to do it. Her distinguished father would be an emotional wreck. She might be too, though, just seeing him cry. Miriam had always been a daddy's girl.

She smiled thinking about it as she watched the cars park. She'd only visited a few times since she'd graduated high school, but still, most of the faces going into the small country building were familiar. It was nice that after all the chaos she'd been through, some things actually never changed.

Even without going in, she could conjure the oiled smell of the pews that diminished as the perfumed bodies filled them. There would be hymns and then newer, faster songs, shouts and sighs, and women fanning themselves with their bulletins—hot despite the cool temperature the building was kept at. Then Reverend Jones would ascend to the pulpit. He would start off soft, with a slight tremble to his tenor, and then build in volume with each point. It wasn't a quiet church. The congregants urged him on in every breathy pause he took. There was a bit of theater to it. The whole ordeal was loud, sweaty, and touchy, but there was also something in its ritual chaos that soothed the body.

And she only realized now that she missed it.

The parking lot was nearly full now. Greeters shut the front doors, but she hadn't seen her parents. They normally came early for Sunday School, but the doors stayed open until service started. Despite the nostalgia, Miriam hadn't wanted to go in. Nearly a hundred people seeing her was not ideal when she still wanted to lay low for a little while. Ideal or not, she must have missed her parents somehow. She hadn't seen their car, but it was more likely they'd purchased a new car than they were skipping church.

The Dark Hours 149

Standing, Miriams's legs protested at being straightened after crouching for so long. As she got closer, the muted sound of music and voices escaped the building, but she made her way down and around to the basement door that opened to the fellowship hall. There was a better chance of her getting in unnoticed that way. She still wasn't sure how she would find her parents, but one thing at a time.

And now that she was in here, that one thing was a cup of coffee and a donut. She'd trained for wilderness survival enough that she was used to layering and waiting, but the warmth of the hall and the smell of coffee called to her like a siren...

Hmm. Maybe those were real too. Sirens. Mermaids. Tinkerbell. Bigfoot. Didn't really matter. The coffee was real, and it was glorious.

She sipped the revitalizing brew and listened to the thumping of music that came from the sanctuary above. Miriam couldn't be sure if it was the coffee or the beat, but her little growing bean started fluttering inside her. Despite everything going on, in this moment, she was warm, and fed, and safe.

As if triggered by her mood, the music slowed, and she could pick out the strains of "It Is Well with My Soul." Miriam hummed into a bite of glazed donut, and her eyes fell on a bulletin probably left after Sunday School. She flipped it open and read about an upcoming fall retreat and the continuing food drive. Then she turned to the back page.

The back of the bulletin was supposedly for prayer requests, but she and her momma joked that it should have been titled Church Gossip Column since more often than not it was sprinkled with such gems as: *Please pray for Sister Rita's husband's brother, who's taken with the drink again* and *Keep the Smith's in your heart as they try and reconcile their marriage after his recent indiscretion online.* It was almost always good for a chuckle.

The faint smile died on her lips as she read and the donut turned leaden in her stomach. Numbly, she set the coffee on the table and dropped into a chair, its metal feet scraping across the linoleum. Her eyes stayed fixed on the single damning item that glared up at her from the otherwise innocuous page.

Continue to remember the Walkers. Brother Ben was taken to the hospital in Roanoke last night for a suspected stroke.

Whatever peace she'd felt a moment ago was shattered.

This was her fault.

She'd been missing without a word, and her father probably lost his mind. It would be so easy to blame Meg, the Therians...hell, even Perry.

Anyone but herself.

But she'd made a choice. She chose Perry, and she'd be lying to herself if she tried to pretend she didn't know something like this could happen. Miriam had imagined all kinds of scenarios, but in one like this, she was already dead. She'd never allowed herself to think past that to all the damage she'd leave in her wake. Because, ultimately, she hadn't believed it would happen. She was in love, and that had colored all her judgements.

She had to make this right. Somehow.

But getting to Roanoke wouldn't be easy. It was an hour and a half from here and finding a ride to the city was a lot harder on a Sunday morning. If she went into the church service to find someone to take her, she might be endangering everyone, and she wasn't going to make any more flippant decisions.

The preacher's voice was echoing down from the sanctuary above when Miriam walked back out into the parking lot. If she could choose anyone, it would be Marquees. He was calm, quiet, and intelligent. She went over to his blue Audi. Naturally, his car was locked. She checked Tori's car next. She would be an excellent ally. Tori was older and seemed to have keen eyes for a situation. Also locked.

Miriam let out a breath.

Anyone who was responsible was going to lock their car. Which meant she needed to choose the best of the worst. Rashand was not ideal. He was flighty and would probably tell everyone the moment she left his vehicle that he'd seen her. But maybe she could impress upon him the danger of the situation enough that he'd keep his

The Dark Hours 151

mouth shut. She'd have to hope he enjoyed life too much to want to endanger it.

Walking over, she peaked into his car and could see the lock button of the red Honda was indeed in the unlocked position. She slipped into the back seat littered with pizza boxes, empty fast-food bags, textbooks, and old homework. Miriam picked through the flotsam and jetsam until she found a jacket crumpled under a college text on business theory. It wasn't much, but it might help her blend in. She tugged it over her and settled in to wait.

If she thought the reverend was long winded when she was sitting in service, it felt like forever waiting in the car. The sun-warmed interior was making her drowsy when a sudden increase in noise snapped her back to attention. The church doors had opened, and people were lingering and chatting as they exited.

Miriam sank down on the floor behind the driver's seat, throwing the jacket over her head. Rashand was a talker, and it was several more minutes before she heard him near the car shouting promises to meet up with his friends. Body tense, she held her breath as he got in and started the engine. Country music blasted through the speakers, making her jerk in surprise, but he didn't notice. The vehicle started moving, and Miriam let herself breathe. He was heading in the direction of town, but she would still wait until he pulled into whatever restaurant he was going to.

Finally, the car took a turn and slowed. She'd probably only get one shot at keeping a low profile. As soon as he turned the engine off, she tossed the jacket aside and spoke.

"Rashand—"

He screamed, and the drivers' seat lurched as he grabbed the door handle to escape.

"Wait! It's me. Miriam."

He jerked around, eyes wide. "Don't you ever do that—Miriam!"

"Yes."

"Oh my God! Where have you been? Everyone's been looking for you. Your parents have been worried sick. Your dad's in the hospital and—"

"I know. Would you just give me a moment to explain." He looked annoyed at the interruption but was silent while she tried to spit out her poorly constructed story. "I was in the woods, and something happened."

"You found a secret government base."

She blinked. Wow. That was definitely better than the story about hitting her head and getting disoriented she'd been planning on telling him.

And a lot closer to the truth.

"How did you know?"

"I knew it!" He glanced around and lowered his voice. "There've been rumors for years that the government found something to do with the lost colony of Roanoke and has been hiding the secrets. When no one could find your campsite, I kept telling people that it was because you got into something."

More than he could possibly know, but maybe it would keep him quiet about helping her.

"You were so right. I only barely escaped, and then I found out about my dad. I *need* to go see him, to let him know I'm okay, but no one can know."

Rashad glanced around, seeming to take in the Cracker Barrel parking lot for the first time. He lowered his voice. "I get that, but isn't your dad's hospital room the first place they'll look for you?"

"I'm not sure they've traced me back to my folks yet, but if you were willing to help, you could go in first and scout it out for me."

"Oh! I see where this is going." Really, just now? But she let him talk. "You gotta lay low, can't use any credit cards or anything, but you know you can trust me."

"Exactly." She took a deep breath. Time for honesty. "I'm not going to lie. This is very selfish of me. Just talking to you could be putting you in danger, but you seemed like my best option." The only option in the parking lot at least.

For once, he didn't say anything right away. Then, he let out a low whistle. "All right. I got you. Let me go drop my phone off at the apartment. Can't have them listening in."

The Dark Hours 153

This was going better than she could have anticipated. She stayed on the floorboards as he sent a text to his friends about missing lunch and then drove home. She let him ramble on about government conspiracies, and how he'd always suspected them but never actually thought he would be involved.

When he got to his apartment, he was inside for a good ten minutes, way longer than it took to drop off a phone, and she really had to pee. Looking both ways, she hurried into the building. He was just opening his door as she was about to knock. He dropped the plastic bag in his hands, spilling out sandwiches and snacks.

"You've got to stop that!"

"I'm sorry. You were gone a while, I was starting to worry, and I really need to use the bathroom," she said.

He chuckled and stooped to pick up the stuff. "You're on edge! Go on in. Just don't mind the mess."

And it was a mess. She'd thought Perry had a bachelor pad, but there was actually some sense of semblance and order to his clutter. This looked like a clothing store threw up fast food and frozen dinner containers. The bathroom wasn't much better, but the sink was mostly clear, and it didn't stink. That had to be better than she'd find out on the road.

As she was leaving the apartment, her eyes fell on a note left on the coffee table.

If I turn up missing too, the government's behind it, like I've been trying to tell you. Love you all.

Her stomach turned, but when she met his eyes, Rashand smiled and shrugged. "Just a precaution. Come on. Let's get you to your dad."

23

EXPLANATION

Clare's Notes:

If I could tell my dad any of this, would he believe me?

Rashand chattered the entire hour and a half drive to Roanoke. First, he asked about the government base. She fed him a story about how they'd given her something to interfere with her memory, and the only thing she recalled was blips of interrogation by an intimidating woman with some official title that was now lost to their drug. Miriam figured the closer she could keep it to the truth, the better.

Next, he asked about how she escaped. That was easier—she'd mapped the place and gotten some help from a person she befriended on the inside.

After that, he went on and on about what he imagined they were hiding up there. Prime on his list was a UFO. Because did she know that every civilization had a town or people that just vanished? It only

The Dark Hours   155

made sense that they were being visited every couple hundred years for alien research purposes and...

His voice faded to the background as she finally thought about the things he'd been saying. Here she was dismissing his far-fetched theories when she knew for a *fact* that there were large organizations operating in the shadows of human existence. Just because he was too smart to ever think it was vampires and werewolves didn't mean he hadn't keyed in on something.

Miriam had always thought that things like the disappearance of Roanoke didn't need an explanation. Clearly, they'd been welcomed in by a nearby Indigenous tribe to help them survive. Her dad liked to quote Occam's Razor: "The simplest explanation is usually correct." So, she'd thrown out complicated conspiracy theories, especially since there was always a more straightforward explanation for the collapse of an ancient town—like famine, war, or illness.

But what if she'd been wrong?

There could be an even more simple explanation that she'd never known was part of the equation.

Immortals.

And why not? After all, Therians were the simplest explanation for things like the chupacabra, the yeti, and Bigfoot. Hell, what if every Bigfoot sighting was just Perry having fun with the locals he'd found too close to his den before he moved South? Sounded like something he'd do.

Miriam tried to key back to what Rashand was saying. He was talking about how, according to patterns, they were overdue by a couple hundred years for a visitation, if you didn't count Area 51. And there was a lot of debate over whether to count it. Not because they didn't think that was aliens, but rather it had to do with the crash area and trajectory. Apparently, it didn't fit with other patterns.

Great, maybe she could add aliens to her list of things that existed. Though, if she were honest with herself, Miriam had always thought those were possible.

Regardless, there was a pattern, at least according to Rashand, and it'd been broken. So, what did that mean? Perry said that Therians were rarely responsible for human deaths. That would put vampires as the culprit for missing towns. Made sense that they'd pick small, out of the way towns to occasionally decimate. But why stop?

That too had a simple explanation.

Visibility.

The vampires depended on the fact that no one believed in them, and as the world developed more and better ways to communicate, vampires couldn't make large hits without being exposed. That's why the *Survivors' Handbook* had been such a big deal.

"Do you think your capture was at all related with the string of murders in Richmond? Some people've been saying those look like a government silencing."

His comment dropped into place, and suddenly, things connected. The vampires depended on secrecy as a whole. Richmond had been drawing attention to them. They would have to silence it one way or another. It was too big and visible for something like what must have happened at the missing towns, but something would be done.

And soon.

"Hey, girl. Hey. You all right? I didn't mean to remind you of it. I'm sorry. I was just talking."

She shook her head, but her words came out less confident than she'd like. "No, it's fine. I just need to think a little."

After a compassionate glance, his relentless chatter stopped, and she found herself again looking out a window at the passing landscape trying to pull her thoughts together. She knew she wouldn't have to tell Meg. The bitch was into everyone's business and probably saw this coming the night they'd gone on the offensive.

But Miriam couldn't hold onto her anger. She wanted to. Meg deserved it. But just like Miriam'd been able to see, almost as if from above, that the vampires were going to silence what was happening in Richmond, Miriam could now see Meg's actions.

Meg had lost Perry and a lot of her people in a battle that Miriam didn't understand the scope of. Skirmishes were happening in Rich-

The Dark Hours

mond now, like warning tremors before an earthquake, but true war was coming. And Meg had to decide if her people were staying or going. She'd decided for Miriam because she didn't want that loss on top of all the others.

And Meg *had* done it wrong. The gravity and emotional processing of what Miriam had to decide couldn't be forced just because it would make Meg's life easier.

But Miriam could still feel the squeeze of guilt in her chest. War was coming to Richmond, and Meg's attention was on her instead.

THE DARKNESS as they entered the hospital parking deck pulled her from her thoughts.

"Will you go up and let me know how it looks? Just keep an eye out for anyone who seems a little too alert," she said.

"Is that the best you got for this? 'Anyone who seems too alert'?"

Miriam smiled. "Lame, I know, but yes. It's the best I've got. I have to see my dad. He needs to know I'm okay." Her voice choked, and any resistance in Rashand's face flitted away.

He nodded. Then nodded again, as if to himself. "Okay. I got you."

Without another word, he was out of the car heading to the elevators. Miriam couldn't help the feeling of warm affection as she watched him go. They weren't close, but he was knowingly risking everything to give her this. There was still good in the world, and it sprouted up in surprising places.

That made his absence seem all the longer though. What felt like an eternity of tight guilt and worry before he returned was probably only twenty minutes, and then he was walking back to the car. She looked at his eyes, and they managed a whole conversation. Her look asking if it was safe. His answering that it seemed to be, but who knew. She was out of the car with her bag before he got to it.

"Thank you."

He shrugged.

"You should go." Rashand opened his mouth to protest, but she stopped him. "No. Trust me. It's better. If I run into trouble, there's nothing you could do against these people to help. You'd just be pushed in the middle of it with me."

"Girl—"

"Don't you 'girl' me. I'm a grown-ass woman, and I know what I'm doing and what I'm not. What I'm not doing is endangering your life any more than I already have."

Rashand looked like he'd just swallowed something bitter, but it didn't matter. What mattered was that he was as small a suspect to the Therians as she could make him.

"Look, you don't get to know how this story ends. I'm going to go up to find my dad, talk to him, and then probably disappear again. And the less you know, the better it is for you. It's bad enough that I involved you at all."

He rolled his eyes and opened his mouth again, but she cut him off one last time. "No. I appreciate your help more than you can know, but still, no."

Miriam hugged him quickly and then walked away before he could argue anymore.

His voice followed after her. "He's on the fourth floor, room 419."

She turned back to see him standing, shoulders drawn in with concern. If he had any sense at all, that concern would be for himself, but he'd never struck her as the sensible type.

"Thank you. Now go home. Please."

THE STERILE SMELLING building was at least well marked. After getting a visitor's pass, she found the elevator easily and was up to the fourth floor. The doors opened, but no one even looked up from the nurse's station. That was a good sign. Miriam followed the marked doors but walked past 419 on the first pass, keeping an eye out for anyone familiar or too watchful.

Seeing no one, she doubled back. Standing at the door, her heart began to pound. What could she even say when she went in there? What if the shock of seeing her made things even worse for his health?

The Dark Hours

Her tiny Phoenix chose that moment for a light flapping inside her.

"You're right," she whispered back to her belly. "But don't you go making a habit of it. You're too like your daddy already."

Miriam took a slow breath to steel herself, then entered.

Jem Walker had always been a pleasant woman. While inhabiting a hospital room with her sick husband, there still seemed to be a peace about her. Silver hair streaked playfully among her black curls, and red glasses perched on her nose. She sat close to Benjamin's raised bed, and they were absorbed in a game of cribbage set up on his food tray. Despite the droop to the left side of his face, he looked good. His words were slurred, but he was still managing to trash talk.

"Can't even beat me when I'm laid up in the hospital," he said slowly.

"I've been going easy on you. Wouldn't want you to give up all hope and die on me, would I?"

He chuckled, but it was cut short by her mom's gasp. She'd glanced over to the door. The playing cards slipped from her fingers and fluttered to the floor. Her dad followed her gaze, his eyes locking onto Miriam's. The cards in his hands began to tremble.

"Please—" She couldn't get out any other words.

Her mom stumbled up, nearly tripping over cords, and wrapped her arms around her. "You're alive! My baby's alive!"

The familiar scent of her cocoa butter lotion washed over Miriam, and all her defenses melted away. She let out a sob in her mother's arms, allowing herself to feel helpless and lost and afraid...if only for the moment. For a breath of time, she was held in the strong arms that had always been a safe haven.

Then Miriam pulled away and went over to her dad. Tears streamed freely down his face, and his mouth worked up and down but no sound came out.

"Please, Daddy. Please try not to get too excited." She grabbed his hands in hers. "I'm so so sorry."

"Where?"

The word came out thickly, but she knew what he wanted to

know. They'd probably searched all over where she'd told them she'd be surveying. Oh, and she'd been there during the day, and then drove twenty miles in the other direction to spend the rest of the night with Perry. It had become part of their rhythm when she came on long visits, working during the day and coming home at night.

"I was up in the mountains."

He shook his head firmly.

"Daddy, I was."

How to tell them this... She'd had this conversation a thousand different ways in her mind. She needed them, and they couldn't be there for her if they didn't even know what was going on. Still, they weren't ready for all of it.

"Perry lived up there."

Both her parents were sharp despite growing older, and her mama grabbed at the implication of her words.

"'Lived' not 'lives'?"

Miriam nodded, bitter heat closing her throat as she managed to say, "He died in the big fire just outside of Richmond."

She felt her dad's gentle squeeze on her hands, and she let her body sink into the chair by his bed. Jem came and stood next to her, wrapping an arm around her.

"Baby, I'm sorry. I know you loved him..."

Her mama stopped speaking, but Miriam could hear the questions dangling unsaid in the air. And she owed them answers after everything they'd been through.

"He was part of a sort of counter-terrorist group. The Richmond fire was a direct attack against...a hostile entity on American soil."

THE CONVERSATION with Miriam's parents had been difficult despite the fact his tests were coming back positive, and he'd likely only need to start a cholesterol medicine after all this. Her dad's diagnosis was a TIA. It wasn't fully a stroke, but she knew the stress of her disappearance had contributed to it.

Not that either of her parents said that.

The Dark Hours

They seemed to be trying to be as careful with her as she was with them. Probably half afraid she'd vanish again. It was a valid fear.

The last thing she wanted to do was add more stress to her dad, but her parents had always been able to see through her bullshit. Half-truths were the most she could get away with, and even those were stressful.

She'd told them that Perry worked for a clandestine counter-terror group that she couldn't talk about, that neither Perry or the group existed as far as the government was concerned, and Perry had died in the line of duty. They seemed to accept this with tight lips and raised brows.

As for her disappearance...that was harder.

"So let me get this straight," Jem's soft voice was nonetheless sharp. "This group kept you up in the mountains because they think this other 'terror organization' is going to target you? But then, *you* decided you couldn't live like that and left anyway?"

"It's so much more complicated—"

"Then simplify it for me." It was a plea, not a demand.

"Is this a cult?" Despite the slurred words, it *was* a demand. Her father wasn't buying it.

"No, Daddy. It's not a cult."

"Then what aren't you telling us?" Jem asked.

She closed her eyes and felt a hot wetness threatening. Damn hormones. She'd wanted to seem strong and confident when she said it.

"I'm pregnant."

She heard the gasp and looked up to see her mama's hand floating mid-way to her mouth. Her father began shouting, but it was hard to pick out what he was saying. Her mom did a better job of it.

"Stop. Stop it! What's done is done. Your words won't hurt that poor boy. They'll only hurt Miriam, and pitching a fit will make you a world worse."

Benjamin covered his face with his hands and let out a low sound. Miriam put a hand on his arm. She was a lot like her dad in that neither of them liked to appear weak. Just being stuck in the hospital bed had to be killing him.

Finally, his breathing slowed, and he covered her hand with his own.

"So, I'm going to be a grandpa." He made his words clearer this time.

She let out her own held breath. "Yes."

"When?"

"I don't know. I—" She looked down at her belly. So much she didn't know. "I found out right before Perry died, and everything was chaotic. I haven't been to a doctor, and honestly, I wasn't sure I wanted the baby."

"Oh, my sweetie." Jem grabbed her other hand, and Miriam let herself be drawn back into her mama's arms. "If you're afraid of doing this alone, you don't have to be."

Through the whole convoluted mess, her mother saw to the heart of the matter. But there was so much she didn't know. If her baby was Therian, raising it alone would bring more challenges than she could even imagine. She was crazy for doing this.

Miriam drew in a shuddering breath. "I might have to do this alone. If I go back to this group for protection, I don't know if I'll get to contact you, and I don't want to do it without you. I want my baby to know it's grandparents and uncles. I want my mama in the room when I'm in labor and my daddy to cry when he sees his first grandchild."

Her father didn't bother to wipe his tears. He squeezed her arm and said, "And I want that grandbaby to live. If you're truly in danger," he gave her as firm a stare as his half-slack face could manage, "you get yourself to safety."

"But what about you?"

"All I needed was to know my little girl's alive."

Her mom kissed her forehead. "I know *my* baby. You're strong and brilliant. You'll find a way to get what you want if it's at all possible, but in the meantime, your father's right: You have to make sure you're safe, for all of us."

24

REASONS

Clare's Notes:

There have to be humans who know about and cooperate with the vampires. Are there thralls, like Renfield to Dracula? Does the government know? The president??

Meg and Adrian were being called back to Richmond, and Meg was barking commands at a higher rate than normal.

Not that Clare was surprised though. She was self-aware enough to recognize a fellow control freak when she saw one. And when things were chaotic, when she should be delegating the most, that was always when Clare found herself the least able to.

So she watched Meg scramble, torn between her two realms—family matriarch and Therian leader—with as much composure as any control freak can show when forced to hand over the reins to someone else. Which is to say, she was operating under a thinly veiled panic. Whether she liked the woman or not, Clare could understand that. So despite the fact that Meg had threatened to feed her to the invading vampires, Clare found herself trying to be as helpful as possible. At least until it was nearing time to go.

Because she *was* going.

Which was why she was currently sitting with her bags on her lap in the truck waiting for the impending Hurricane Meg.

There was zero chance that either Meg or Adrian would miss her smell on the way, and if it came to a forcible removal, the immortals would surely win. But they could kiss her mortal butt, because she was going. And she had her arguments all ready.

One: Richmond was the better location to continue research on her abilities and her blood. Wouldn't they want to do that with possible vampire armies at their doorstep? Two: She would stay in the warehouse. Three: Clare could keep Meg updated with how Miriam was doing.

They were solid reasons. They weren't Clare's real reasons, but they were solid. She wasn't about to divulge a weakness and admit to the old bag that the claustrophobia, bugs, dirt, and the constant musty smell that now permeated everything she owned was going to undo her sanity. And showing weakness in front of Adrian? Ha! Not a snowball's chance in hell.

Nope. It was definitely that she wanted to be helpful. That's all. And vampires be damned. She'd risk going back to Richmond over staying here.

The driver, a bronze, dark eyed man who could have been from a myriad of ethnicities, had glanced at her only once, and then ignored her. It was par for the course. She was still very much an outsider.

She fidgeted and spun the ring on her finger. Despite how it felt, it wasn't long before Meg was striding down the leaf strewn hill with a speed and ease that Clare would never know. Though shoe choice probably would have helped matters some, to be honest. She'd been more unprepared than she realized for a trek and stay in the mountains. This pair of Adidas would never recover. Clare flicked a gob of mud from the canvas and rolled her eyes. She was such a city girl.

Meg's lips were pursed and her eyes narrowed as she opened the front passenger door, but she said nothing. Adrian was only a minute

The Dark Hours

behind her. Stoic acceptance had never been his forte, and it didn't appear he was going to start now. Clare could hear his ranting before he even opened the door. He switched from Italian to English and addressed Meg.

"You can't approve this! She'll—"

"Get herself killed most likely, but she's shown herself valuable, and perhaps a little capable." Clare shot a smug grin at Adrian. "If she insists on recklessly endangering her own life, she can be my guest." Meg turned her intense glare on her, and Clare's grin faltered. "But if you endanger my people, I'll gut you myself!"

Meg turned around in her seat while Adrian jumped in and slammed the door with enough force to shake the truck.

Well, all in all, that went much better than Clare'd expected.

It was 5:16 by the time they pulled into Bay Three, and Clare was going to miss that little truck clock. Not that time mattered much. The days all blurred together. This day had been spent in preparation and driving, and it was remarkable how long a couple hours felt when spent in tense silence without a device for distraction.

Before the engine was off, Meg was out of the vehicle and marching over to a Therian with an outstretched printout. The driver exited next, leaving her with Adrian. This felt familiar, sitting in a Therian bay alone in a vehicle with a vampire. She reached for the door handle—this scenario didn't play out so well last time—but stopped at Adrian's voice.

"Are you trying to get yourself killed?"

Clare bit back a sarcastic and sadly clichéd comment about pots and kettles. She was beginning to understand Adrian, and there was actual concern behind those angry words.

"I appreciate that you don't want me to get hurt, but you're not responsible for my safety or my life." She let out a sigh. "I'm not sure where I belong anymore, but it wasn't at the caves. It might not be safer here, but it's definitely better."

He drew in a deep breath for a retort, but she left the car without giving him a chance to deliver it.

. . .

SHE'D NEVER SEEN so much bustle at the warehouse and so much evidence of shape-shifting. Clare had been told that it could be easier for them existing in their animal forms, but she hadn't been expecting this. A stream of Therians was coming, going, talking. None of them were fully phased, but there was a motley of animal traits being expressed for no reason that she could see. Claws or fangs were the most common, but a light coat of fur was a close second. Elongated noses and bulked muscles straining at clothing were prevalent, as were animal eyes.

Her internal journalist was buzzing with questions, but Clare was met with cold gazes, so she kept them to herself. Contrary to certain vampiric opinions, she did have some sense of when it was better just to shut up. But that didn't mean she had to turn off her ears. She'd intended to go to her room and shower away the cave before getting to business, but then she might not learn anything about what was happening. Crowded, busy people were great for leaking tidbits of information.

Peeking in the busy Control Room revealed an absence of her best chance at information: David. So, Clare made her way down to the cafeteria. It was dinner time, but there were relatively few Therians there, and still no David. Before she could leave, the smell of chicken curry reminded her that her body had needs outside of her perpetual curiosity. And despite a prevalence of bloody, barely seared meat, these people knew how to cook.

Clare chose a table near a few Therians in hopes of overhearing conversation, but with ears far more sensitive than hers, they seemed to be aware of how easy sound could travel. Outside her own chewing, she only caught a susurrus of conversation.

Halfway through a surprisingly spicy curry, Aberdeen came in with a little cooler and headed right for Clare. The red-haired woman was conspicuously human looking, but her expression was tight and hard to read. Sitting down across from Clare, she motioned at the arm that had been the bleeder. "How are you?"

The Dark Hours 167

"A little purpler than I was before, but I've always liked purple," Clare said with a joking smile. But Aberdeen didn't smile back. She let out a short, frustrated huff and shook her head.

"I wish you hadn't come back. My people aren't at their best right now." She rubbed her temples for a moment. "But I'm glad to see you're better, and we could use your help."

Clare lowered her voice. "It's Jonathan, isn't it?" She hadn't felt any emotions coming from him, but knowing she was coming back, she hadn't reached out either.

Aberdeen frowned and filled her in on the increased tension from vampire attacks and the fight between Jonathan and Akito. By the time she finished telling how the Therians were on edge and Jonathan hadn't left his room since, Clare was on her feet and moving.

"Meg asked me to find you so you could check in on him and give him this." Aberdeen thrust the cooler at her, and only as she took it did Clare realize what was in it. "But you need to be careful...of us and of him. He's in pain, and the sun's low."

The dark hours. It felt more ominous now than when Meg had first called it that.

In the upstairs hall, a few Therians turned to watch as they neared Jonathan's door.

"Thank you for your help and for your concern." Clare closed her eyes for a moment, unsure of how to untangle what she was trying to say. "I realize I haven't done a lot to inspire trust, but you've always been gracious." Aberdeen offered her a small smile, and Clare continued. "I'll be careful, but I'm learning I'm made of tougher stuff than even I thought I was."

"It's not only your safety. If he...hurts you, the Therians will kill him."

Right. So no pressure. Clare turned and knocked on Jonathan's door. Nothing stirred from within.

"Hey, it's Clare," she said and knocked again.

The bustle in the warehouse slowed, like a collective breath being drawn in and held. As the silence stretched on, she glanced at the cooler. The blood inside wasn't an appealing thought, but sometimes hunger worked when nothing else did.

"I brought you dinner." She could only hope her voice sounded light.

Aberdeen took a quick step back, but when Clare turned to see why, she heard movement and the soft click of the door. The tight line of the other woman's mouth was not encouraging. So, this was her life now. One crisis after another that she managed to stick herself into the middle of. Still, it was better than the life she was pretending to live before.

Jonathan's door cracked open...and stopped. Looked like that was the only invitation she was going to get. Pushing the door wider, she squinted. The dim interior was faintly visible, but she didn't see him...didn't see the hungry, wounded vampire. And suddenly, the irony of bringing him dinner versus being dinner raised a nervous half chuckle from her throat. But this was Jonathan. She'd seen inside his soul, and he wasn't a monster.

Shaking her head at the craziness of it all, Clare plunged into the darkness and shut the door behind her. As her eyes adjusted to a room lit only by the light coming from the bathroom, she could see Jonathan had taken a seat at a small table in the corner to her left.

And finally, she was afraid.

There was no sign of wounding, neither physical or emotional. There was no sign of anything. He sat looking at her like one might look at a lamp post. His face, while blank of pain, was also blank of anything else. His posture was straight with an unnerving motion-lessness, but there was no hint that he was *stretching*.

Something was very, very wrong.

With slow, deliberate steps, Clare placed the cooler on the table in front of him. His vacant eyes followed her as she stepped back and sat on the edge of his bed. There didn't seem to be anything more she could offer, but after several minutes of silence, she asked, "Won't you talk to me?"

His head tilted ever so slightly, like he was listening for some-

The Dark Hours 169

thing. Finally, Jonathan said, "Did you know that I remember everything?"

His voice was soft, perhaps dreamy.

"I took a nasty blow to the head when I was a child, courtesy of my father, and spent two days in the hospital. Despite the rosy prognosis, I never fully healed. The new trait was definitely an injury. People think it's such a gift to be able to remember everything. The closest they come to it is the traumatic situation where every detail is recorded in crystal clarity. And they push away that 'gift' every bit as much as I push away mine.

"But push all I want, I can't truly forget. It's all there the moment I reach for it, like opening a door. When I shut the door, it becomes far away, like it doesn't belong to me. It's still there though. I could open my memories and walk through any day I've lived since my head injury. It seemed like a cruel trick until I met Tam. I would go home from our dates and relive every moment. And now, it's the only way she still lives. I can bury my reality and trace every line on her face, smell the strawberry shampoo in her hair. If that becomes too much, I can take myself to memories of art galleries and museums. Be anywhere but here."

His eyes seemed to focus on Clare then. "Why are you here?"

"I..." What could she even say after all that? After everything that had happened to him? "I'm sorry."

"Pity's the worst," he spat out. "It doesn't solve anything, help anything. It just reminds you that you're literally pitiful." He ran his hands over his face. "And you still haven't answered. Why are you here?"

"You weren't answering your door. So, when I came back to the warehouse, Aberdeen asked if I wou—"

He pushed away her words with a gesture. "No. Here, as in, why did you come back? I don't have a choice, but why do you stay?"

His voice was edged, though not raised, and Clare felt the building of energy in the room that happened before an immortal changed. Somehow that was better than the soul-less thing that had been sitting there a moment ago. And it might be foolish, but despite their warnings, she couldn't find it in her to be afraid of Jonathan, not really. The only thing that kept her from reaching out and touching him was the knowledge that it would physically hurt him.

"They can't keep you safe, if that's what you're thinking."

He rose with the grace and power that seemed innate to all immortal movement. She stood and faced him in return. Despite the crackle in the room, his eyes were gray.

"It's not that," she said, voice low.

Maybe it was at first, but everything that had happened since she broke out of the mansion had taken her farther from that fear. There were so many little reasons why she wanted to be here, but one suddenly seemed to come to the front.

"Somehow, I feel like I belong here, in this world."

There was a brief flash of emotion on his face, and then he turned his back to her and leaned against the table with the cooler.

"I'd like to eat now. You should go." Clare tried to protest, but he kept talking. "Let the Therians know I'm fine, but until they resolve their very important turf war, I think it's best for all of us if I don't work with them in the Control Room."

She wanted to disagree with him, but the Therians, partially phased and ready for action, couldn't really be argued with.

"I'll be here if you need anything," she said.

The lines of his back and shoulders tensed as he growled, "Please, just go!"

25

BROKEN

Clare's Notes:

I'm attracted to Adrian. I think. Am I really? Maybe it's just an extreme version of opposites attract. Two weeks ago I would have said I hated him. So, I don't know what this is, but I'm voting for a case of latent teenage angst and rebellion. It's that or I need my head examined.

Siri gripped the wheel of a disgustingly plain black sedan, then drew her hand back with a hiss of pain. She still hadn't figured out what to do about the burn left by that bitch's blood, not that she'd had much time with everything in chaos. And now this.

Even without a summons, she knew this place by any route. She and Deval had seen revolt before, in India. When they came here, aside from buying antiquities, her father had bought land around the growing city. As the high rises went up, he made sure there were safe places for their people to go to ground if needed.

And he'd trusted her with both their construction and their secret. Keeping them secret was easy enough. She came and went as she pleased, did whatever she liked, and no one questioned the princess. No one would dare follow her or cross her.

The safe houses weren't hard to maintain once they'd been built either. Siri occasionally went to install new tech or update the decor. Every now and then, she'd catch a meal and have them clean before she ate. She had no intention of staying in a rat-infested bug-out hole if they needed to flee.

And Siri had fled before.

She whipped the car through a turn at a yellow light. Since the attack, she'd been staying with a different group of their vampires than Deval because who else could he trust to help run what was left of them? Even after all their losses, they were still too big to hide in one location. They'd been communicating by their soul bond, but something of her personal agenda must have leaked through as well. Her father had summoned her.

She'd always been close with him, and while he'd given her pointed advice, he'd never forced her to do anything. But the attack on the mansion had changed things. He could have asked her to come or sent a messenger, but a summons was like a dragging shackle. She couldn't refuse it.

Even more infuriating was the tinge of fear she felt.

No one among their coven now was there at the time of Kali, besides her and her father, but she remembered awakening in the chamber of the great goddess who had given Deval his power. Meg and Adrian were being called back to Richmond, and Meg was barking commands at a higher rate than normal.

Not that Clare was surprised though. She was self-aware enough to recognize a fellow control freak when she saw one. And when things were chaotic, when she should be delegating the most, that was always when Clare found herself the least able to.

So she watched Meg scramble, torn between her two realms— family matriarch and Therian leader—with as much composure as any control freak can show when forced to hand over the reins to

The Dark Hours 173

someone else. Which is to say, she was operating under a thinly veiled panic. Whether she liked the woman or not, Clare could understand that. So despite the fact that Meg had threatened to feed her to the invading vampires, Clare found herself trying to be as helpful as possible. At least until it was nearing time to go.

Because she *was* going.

Which was why she was currently sitting with her bags on her lap in the truck waiting for the impending Hurricane Meg.

There was zero chance that either Meg or Adrian would miss her smell on the way, and if it came to a forcible removal, the immortals would surely win. But they could kiss her mortal butt, because she was going. And she had her arguments all ready.

One: Richmond was the better location to continue research on her abilities and her blood. Wouldn't they want to do that with possible vampire armies at their doorstep? Two: She would stay in the warehouse. Three: Clare could keep Meg updated with how Miriam was doing.

They were solid reasons. They weren't Clare's real reasons, but they were solid. She wasn't about to divulge a weakness and admit to the old bag that the claustrophobia, bugs, dirt, and the constant musty smell that now permeated everything she owned was going to undo her sanity. And showing weakness in front of Adrian? Ha! Not a snowball's chance in hell.

Nope. It was definitely that she wanted to be helpful. That's all. And vampires be damned. She'd risk going back to Richmond over staying here.

The driver, a bronze, dark eyed man who could have been from a myriad of ethnicities, had glanced at her only once, and then ignored her. It was par for the course. She was still very much an outsider.

She fidgeted and spun the ring on her finger. Despite how it felt, it wasn't long before Meg was striding down the leaf strewn hill with a speed and ease that Clare would never know. Though shoe choice probably would have helped matters some, to be honest. She'd been more unprepared than she realized for a trek and stay in the mountains. This pair of Adidas would never recover. Clare flicked a gob of mud from the canvas and rolled her eyes. She was such a city girl.

Meg's lips were pursed and her eyes narrowed as she opened the front passenger door, but she said nothing. Adrian was only a minute behind her. Stoic acceptance had never been his forte, and it didn't appear he was going to start now. Clare could hear his ranting before he even opened the door. He switched from Italian to English and addressed Meg.

"You can't approve this! She'll—"

"Get herself killed most likely, but she's shown herself valuable, and perhaps a little capable." Clare shot a smug grin at Adrian. "If she insists on recklessly endangering her own life, she can be my guest." Meg turned her intense glare on her, and Clare's grin faltered. "But if you endanger my people, I'll gut you myself!"

Meg turned around in her seat while Adrian jumped in and slammed the door with enough force to shake the truck.

Well, all in all, that went much better than Clare'd expected.

It was 5:16 by the time they pulled into Bay Three, and Clare was going to miss that little truck clock. Not that time mattered much. The days all blurred together. This day had been spent in preparation and driving, and it was remarkable how long a couple hours felt when spent in tense silence without a device for distraction.

Before the engine was off, Meg was out of the vehicle and marching over to a Therian with an outstretched printout. The driver exited next, leaving her with Adrian. This felt familiar, sitting in a Therian bay alone in a vehicle with a vampire. She reached for the door handle—this scenario didn't play out so well last time—but stopped at Adrian's voice.

"Are you trying to get yourself killed?"

Clare bit back a sarcastic and sadly clichéd comment about pots and kettles. She was beginning to understand Adrian, and there was actual concern behind those angry words.

"I appreciate that you don't want me to get hurt, but you're not responsible for my safety or my life." She let out a sigh. "I'm not sure

The Dark Hours 175

where I belong anymore, but it wasn't at the caves. It might not be safer here, but it's definitely better."

He drew in a deep breath for a retort, but she left the car without giving him a chance to deliver it.

She'd never seen so much bustle at the warehouse and so much evidence of shape-shifting. Clare had been told that it could be easier for them existing in their animal forms, but she hadn't been expecting this. A stream of Therians was coming, going, talking. None of them were fully phased, but there was a motley of animal traits being expressed for no reason that she could see. Claws or fangs were the most common, but a light coat of fur was a close second. Elongated noses and bulked muscles straining at clothing were prevalent, as were animal eyes.

Her internal journalist was buzzing with questions, but Clare was met with cold gazes, so she kept them to herself. Contrary to certain vampiric opinions, she did have some sense of when it was better just to shut up. But that didn't mean she had to turn off her ears. She'd intended to go to her room and shower away the cave before getting to business, but then she might not learn anything about what was happening. Crowded, busy people were great for leaking tidbits of information.

Peeking in the busy Control Room revealed an absence of her best chance at information: David. So, Clare made her way down to the cafeteria. It was dinner time, but there were relatively few Therians there, and still no David. Before she could leave, the smell of chicken curry reminded her that her body had needs outside of her perpetual curiosity. And despite a prevalence of bloody, barely seared meat, these people knew how to cook.

Clare chose a table near a few Therians in hopes of overhearing conversation, but with ears far more sensitive than hers, they seemed to be aware of how easy sound could travel. Outside her own chewing, she only caught a susurrus of conversation.

Halfway through a surprisingly spicy curry, Aberdeen came in with a little cooler and headed right for Clare. The red-haired woman was conspicuously human looking, but her expression was tight and hard to read. Sitting down across from Clare, she motioned at the arm that had been the bleeder. "How are you?"

"A little purpler than I was before, but I've always liked purple," Clare said with a joking smile. But Aberdeen didn't smile back. She let out a short, frustrated huff and shook her head.

"I wish you hadn't come back. My people aren't at their best right now." She rubbed her temples for a moment. "But I'm glad to see you're better, and we could use your help."

Clare lowered her voice. "It's Jonathan, isn't it?" She hadn't felt any emotions coming from him, but knowing she was coming back, she hadn't reached out either.

Aberdeen frowned and filled her in on the increased tension from vampire attacks and the fight between Jonathan and Akito. By the time she finished telling how the Therians were on edge and Jonathan hadn't left his room since, Clare was on her feet and moving.

"Meg asked me to find you so you could check in on him and give him this." Aberdeen thrust the cooler at her, and only as she took it did Clare realize what was in it. "But you need to be careful...of us and of him. He's in pain, and the sun's low."

The dark hours. It felt more ominous now than when Meg had first called it that.

In the upstairs hall, a few Therians turned to watch as they neared Jonathan's door.

"Thank you for your help and for your concern." Clare closed her eyes for a moment, unsure of how to untangle what she was trying to say. "I realize I haven't done a lot to inspire trust, but you've always been gracious." Aberdeen offered her a small smile, and Clare continued. "I'll be careful, but I'm learning I'm made of tougher stuff than even I thought I was."

"It's not only your safety. If he...hurts you, the Therians will kill him."

The Dark Hours

Right. So no pressure. Clare turned and knocked on Jonathan's door. Nothing stirred from within.

"Hey, it's Clare," she said and knocked again.

The bustle in the warehouse slowed, like a collective breath being drawn in and held. As the silence stretched on, she glanced at the cooler. The blood inside wasn't an appealing thought, but sometimes hunger worked when nothing else did.

"I brought you dinner." She could only hope her voice sounded light.

Aberdeen took a quick step back, but when Clare turned to see why, she heard movement and the soft click of the door. The tight line of the other woman's mouth was not encouraging. So, this was her life now. One crisis after another that she managed to stick herself into the middle of. Still, it was better than the life she was pretending to live before.

Jonathan's door cracked open...and stopped. Looked like that was the only invitation she was going to get. Pushing the door wider, she squinted. The dim interior was faintly visible, but she didn't see him...didn't see the hungry, wounded vampire. And suddenly, the irony of bringing him dinner versus being dinner raised a nervous half chuckle from her throat. But this was Jonathan. She'd seen inside his soul, and he wasn't a monster.

Shaking her head at the craziness of it all, Clare plunged into the darkness and shut the door behind her. As her eyes adjusted to a room lit only by the light coming from the bathroom, she could see Jonathan had taken a seat at a small table in the corner to her left.

And finally, she was afraid.

There was no sign of wounding, neither physical or emotional. There was no sign of anything. He sat looking at her like one might look at a lamp post. His face, while blank of pain, was also blank of anything else. His posture was straight with an unnerving motion-lessness, but there was no hint that he was *stretching*.

Something was very, very wrong.

With slow, deliberate steps, Clare placed the cooler on the table in front of him. His vacant eyes followed her as she stepped back and sat on the edge of his bed. There didn't seem to be anything more she could offer, but after several minutes of silence, she asked, "Won't you talk to me?"

His head tilted ever so slightly, like he was listening for something. Finally, Jonathan said, "Did you know that I remember everything?"

His voice was soft, perhaps dreamy.

"I took a nasty blow to the head when I was a child, courtesy of my father, and spent two days in the hospital. Despite the rosy prognosis, I never fully healed. The new trait was definitely an injury. People think it's such a gift to be able to remember everything. The closest they come to it is the traumatic situation where every detail is recorded in crystal clarity. And they push away that 'gift' every bit as much as I push away mine.

"But push all I want, I can't truly forget. It's all there the moment I reach for it, like opening a door. When I shut the door, it becomes far away, like it doesn't belong to me. It's still there though. I could open my memories and walk through any day I've lived since my head injury. It seemed like a cruel trick until I met Tam. I would go home from our dates and relive every moment. And now, it's the only way she still lives. I can bury my reality and trace every line on her face, smell the strawberry shampoo in her hair. If that becomes too much, I can take myself to memories of art galleries and museums. Be anywhere but here."

His eyes seemed to focus on Clare then. "Why are you here?"

"I..." What could she even say after all that? After everything that had happened to him? "I'm sorry."

"Pity's the worst," he spat out. "It doesn't solve anything, help anything. It just reminds you that you're literally pitiful." He ran his hands over his face. "And you still haven't answered. Why are you here?"

"You weren't answering your door. So, when I came back to the warehouse, Aberdeen asked if I wou—"

He pushed away her words with a gesture. "No. Here, as in, why did you come back? I don't have a choice, but why do you stay?"

The Dark Hours
179

His voice was edged, though not raised, and Clare felt the building of energy in the room that happened before an immortal changed. Somehow that was better than the soul-less thing that had been sitting there a moment ago. And it might be foolish, but despite their warnings, she couldn't find it in her to be afraid of Jonathan, not really. The only thing that kept her from reaching out and touching him was the knowledge that it would physically hurt him.

"They can't keep you safe, if that's what you're thinking."

He rose with the grace and power that seemed innate to all immortal movement. She stood and faced him in return. Despite the crackle in the room, his eyes were gray.

"It's not that," she said, voice low.

Maybe it was at first, but everything that had happened since she broke out of the mansion had taken her farther from that fear. There were so many little reasons why she wanted to be here, but one suddenly seemed to come to the front.

"Somehow, I feel like I belong here, in this world."

There was a brief flash of emotion on his face, and then he turned his back to her and leaned against the table with the cooler.

"I'd like to eat now. You should go." Clare tried to protest, but he kept talking. "Let the Therians know I'm fine, but until they resolve their very important turf war, I think it's best for all of us if I don't work with them in the Control Room."

She wanted to disagree with him, but the Therians, partially phased and ready for action, couldn't really be argued with.

"I'll be here if you need anything," she said.

The lines of his back and shoulders tensed as he growled, "Please, just go!" a boon of the highest kind.

As the firstborn in his line, Deval's anger was not to be taken lightly, not even by his daughter. A thrall might break their bonds from their creator, but Deval's bond to her was part of the gift of the goddess. It would last as long as he still lived.

She would always be his.

That was all she'd wanted of Adrian. Her father's refusal to understand that was unfathomable, but she tried to put those thoughts away as she drove into the lowest parking deck of the upscale condominiums. As the owner, access to the basement suite was exclusive. Not that most people even noticed the nondescript locked door in the parking garage.

Siri kicked the door on the piece of shit "invisible-looking" car shut and chirped it locked. Not that anyone would want it, but she wasn't about to need a ride from some peon thrip here.

She gingerly placed her hand on the small metal panel beside the handleless door that could easily be ignored for conduit access. The burn didn't hurt too much, but every twinge of discomfort only made her more irate. After a small whirring click, the door swung inward to a white foyer lit with gold sconces then stepped down into an open living area. Black leather couches with deep red pillows made a large "U" shape around a fireplace of black marble. She'd sometimes regretted her choice of thick white carpet, but keeping blood off it had almost become a game when she fed here.

Across from the lounging area was a white tiled kitchen with a long black island. It amused Siri to make it look conventional. Sure, it was probably practical on the rare occasion when an inspector needed to see the premises, but the hanging rack over the island, complete with knives on a magnetic strip, was hilarious. And fun. She was an excellent aim with the smaller knives.

Even with twenty-three vampires taking up space here, it didn't seem too crowded. Doubtless there were infractions. Those were unavoidable, but they all looked away as she swept into the room.

So power was still being maintained and respected. Good.

Siri ignored the posturing lot of them and strode to the master suite. It was lavishly done. The carpet here was deep and black. White wainscoting trimmed in gold came up to ebony wood walls. In the center of the tray ceiling was an ornate gold chandelier. That fixture hung over a mahogany wood sleigh bed with red silk sheets and a black Icelandic Eiderdown comforter. Antique cream and gold chairs nestled in the corners.

A thread of incense hung visible in the soft light. The office was just off the bedroom, and the door was open. Her father, dressed in a

The Dark Hours

rich black suit, sat at the carved cherrywood desk and was framed by the built-in bookshelves that filled the back wall. An old leather volume was open on the desk in front of him. He didn't even look up at her approach.

"I've received a communication from the international grand council. The activities in Richmond are attracting too much attention. They said they will cleanse the area if necessary."

Siri ground her teeth. This wasn't a reason to summon her.

They'd expected interference from the grand council when a rogue vampire started displaying his kills for the humans to find. So, the Nidhi coven had not only been fighting Therians and encroaching covens, they'd also begun hunting for the thrip responsible. Theories abounded, but it had to be a newly made vampire, one who didn't understand that visibility meant death. And one who had a particularly sadistic bend.

That last bit ruled out Adrian. As unthinkable as it was that he'd teamed up with the Therians, slaughtering humans for fun was contrary to his nature. That had always been part of his problem.

Finally, Deval looked up from his tome. "With all that's going on, I find it irresponsible that you're distracted by other things, things that you haven't shared with me. Everything I've built is for you."

Siri dug her nails into her palms. As if she hadn't participated in the building all these years. "And yet you summon me here like a disobedient child to scold me. I've lived for centuries. I could have an empire of my own if I wanted it."

"Do you?"

Did she? Where would she go, and why? She had everything she wanted. Everything except Adrian. And as her jealous longing rose, she felt her father's quiet presence inside her by the flash of his surprise.

She jerked back. As powerful as his bond to her soul was, he'd never before used it against her!

"How could you violate *me*?"

"I needed to know what could be so important as to capture your attention while our world was on fire. How can this still be about him? Are you trying to take further vengeance on the Therians for his death? Let it be!"

As her father stood, she hated how she felt small before him. He was as soft and powerful as pitch blackness. When he wanted to comfort her, it was a welcome blanket. When he wielded his authority, there was nothing that could pierce it.

Damn him.

His jaw clenched, and there was no telling how much he was perceiving from her. His abilities as a firstborn exceeded that of any normal vampire. Even knowing that, she'd lived unafraid. He was her father. He was cunning and brutal with others, but he'd rarely even been angry with her.

Until now.

"Adrian lived."

Siri didn't have to say anything else. She could watch all the implications fall into place in her father's eyes.

After a moment, he asked, "And you know this how?"

This was what she'd truly been hiding. All of it. From partnering with Lachlan and trying to turn Adrian again to wipe his engram, to the light-bearer and holding Jonathan's son. There wasn't even a good place to begin, and she could feel his anger rising. He wouldn't froth and rage when her story was done. That wasn't his way, but she couldn't predict how his fury would come out.

Siri sank onto the bed, and as ancient as she was, it somehow managed to make her feel young. As she told her story, he was still. He moved only to sit back down in his own chair, fingers steepled in front of his mouth. When she finished, he leaned back and regarded her coolly.

"In the greatest crisis we've had in over two centuries, you decided to keep this from me. How can you be so spoiled, so short-sighted? And all this over someone who didn't want you."

He always did know how to cause the most pain.

"You of all people should understand what it's like to desire someone and be kept from them," she snapped back.

He stood and advanced, voice infuriatingly even. "The love of a

The Dark Hours

parent doesn't compare with the lust you feel for Adrian. I ripped myself apart in order to have you, but you've ripped apart everything *I've* done for a man who's unworthy of you. I've misjudged your maturity and your character. And now, I need to clean up the mess *you've* created."

"What are you going to do?"

He sat down on the bed next to her. "First, we must alert the others about this light-bearer. Their blood is rarely so powerful as to leave lasting damage, and I clearly can't trust you to deal with her without your emotions getting the better of you." He gestured at her hand. "You'll need to excise the wounded area for it to heal."

The very idea only made her anger at the light-bearer rise more. But Deval continued before she could object.

"I should have killed Adrian when he first showed his engram, but you were so enamored. My love for you clouded my judgment and led us to this point. Even if I manage to salvage our coven, it will be decades, at least, before I recover the honor I've lost from losing control of the region. I can't allow any more lapses in judgment."

Kill Adrian. He was going to kill Adrian.

"Please. Just let me try one more time."

No!

The word ricocheted through her, becoming louder and louder as it filled her soul. In the increasing wave of anger that assaulted her, she was vaguely aware of clenching pain as her father gripped the back of her neck.

For a moment, there was silence, then he whispered into her ear, "I've sacrificed everything to have you, but I'll kill you myself before I see you whore yourself into death's maw and take all of us with you for that piece of shit. Have I made myself understood?"

Deval had never *stretched* to her to punish her. But now, he filled her soul with his heavy presence, pushing her down, down into herself. Searching her. She pushed back, not against the search as much as to maintain the boundaries of her own being. The physical pain on her neck increased along with the crushing invasion of self.

"Have I?"

His voice was hushed like a forest after an ice storm, and Deval froze the life in her body. She'd done it to others, but to feel the loss of control in her own body was more terrifying than she could have imagined. She couldn't so much as twitch a finger, and she didn't doubt his intent.

Siri yielded, and he poured himself into her. For a moment, it was suffocating, like breathing in water when you'd been holding your breath against it. It filled you with a deadly wrongness. In her endless days of toying with her own creations, she'd never been able to penetrate a soul so fully. Deval went through her intentions and secret places. Everything was bare under his probing.

Then he was done. He released her neck, and her life-force back to her. She fell back on the bed, gasping.

"I'm glad you didn't make that harder than it had to be. Please don't make me have to do it again." He stood and returned to his desk, picking up his book once more like he hadn't just violated every ounce of her being.

"Contact Jonathan and direct him here instead of your drop zone. You've done well in breaking him."

When she didn't move, shock still freezing her mind and body, he added, "Now."

26

RIDICULOUS

Clare's Notes:

I finally feel like I belong somewhere. I just wish it wasn't here.

C lare sat on the bed in her room and chewed on the end of a hard plastic pen. It had no give and wasn't satisfying in the least, just like her current situation.

Adrian was gone again, hunting down vampires with a cadre of Therians. They were looking for one in particular, and it wasn't Deval or Siri. Apparently there was some rogue vampire flaunting his human kills. Aberdeen had to explain why this was a bad thing because Clare was under the impression that the whole point of what they'd been doing was trying to expose vampire activity to the humans.

Which it was, but on a small hard-to-trace scale, since there was apparently far more to the vampire kingdoms than she'd been aware of. According to her very reliable source, the vampires were more inclined to start the next World War than be exposed, and dropping bombs and blaming it on foreign entities was definitely in their playbook. Though, they probably wouldn't start there since that took a lot to execute.

Fantastic.

Like awful background music in a shopping mall, Jonathan's discordant pain lightly flitted through her awareness. She tried to tune it out with work. It had always done the trick in the past when she wanted to avoid whatever problem was nagging at her.

This time, not so much.

With her notebook on her lap, she tried to piece together an article that didn't sound like she was completely insane.

It was impossible. She couldn't convey this information in a way that was even passably believable. No wonder vampires were able to exist under the radar. Just writing, the words "secret vampiric empire" made her roll her own eyes. It was ridiculous. She would have to try though, and if nothing else, the heliophiles would believe and act on the information she got out.

But putting it out there was a whole different set of problems. From the moment they returned to the warehouse, Meg was as inaccessible as a queen on her throne, and so was the Control Room. It was more of a War Room now, and clearance didn't include nosy humans who were just extremely curious about what the hell was going on.

If she ran into David, she could ask him if he would leak it on the web while he was working. He had to still have access to *You Know It*'s website, and there were countless forums that would do, but she hadn't figured out his schedule to be able to reliably run into him.

One problem at a time. She had to make this sound as believable as possible first. It was late, but who knew how much time they had to warn people. Even if the vampires didn't decide to just nuke the city, it wasn't safe.

Clare yawned, scribbled out a line, and started again.

. . .

The Dark Hours 187

HER MOUTH WAS dry when she woke some time later leaning against the headboard with her neck kinked. Clare glanced around, but no, she'd broken the clock, and they hadn't replaced it. It was entirely possible that Meg was just being petty.

Sighing, she rolled off the bed and proceeded to change out of the clothes she'd slept in. Pulling on a white long-sleeve shirt, she wondered what the woman she'd been two months ago would think of the woman she was now. No shower, no clear goal, and white after Labor Day—to say nothing of her questionable whereabouts and taste in men.

With another sigh, Clare went down to breakfast. Unlike the night before, the cafeteria was busy, and the clock on the wall read 8:11. So, she'd gotten around seven hours of sleep.

Felt more like five.

She skipped the hot food line. There was only one thing she needed: coffee.

Well, and the waffle maker next to the coffee station. She might need that too.

Once she was armed with the necessary weapons against the morning, Clare scanned the bustle looking for somewhere to plop her semi-conscious butt.

"Welcome back."

The voice behind her made her jump, and coffee sloshed over the rim of the cup, scalding her fingers.

"David, you about gave me a heart attack. And you don't have to look so pleased about it."

"It's just you're normally the chipper one in the morning while I look like yesterday's pizza. I like the role reversal."

She growled at him, and David chuckled.

"Picking up the local language through osmosis I see. No need to scowl, we both know that was funny. Now, come on. There's a spot over here."

They sat down, and Clare had to admit she'd never seen him look so bright-eyed in the morning.

"How long have you been up? Even when you came in to work at nine, you didn't seem to wake up until eleven."

David dipped some toast into his egg yolk, "Since about five—p.m., not a.m.—which, come to find out, that's not such a bad time of the morning if you're already awake."

She just shook her head at him. "You actually seem to be enjoying this. We've worked together for years, and the only thing you ever showed any excitement about was gaming."

"And my favorite games were always the zombie apocalypse types." He poked her arm and gave her a slight smile.

"Okay. Now you're making jokes and looking borderline happy. We've officially swapped roles. So does that mean I get to act moody and steal your food."

His smile broadened, but he shook his head. "It's crazy here. Legitimately. But all my life, I must have missed my calling. I didn't know you could actually be happy at work. I mean, my God, they aren't even paying me, but all this is so much bigger than me. I'm not thrilled about the *constant* threat of death, and I reevaluate my life choices by the hour, but I feel like what I do actually means something."

She knew that feeling. This immortal world sucked you in, and everything about it seemed more real and more important than life before. Even if she went back, how would she make friends? The most life-altering thing that had ever happened to her was something no one else would understand or even believe.

No one else except the people in this world.

They ate, both lost in their own thoughts for a few moments, and then Clare said, "So, if I was trying to write another article, or a warning, for the heliophiles, would you be able to type it out and post it from the Control Room?"

"We're literally working with "were-people" in a secret base, and you're still trying to get favors out of me. Our apparent role-swapping is definitely incomplete."

"But could you?"

The Dark Hours   189

"I absolutely *would*. You know low-commitment subversive actions are totally in my wheelhouse, but we have people who put out information from various locations across town. The amount of security that goes into something like a post is ridiculous. The vampires would work on cracking where it came from immediately. We mostly do monitoring and command from Control."

She couldn't miss the plural pronouns. It was as conspicuous as if he'd grown an arm out of his chest. Working at *You Know It*, David never included himself in the organization. *He* was always doing something for *them*. There was never a *we*.

Clare had told Jonathan she felt like she belonged here, but she was a light-bearer. She was different, and this world seemed to call to her. It was surprising that David should feel the same thing. Sure, he didn't fit in at *You Know It*, but he'd at least found a community with the online gaming crowd. And yet, he'd given up everything in his old life, almost instantly, and traded it for this chaos. Just like she had.

That had to be the way Jonathan saw it when he'd asked her why she was here. It didn't seem to make sense on the outside. Maybe the most important things never did. Like attraction.

And no.

She was not going there. At this point there was no denying how she felt, but that didn't mean she had to brood on it. Or do anything about it for that matter. Immortal life was so unpredictable. Who knew if Adrian would even come back from whatever mission thing he went on last night.

Oh God.

What if he didn't come back?

"Have you heard from the team that went out last night?"

David arched an eyebrow at her. "No. They don't take anything that can tie them back to operations here. And they're likely to stay out for a while. They don't need sleep the same as we do, and if they've tracked a target back to a nest, they'd want to attack during the daytime anyway."

He declined to mention the very obvious reason she was asking or to gloat about his assumptions earlier being correct. That was as out of character as the rest of him this morning, and then she got it.

"Oh! You like someone here!"

"What? Why would you even think that?" He'd always had an excellent poker face, but she wasn't buying it.

"You're cheerful, legitimately cheerful, at eight in the morning. You're sticking around, endangering your life, and enjoying it."

"That doesn't mean anything. I like the work I'm doing here."

"*And* you totally let an 'I told you so' moment pass un-utilized. The last time we were in the cafeteria you insinuated that Adrian and I were interested in each other. Now I hand you a moment to boast of your superior correctness, and you let it slide. Why would you do that unless you had your own attraction you didn't want to get caught in?"

"Look. Catty gossiping was fun and all at the magazine when there was literally nothing else worth doing, but I would have to be a complete idiot to get involved with someone here." David said it with maybe a little more heat than was entirely necessary, but years of interviewing had taught her not to be distracted by things like that.

"That's not a denial."

"We're not having this conversation," he said, taking his mostly empty plate to the trash.

"Your secret's safe with me," she called after him, but the feeling of triumph was short-lived.

She'd been teasing, but David was a private person. Clare felt heat rise up her neck. He definitely liked someone and was probably mortified that she'd mentioned it. Leaving her own plate, she hurried after him. The stairwell to the ground floor was quiet after the noise of the cafeteria.

"Hey, I'm sorry. I was just playing around. Easier than worrying, right?"

He shrugged and kept going. "Whatever. It's fine, Clare."

So, she had two choices: Make a joke about him clearly not being a furry, in hopes of lowering the tension. Or just be awkward and let it drop. Not that it wasn't already awkward walking down the ground floor hall not talking.

The Dark Hours

"Okay. Well, I'll be around, you know, trying to write that article." He walked past her to his door. "Sweet dreams," she called after him, and he gave a little wave without looking back.

So that went great.

Clare walked down the hall to her own room but left the door open as she went in. Not that anyone was going to need her or anything. Or that she'd miss the commotion of a returning team. She'd only been gone a few days, but she'd forgotten how small the warehouse could feel sometimes.

Sinking onto her bed, she faced the hall with her notebook on her lap and tapped a pen against it. The sound wasn't quite like the tapping of a keyboard, but it soothed her nerves a little anyway. With everything else going on, having a piece to write added a sense of normalcy to the chaos. Even in this place, and despite the shifting she could feel inside herself, she still had this.

And she couldn't focus on it.

The information she had might literally make the difference between life and death for someone, and her mind kept slipping back to David. She wasn't even worried that he might be mad at her. He was perpetually mad at someone. It gave him fuel to get up in the morning. Rather, she was going over a list of immortals that might possibly be of interest to him.

He didn't actually like a lot of people. Anyone that seemed fake or pretentious was out, and pretentious definitely eliminated Adrian.

Not that David had shown any inclination toward him at all. From what she'd been able to gather of his type, he liked them intelligent and male. Beyond that, he didn't seem too picky about exteriors.

So, despite his asocial nature, David had found someone he enjoyed. And it had to be killing him.

As he wasn't a "complete idiot," he'd probably choose to squash the feelings. Maybe he'd have better luck at that than she'd had. Should he want to pursue it though...

What were the chances that the immortal in question would be interested in a cranky, human lover?

Her very short experience told her those relationships both

happened and were a bad idea. Not that such facts were stopping her from considering it for herself, but one would have to suppose that much longer-lived entities had better sense.

God, she hoped not.

Clare threw herself back on the bed with a small groan of frustration. What the hell was wrong with her?

27

CHOICE

Clare's Notes:

What do I think I even can accomplish here? I'm in the way of the immortals, and even if I get a story out to the humans, it's not like anyone will believe it.

Miriam had spent the night in the hospital room with her parents, but in the morning, the last of her father's tests came back normal. He could be discharged.

And she couldn't delay any longer.

"Baby, can we take you somewhere?" Jem asked as she gathered their things. "I can't imagine just leaving you here."

Miriam shook her head. "I'll phone Perry's people, and we'll figure things out from there. It's better if you're gone anyway. I don't want you dragged into this too."

The slackness of her father's face was already resolving, and he looked healthier dressed in his regular clothes. Without any signs of weakness, he walked over to her, put a hand to her cheek, and drank in the sight of her.

"Promise you'll be safe."

She couldn't meet his eyes, so she just lowered her head against him. "I promise, daddy." The sound of his heartbeat in his chest was steady and strong, and he held her tight.

Then, the nurse was in the room with a wheelchair to see them out. Her father tried to wave it off, but it was still time to go. She gave her mama one last hug and kiss as her father complained that there was nothing wrong with his legs while being settled in the chair. She watched them leave with the ache of not knowing when she'd see them again, but she knew she couldn't linger.

There might not be much time before the nurse came back or someone came to clean the room. Miriam dug out her journal to double check the number she'd written and then grabbed the phone in the room.

"You've reached Winchester answering service. Please leave your contact information, and we'll get back with you." A long beep followed the message.

"This is Miriam. I'm fine. The baby's fine. But you don't own me. You don't own my body, and you sure as hell don't own my future. I'm going to determine that myself. You don't get to decide whether or not I come back. If you want to meet to discuss things, I'll be at the Biscuit Barn near the hospital in downtown Roanoke."

THE WIND WAS cold as the sun spilled early morning light that didn't seem to give any warmth yet. The drive would have only taken a few minutes, but the walk was twenty minutes—which felt like an hour with all the cement and cars and grumpy commuters. Her small town was fine, but the city had always felt a bit much. Give her the woods any day.

When Miriam finally got to the cozy little restaurant, the person at the register shot her a strange look. Probably didn't get too many people in hiking boots and duffle bags coming in. Could also be the dark rings and exhaustion on her face too. Oh well.

Miriam had been here a couple times before when she came to

The Dark Hours

Roanoke with friends. It was small and quiet enough that someone threatening her wouldn't go unnoticed. Which was a plus. And their food was amazing.

Just the smell of biscuits and coffee was making her stomach growl, and how long had it been since she'd been able to eat a good meal? Hospital food definitely didn't count. Well, the baby was hungry today, and if salivating at reading the words was any indication, baby wanted a large homemade biscuit, a cup of fruit, and probably the chicken and waffles.

Miriam sat down to wait for her food and her guest. It'd been a little over an hour since she'd called. If they drove from Richmond, it would be about another two hours before her guest showed. But maybe no one would come. And what would she even say if they did?

Her breakfast came, and she could swear her taste buds were more sensitive. The nausea was barely registering, and nothing had ever tasted so good. She devoured every last bite.

An overly full stomach and the soft murmur of people was making her feel a little sleepy despite the coffee. As the food settled, a light fluttering low in her belly spread a warm happiness through her.

Good morning little Phoenix, she thought at it. *Enjoying your breakfast too, huh?*

She hadn't been paying attention to the door, it hadn't been long enough yet, but it was hard to miss the woman who walked in next. Her skin was a rich balsamic color. Tall, lithe, and stunning in her bright makeup and chic clothes, she looked like she belonged in the city. The woman's gaze fell on Miriam, and she felt a tingle at the base of her skull.

Therian.

Somehow even without yellow eyes or any other tells, her own animal instincts had learned to spot danger. Survival training had taught her to listen when alarm bells were going off in her body. Heart racing, fingers itching, and an arm instantly over her stomach, Miriam watched as the woman made her way over and sat across the table from her. No one looked their way.

"I'm Sadé." The woman's voice was deep and rich but didn't have any of the African timbre that Miriam had been expecting based on her appearance.

"Miriam."

"I know. I have a phone call for you."

The woman pulled a small phone out of a yellow purse big enough to hold a week's worth of backpacking supplies. She dialed a number Miriam couldn't make out and handed the phone over.

"What the fuck are you thinking—" Meg didn't wait for a greeting before starting in.

Oh no. This was not how things were going to go down.

"No. You will *not* talk to me like that. I don't care who you are or how much power you have. I'll hang up the phone and be on the first ship to the middle of the ocean before you can shit yourself over it."

There was silence on the other end, but Miriam would wager a week's earnings that it was only because of shock. She needed to get her words out before she lost her nerve. Or the advantage.

"Look, I need my people, so I know it wouldn't be right to keep my baby from its people either." Miriam could hear the heavy exhale on the other side. "I realize this is happening at the worst possible time, and...I'm sorry for that. I don't want you to have your attention divided when your people need you. But I'm not going back. If you've got an idea that could work for both of us, I'll listen."

"You have more nerve than is healthy for a human." Miriam felt her fingers curl into a fist, but Meg sighed and her voice lost a little of its steel. "Would you consider staying with a group of survivors at a Therian monitored site?"

It was Miriam's turn to sigh. "For how long, and would I be able to see my family?"

"It would be better if the baby was born with us."

Who knew what Meg wasn't saying. There could easily be complications with the pregnancy or other difficulties that she was hiding. Then again, maybe she was just planning on stealing the baby.

"Why?"

The Dark Hours 197

"If it's Therian, there will be anomalies when its blood is drawn that will trigger vampire attention," Meg said.

That sounded legit, but that didn't mean there weren't other reasons. "Anything else?" Miriam asked.

Meg gave a snort that could have been an attempt at a laugh. "Of course Perry would pick a woman who could vex me in his absence. There's a hundred more reasons, but as you said, this is the worst possible time. I'd prefer to know you're safe and then discuss logistics."

"How can I trust a single word you say?" Someone turned to look, and Miriam lowered her voice to a fierce whisper. "How do I know you won't just take the baby or turn me?"

"I earned that. I've earned your suspicion."

It wasn't an apology, but it was something.

There was silence for a moment longer, and then Meg said, "Maybe we have to believe in Perry, in the trust he had in each of us."

Miriam swallowed at the sudden thickness in her throat. Perry saw the best in anyone. He saw what they could be. And he'd better be right about his grandma because if she turned out to be psychotic, Miriam would find him in the afterlife and thrash him for the rest of time.

"Okay." This definitely did not seem like a smart survival decision. Her brain screamed against it even as her heart was strangely at peace.

"Okay," Meg echoed.

"Now what?"

"There's a small group that's settled in the area north of you there in Roanoke. Hippie types who like living off the land. The locals think they're a commune. The Therians who run it are friends but not part of my tribe. I would know you were safe and could contact you as soon as I was able."

She didn't know much about Heliophiles, but living off the land had always appealed to her. It was a surprisingly decent suggestion.

"What about my parents?"

"I doubt there's any immediate danger to them, but whatever kind of contact is to be risked will have to be decided by that community. I don't have jurisdiction there, just friendship."

As vague of an answer as that was, knowing Meg didn't have jurisdiction gave her some comfort.

"I can work with that," Miriam said finally.

There was a huff on the other end, but Meg said, "All right. I'll make the arrangements and have Sadé transport you."

Miriam glanced at Sadé. With Therian hearing, she had to have heard every word of the conversation, but she'd pulled a smart phone out of her cavernous bag and had been looking at it while Miriam talked.

"Okay."

"Good," Meg said, and the line went silent as she ended the call.

Miriam handed the burner back to Sadé. "I'm surprised you carry tech on you. Most of those I've met in your...organization seem phobic of stuff like that."

"I'm a courier," she said with a shrug. "But my purse is insulated to keep my phone from being turned on or accessed when it's in there."

That sounded about right.

"Not all of us are like that though." Her eyes searched Miriam's. "Many of us have normal lives. It's those of us that feel a greater social responsibility that have to be more careful."

A normal life seemed the furthest thing from possible, but Miriam just nodded.

There was a ping on Sadé's phone. She typed back, and then motioned to Miriam as she stood.

"They've agreed to have you."

THEY DROVE for around an hour in a sleek old Toyota that handled the mountain roads surprisingly well. If nothing else, the fall display of colors was stunning in the afternoon sun. Miriam had been holding her body tight and ready for weeks, and a little sunshine and hope threatened her with a melty drowsiness. Driving to a new

The Dark Hours

Therian location was no time for contentment, and yet a gentle bump in her belly disagreed.

Miriam felt the smile on her face. It was so irrational, the love she felt for the little life growing in her. She didn't know if it was a boy or a girl or even if it was human or Therian. But she knew she would spend her last breath to protect it. More than that, she was trading the life she thought she'd have, all her hopes and dreams, and it was worth it.

She hadn't fully known the cost when she chose Perry, and she still didn't know. Her heart might never recover. But she knew that with this choice the cost was everything, and she was all in.

Sadé turned from a paved road to a dirt one in a tree-filled holler, the jolt bringing Miriam out of her thoughts. They passed a sign announcing Peaceful Acres followed by several No Trespassing signs. No wonder locals thought it was a commune. But for all that, there was a calm sort of beauty. The trees and shrubs felt purposeful despite a lack of anything that suggested an ordered farm. The forest cleared about a half mile in and a cluster of cabins were sprinkled about well-tended plots.

If the people weren't bat shit crazy—fingers crossed—she could probably be content here. At least until the baby was born.

28

SOOTHED

Clare's Notes:

Seeing people normally is like seeing the topside of an embroidered fabric. Everything is neat and makes sense. Stretching is like seeing the underside. It's chaotic, but you're seeing so much more of what goes into it. Also, you could pull on the smallest thread and affect the whole picture. Or make it unravel.

There wasn't even a clock in Clare's room, and she could still feel the minutes crawling eternally by. Time could fly when she was in the zone with a piece, but this one wasn't coming together at all. The more earnestly she tried to convey the danger the more it sounded like the assertions of a paranoid crackpot who'd invested in a lifetime supply of tinfoil hats.

But seriously, was there actually a way to say "don't go out at night because of marauding gangs of vampires" without sounding insane?

If the field of wadded up paper that littered her bed and floor was

The Dark Hours 201

any indication, probably not. Clare sighed. It would have to be good enough.

That wasn't the only problem though. Meg's tribe was well coordinated, but internet influence wasn't one of their in-house specialties. Even if she managed to piece together something semi-coherent, she wasn't going to be able to get it on the web from here. David had been no help, and while Adrian had come back, he and any Therian she might wheedle about assisting her were in a meeting with Meg.

It didn't help that she could feel the anxiety in the building. It seemed to crawl palpably over her.

A ripple, like a moan, pushed through her spirit. Jonathan was awake. His pain was quieter now, but even so, its constant presence was like a weight in her consciousness. Add that to the tension already filling the place, and it was overwhelming.

There had to be a way to shut it out.

Clare got up and closed the door to her room, paced a time or two, and then lay down. Slipping over the edge of herself into that liminal place happened as easily as an unintentional prayer. Her Watcher wasn't directly with her, but that meant little here.

"Hey. Can I ask you something?" Clare sent the question out along the thread that connected them.

There was quiet in the dark richness while she waited, and then, the presence of flame. The heat was in her soul, but its burn was different somehow, and Clare could feel her heart in her body begin to drum faster. She didn't know what was wrong, hardly knew anything about this creature at all, but something wasn't right.

And it made her afraid.

"Don't fear."

And suddenly, it was like she was lying in the sun on a perfect day. Everything in her body relaxed. It should make her suspicious that this being could just snap her into this state of mind, but she felt too safe to be worried. If this was what being *soothed* felt like, she could make a killing doing it. It was delightful.

"Well, I was going to ask how to shut out all the...feelings? I honestly don't know what I've been picking up on. But it's all gone now," Clare said.

Her Watcher acknowledged the gratitude in Clare's calm being with a pleased feeling. *"Your mind will learn how to tune out the background noise as it does with your other senses, but those things can be blocked out purposely."*

She wasn't afraid anymore, but she was still aware of the difference in her Watcher. Its attention was with her but also elsewhere. If Clare focused, she could almost see what it was.

"No." The command jolted through her. *"Your ability can reach places you aren't ready for, and I cannot be the mentor you should have had. However, I can show you this."*

Her Watcher strummed the connection between her and Jonathan. It didn't frown—not in the sense of a facial expression that a person could see—but Clare could feel the curious displeasure at the connection with its fibers of pain and agitation running through it like an undertow. Then, its attention moved from her.

"I must go. Be careful of that one."

And it pushed against her, the heat backing Clare into herself. It was the opposite of a *stretch*. She was pressed firmly into the corners of herself until she could no longer feel her connections. There was no heat from her Watcher or pain from her friend. There wasn't any excitement strumming through the building, nothing except the physical world around her physical body. It was like having all sound gone after hearing something too loud for too long. It felt like a loss.

And a relief.

Clare felt a faint smile twitch at the corners of her lips.

Probably could write a little better now without all the new stimulation in the background. Ooh, and tea. Tea would be nice. She could just sit in the quiet with tea and write...about vampires wantonly slaughtering in the city. That'd be great for the zen bubble she was still kind of in.

In the calm, she lay there thinking about the *soothe*. She'd done it to David, when they were both prisoners of the vampires, without even knowing what she was doing. Everything was wrong, and yet

The Dark Hours 203

somehow she'd been able to...lie to him? Convince him? Adjust him into rest?

Lying seemed impossible in the liminal realm, and yet when she managed to touch his life, it was like she could move it in the direction she wanted. Her mind itched, like it was on the cusp of understanding but still didn't. Idly she wondered if that was what cult leaders were doing without realizing it.

Clare snorted and then sighed. As nice as the quiet chill she felt was, it was lonely.

Correction: She felt lonely. She'd left her old life purposely once. Changed her name, quit hanging out with the people who knew her "before." This was different than when she ran away from who she was.

It was embracing who she was that'd changed everything, and the people who understood that were all busy with other life-or-death stuff. She could be too, actually. She could be polishing her piece and figuring out how best to deliver it. Instead, she was busy wishing she could talk to people she had no way of reaching.

Except...

She could contact Miriam again. Even the thought of it made her feel less alone.

Now to see if she could reach out selectively without all the other sensations flooding in. Clare didn't want to open the gates, just crack a window.

Staying aware of her body, she tried to search for her bond to Miriam. It was definitely harder, like groping for something she knew was there but couldn't see. And when she latched onto it, she couldn't feel the complexity of life that was Miriam, just the idea of her. Maybe this was more like normal *stretching*. The immortals seemed surprised by what she was experiencing with Jonathan.

Puffing the breath out of her cheeks, Clare let go a little more. And then a little more, until Miriam snapped into focus. She wasn't necessarily calm, but she felt confident, unlike the last time they'd been together. And Clare felt a thread of recognition rise in her.

"Hey girl," Miriam said.

"Hey. You seem good."

"You don't have to act surprised," Miriam said with a chuckle. "But yeah, I'm good. It's actually kinda nice at the survivor colony."

"Oh! I didn't realize you were... How did that happen?"

"Meg doesn't tell anyone anything, does she?"

While Miriam had said she was going to visit her parents for perspective, it was shocking to hear Meg was involved. Clare had no idea what all Miriam could perceive of her in that space, but she responded to Clare's emotion without anything being said.

"We reached a sort of middle ground. If I stay here, I'm not under her thumb, but she knows I'm safe."

"Not gonna lie. I'm glad to know you're safe too. It's crazy here, and I have no idea why I'm even staying anymore."

"And you said you weren't going to lie."

"I—"

"I haven't even known you that long, and I know you're staying because not knowing would drive you crazy. You want to be in the action."

Since when did she become so transparent? Best just to blame it on the wonky properties of *stretching* and not dwell on the thought that everyone might be able to read her so well.

"Okay. Yes. I want to stay, but I shouldn't. It's not logical. It'll probably get me killed, and I don't seem to be helping anything here. Just tell me I'm stupid, and I need to take advantage of the chaos and go make a new life."

Again.

"At the risk of sounding self-centered, I'd like to know there are people like you around as Phoenix is growing up. It's different here. Better, I think, but I can't keep them from Perry's side of the family." There was a pause, but Clare could tell Miriam wasn't done. She seemed to be picking through her thoughts. "Especially if the baby has the Therian trait."

The words hit Clare with a force of emotion from Miriam that was impossible not to be swept up in, like a river flooding over its banks.

The Dark Hours

"The pregnancy is progressing faster than normal, and I'm scared and amazed. And I could do this on my own, just run forever, but I don't think that's what is best for the baby, even if I wanted it. So, I have to believe there is more or better, and that I'm making the right choice and not bringing this beautiful life into darkness. What kind of selfish person would do that? Maybe I shouldn't, but once I decided to keep it, there was no going back. Right or wrong I'm doing this, and I'd feel better if you were around for it too."

It was beautiful, the pure communication of friendship, trust, and fear. Clare had felt feelings like that before, but putting them into words always felt like a trap, and why bother risking that openness not being returned?

Miriam's vulnerability was given like a gift.

With every intention she could find, Clare brought up her own feelings and pushed. She shared her surprise and enjoyment of their friendship, shared her fear of being useless, and shared her desire to be there for Miriam however she could. It wasn't *soothing*. There was no convincing, no twisting or bending someone's emotions into another shape.

Just naked honesty.

Through their bond, she could feel Miriam receive it, and the intimacy of it was startling. But Miriam didn't withdraw from the interaction.

The openness felt threatening. It was easier to write and pour her heart into an article. Strangers couldn't touch her heart. Not really. And she couldn't really hurt them. But she was here with Miriam, directly somehow, with no requirement other than herself. There was no mask or achievement to hide behind, and no need for it. She was seen and accepted.

Wanted even.

It felt like being a little girl on the playground asking the other little girl if she wanted to be friends. And the other girl said, "yes." Simple as that.

"Then I'll be here."

"Thank you," Miriam said. "It's good to know we're not alone in this."

29

LIGHT-BEARER

Clare's Notes:

God. Something's happening to me. I feel too much. It's so loud. And there's no volume button.

The energy in the warehouse had remained tense over the next several days, but it gave Clare ample opportunity to practice opening and closing her awareness. It made her feel like she was at least doing something. So, after breakfast with David—the only time she was sure to run into him—she went back to her room and sat on the bed.

She focused on the in and out of her breath and on the boundary of her body. It was strong and almost solid. On a deep inhale, she created a small opening. The trick had been to push out while opening so the sensations didn't rush in. It was like learning to swim underwater and keeping the air in her nose so that water didn't fill it.

This way, she could reach outside her bubble and choose what she brought in. That was the greater problem: what to choose. She'd *stretched* to Miriam a few times and was pleased to find the woman feeling more at peace staying with the survivors, but she'd been invited to do that.

It would be rude to just *stretch* to someone without reason or invitation. The connection with Jonathan could overwhelm her, and it just saddened her besides. Her Watcher was busy doing God only knew what. Oh, she'd be there instantly if Clare needed her, but she didn't. When she reached out, Clare was met with an almost absent-minded acknowledgment and then a push back—like she came up against her Watcher's own bubble.

With no better ideas at hand, Clare felt out spatially. The Therians were easy to avoid with their bulking life mass. Like having her eyes adjust to darkness, when she was away from the power of their beings, other things came into focus. She could feel the hum of the earth and observe tiny spots of light like a million stars. She chose a larger one of these and brushed its life—a life that hid and explored, life that burrowed and nested.

Her touch startled it, and that startled her.

"No, no. Shhh. It's okay. You're safe."

And it calmed...*soothed* with her unintended influence. Clare could feel both its acquiesce and the gentle use of her energy to cause it.

A sharp noise brought her back to her anchor with a hard snap. She blinked, trying to reorient herself as the rapping on her door continued.

That kind of arrogant insistence could only be one person.

As soon as the door opened, he came in without invitation and turned mid-room to look back with an expression somewhere between irritation and impatience.

"Yes?"

"Aren't you going to shut the door?" Adrian asked.

"Is this one of those visits that requires a shut door?"

She was being playful, but when he answered flatly with a "yes," Clare found her mouth drying.

"Okay," she said, shutting the door softly. It had been days of

The Dark Hours

feeling pent up, of wishing for something to occupy her, and suddenly, she wanted to take back her wishes.

"Sit." Adrian motioned to the single chair in the corner.

"No. Why? What's this about?"

But then she knew, because it was all there imprinted on her psyche: the nervousness, being told to have a seat...being told about her mother. Her world had always pivoted on that point.

"Tell me. Tell me what they found out about her."

Adrian looked to the ceiling and blew out a breath. "The Therians have next to no information on your people."

So, she was a people now? "You mean light-bearers?"

"Yes." He ran a hand through his hair, and a few pieces stayed at odd angles. "So, we started by looking into your mother."

He paused. Unease pooled in her stomach at seeing Adrian flustered.

"She had four name changes aside from when she was just using a pseudonym. They were well done, hard to unravel even with medical records and DNA." He was talking fast now, and Clare was grateful because she couldn't move and wouldn't be able to again until she could see the picture he was trying to paint—like a three-year-old trying to recreate a Picasso no less. "If I'm correct on the first one, and I'm not entirely sure, she was born in Austria to a person clearly using a pseudonym. From there, I only found three hits through her childhood. All involve instances that required medical assistance, and all were in different places. One of them was rural Siberia."

"Siberia?"

He went on as though she hadn't interrupted. "Another was Botswana, and the final was Israel. We lose her there, and the woman she travels with, presumably your grandmother. They're very good at staying off the record. When she shows up again, it's from blood work in a hospital in Louisiana at age 20. This was a car accident, hit and run according to bystanders. Two years after that are the first non-fabricated records of Eliana on a job application in New York. That's where she eventually meets your father. From then, she's a typically documented presence until her death 13 years later. According to Sune, the only reason we were able to tie Eliana to the medical records abroad is that those places weren't reporting to the universal system when her records were previously scrubbed, but they were still advanced enough to include DNA in their panels."

Clare's memories of her mother had been influenced by pictures and stories, she knew that, but she didn't remember a woman on the run. Her mother was quiet but strong, beautiful and kind. She didn't have the hunted look of the survivors...

But now as Clare searched her memory, her mother liked to go to bed early, and she didn't remember close friends. Her mom's life was her children, and that didn't seem strange. Until now. The parallels in her own life were impossible to miss.

"My mom was a light-bearer, and she knew it."

Adrian's nod was slow. "It seems so, and your grandmother too."

"And she was in New York, and then here?" Pieces of information were shifting, reorienting. "Is there a large vampire population in New York?"

"One of the largest," he said.

"And if she knew what she was...in that place..."

Was her kind mother quietly slaughtering vampires in New York? Clare couldn't imagine her hunting them, but maybe she'd perfected what Clare had just been practicing and was able to pick them off slowly enough not to be noticed. There was so much that was speculation. So much unwritten.

"So then she moves here, when she 'settles down' and marries."

Adrian didn't say anything.

"So what, she was killing vampires in Richmond while raising a family?"

"It's possible, but if she was, it was gradual enough that no one at Nidhi was alerted."

With that name, another piece of information shifted. Her eyes fell to the moonstone ring on her finger, and Clare's breath was coming fast now. "How did my father find you? Was my mother alive when he first contacted you?"

"Based on the timeframe...yes."

Her world shrank to a pinpoint, like the nails digging into her palms. "Did you do it? Did your *people*," she sneered the word, "kill her?"

Adrian met her eyes, and she could see it there. "Everything points to it being an accident."

"But."

"But it was after dark, and it wouldn't have needed to be premeditated for a vampire to see her glow and want to run her into the barrier."

"Is there anything else?" Clare asked.

"Not yet."

"Thank you. Now please get out."

"Clare—"

"GET OUT!"

But he didn't.

"What's wrong with you?" Clare was moving toward him now. "Why is it that everything that's messed up in my life points back to you?"

She pushed him then, and his body seemed to absorb the force. And it wasn't right. He should hurt and bow under the blows like she had her whole life.

"It was always you." She was pounding on his chest with the words. "You've taken everything from me!"

But he didn't even raise his hands to ward off her assault because it couldn't possibly hurt him. Meanwhile, her heart was bleeding.

"Why won't you leave me alone!" Her voice pitched into a scream only to fall into sobs.

Clare was crying into his shoulder, absorbed in the shock and pain, and then she felt his arms encircle her. Her body stiffened for a moment, then the fight blew out of her, and she let herself be held as she wept.

30

FAMILY

Clare's Notes:

While both...species??...of immortal phase into different states, I'm told sometimes Therians lose control when that happens. As a huge fan of control, vampires are superior here.

The nondescript blue cover-alls of a general maintenance worker was a very different look from the posh suits Adrian wore when working for Nidhi. Both were more comfortable than being reminded he was the worst thing to ever happen to Clare...and then staying and trying to fucking comfort her.

He scanned the weed strewn parking area as his team cut the chain from the doors of a long defunct brick factory, glad to be anywhere but the warehouse right now. Police had searched the area already, but they'd cleared this part a couple days ago. Not that they'd know a vampire nest from a literal hole in the ground if it grew fangs and bit them on their collective asses.

The thrill of the hunt sang in his blood even as he stared at the black empty space before them. Adrian had been on the go almost continuously since the battle at Nidhi, and in the down moments, he was beginning to feel frayed at the edges...blurry. But he wasn't going to waste Perry's life or this chance to inflict more damage to the Solifugae while they were still reeling from that blow.

His team filed in.

Brad was thick and looked like he belonged in a heavy lifting contest. Adrian didn't need to ask his origin. The man's bearish nature was there even in human form. Emma, he'd met before. The quiet she-wolf was cunning and deadly in a fight. Crazy Mule was indigenous and most definitely not an equine. His turning was later in life, and he looked perpetually hale and around fifty. Unlike the so-called "civilized" cultures, Therians were accepted and respected among most native peoples. Adrian had never asked what had brought him into Meg's fold—everyone had a story, and they were never pleasant—but his reputation matched his given name well.

Akito was the only weak member of the team. He was young and untrained, but after seeing the footage of what vampires were doing in Richmond, he was also refusing to stay put. Faced with his nephew taking things into his own hands, Sune had requested he be put on Adrian's team.

Sure, it was a fucking honor to have Sune put that much trust in him, but working with the pup was *not*. Frankly, it was a headache he didn't need. The kid was new, brash, and purple hair aside, he didn't seem able to blend into any situation. Apart from the scuffle with Jonathan, he'd never been in a real fight with an immortal.

Perry would have loved breaking him in.

The team had done their best to give Akito direction and advice, but without discussing it, they kept him in the middle of the group. At least he had the sense to keep his voice down when they entered the building.

Once inside, they paused as one.

It was so different, the Therian change over the vampiric one. He'd always assumed there was a similar force at work, and maybe there was, but it felt as different as desert and ocean. Maybe that was just the mingling of the blood, but he didn't think so. It felt like he wore his skin like one wears clothing, but moving underneath it was naked, animal truth. There was no need for anger or bloodlust, only a release of the constraints holding him in.

The discomfort in changing was similar, not that he'd allowed himself to fully go into that form. Therians could lose themselves in a change. A lot of the accidental bites occurred that way, and the last thing anyone needed was to have to figure out if whatever Adrian now was happened to be contagious.

No. Fucking. Way.

When things were more stable, he'd experiment with how well he could keep his mind in that form. In the meantime, he held the change in check just past the surface, letting his senses and teeth sharpen. Vampire eyes were better in the dimness, and while he could call up that part of himself during the daylight now, it required a much greater drain of life.

And this was not the time to get sloppy.

The smells of the building rose up around him. Damp concrete, city dust, and sharpest of all, *eau de vampire* accompanied by a tang of blood. A very low rumble came from Akito. Adrian *stretched*, tugging the youth to attention, and the boy fell silent.

That was different too. Loyalty among the Therians wasn't bought with power or strength. He could feel the bonds of their kinship in his being now. A *stretch* along those bonds was like the touch of a family member. It could be soothing or annoying, but regardless, it was family. His touch wasn't quite the same as theirs, but it was familiar enough that when he signaled through it, the tense pack followed.

It had always seemed like a marvel to vampires that the less organized and less advanced Therians could hold out against their influence. Now Adrian had to wonder how the Therians hadn't been even more victorious. If vampires bonded like this, if they used *stretches* to weave individuals into a group instead of as a way to intimidate and command, they would have defeated the Therians long ago.

It was fucking dangerous information.

He banished the thought and focused. If this was a daytime nest, there were only a few places they could be on this level with the light streaming in through broken windows. His team approached what looked like a supply area, a thick door surrounded by cinder blocks. Brad crept forward and snuffled at the crease of the door. He shook his head but then drew in another deep breath. His nose wrinkled, and he followed it past that door into the deeper gloom of the building. Adrian drew air in as well, but whatever the bear's nose was picking up eluded him.

One by one, they followed the big man. At the far back of the structure was a kitchen area. The scant sunlight that filtered to the room still would be too much, but the large walk-in freezer would make an excellent hiding place. The scent of vampire was heavier here and almost rancid. Rusty brown blood smeared the walls and made trails on the floor out a single door on the other side of the room.

Emma jerked her head toward the freezer, and Adrian nodded. She and Crazy Mule already had a light in hand and stood on the far side of the freezer door. Adrian drew his Khanjali dagger from inside his coveralls and twirled it once to feel the balance of it. Then, Emma grabbed the handle and flung the door open.

They were assaulted by the smell of flesh just beginning to decay, mostly vampire, but nothing moved. For a moment, an animal rage rose up. Adrian tightened his grip on the beast, while behind him, Akito made a sick noise. Damn inexperienced pup. Maybe this would teach him to stay home next time. There was nothing glorious about war. Crazy Mule switched on the sun flare, and light flooded into the space.

Cazzo di merda!

It looked like something Lachlan might think to do.

Lined up on old rusting shelves were body parts. They seemed to be set out by some deranged system. There was a calf and ankle split with bone protruding from the gore. A collection of small bits like eyes, teeth, and toes on a baking tray. A torso lay splayed open in a shallow bath of blood, innards rifled through but mostly present.

There was at least one vampire represented, and based on the smell, some of the smaller bits had to be human. A fetid steam began to rise from where the flare hit vampiric flesh. It was hard to tell anything more without close examination, and he'd rather have a chat with a Watcher than do that.

Adrian sheathed his knife, and Emma who'd taken only the briefest of glances, carefully closed the door.

"What the fuck was that?" Akito whispered, eyes accusatory and burning on Adrian.

"Listen," Adrian whispered back, "I know you're young, but if you can't work with me, Sune will have you shipped to the caves. It's what he should have fucking done in the first place."

"He couldn't make—"

Emma cut him off. "You're either in this tribe or you're not. We don't have time to deal with lone wolves right now, but trust me, we *can* make you go. And Adrian's right. That's where you should be."

Apparently, he wasn't the only one put out to have the pup on the team.

Akito drew his lips back from his teeth, fingers twitching, but thankfully said nothing.

"This has got to be the rogue," Crazy Mule said, turning off the light and ignoring the interaction all together. "And those bodies are fresh. This is the trail we needed. He might even still be here."

All eyes went to the blood smear on the other door, and *Madonna Santa*, Adrian hoped he was still here. There wasn't a single part of him that didn't want to rip that creature limb from limb.

"Stay close. It's likely untrained, but since it's taking out other vampires now that means it's gaining strength, skill, or both. Brad, see if you can scent it out."

Brad and Crazy Mule took the front, and Adrian motioned Akito to go in front of him and Emma. The door led to a foyer. There was another door down the small hall with sunlight streaming through its rectangular window and a doorway to the right, opening on a stairwell to a lower level. The smell of coagulating blood wafted up from the dark maw on stale air.

The Dark Hours

Crazy Mule flicked the flare back on and illuminated blood spattered iron steps. Emma took out a flare as well, and as the group descended, they swept the lights back and forth. The space had mostly been emptied. A large machine, with no easily discernible purpose, stood alone in a concrete wasteland. But there were rooms beyond the main one, and the trail of blood thickened to the left towards one.

The door was hanging askew on its hinges, and the closer they got, the more the smell of dead blood clogged his nose. In the absolute stillness, every movement seemed loud.

"I can't take this smell."

Adrian felt his body stiffen with alarm as Akito spoke. He whirled on the pup.

"Then don't fucking breathe or go outside, but don't alert our quarry that we're here with your useless noise." Without waiting to see what he would do, Adrian started back toward the open door, body tense and ready.

When they were near enough that their light shone in, it reflected off a cooled pool of blood and another dismembered body. This one was definitely vampire. Adrian turned his eyes from the flayed flesh and looked around the room. Among the gore was a backpack, open and spilling supplies: flashlights, clothing, and syringes filled with the slight yellow of Z.I.P.s. Had the sick fuck even taken anything?

No one stepped fully into the room. What they were looking for wasn't there any longer. The other rooms in the basement smelled faintly of vampire as well, but that could have been accomplished with exactly what they were doing now: a casual search.

Everything was empty.

When they reached the top of the stairs, Akito pushed past the team and headed for the door that led outside. Adrian motioned for the others to continue the sweep of the building but only to be thorough. He was certain the rogue wasn't here. Instead, he followed the pup out the back door, and found him drawing in deep breaths of the old industrial air.

"Not what you thought you were getting into?"

"Fuck glass you bastard," Akito said in between huffs. "None of that makes sense." He added, slicing the air with his hand, "None of it."

"Two vampires is too few for a nest, but maybe they were an initial scouting party looking for a new location. Could be a sign of a larger group looking for purchase in the area, and they picked the wrong building."

"It's not that." Akito looked across the parking lot to the straggling trees lining a drainage area. "Before my turning, Uncle Sune warned me. He told me about vampires, how they kill us and even each other. This was not that."

"No. It wasn't. I've only met one other vampire that seemed to take such pleasure in..."

For a moment, Adrian could feel Lachlan's hands in his body, ripping. He walked away from the shadow of the building, letting the warm afternoon sun pull him out of the memory. The shock of sunlight landing gentle on his skin hadn't worn off yet.

"But he's dead."

"Are you sure?"

Adrian looked down at his hands, as if Lachlan's bloody head would still be in them.

"Very."

That bastard was dead, and if what happened to Jonathan was any indicator, all of his progeny were too. He couldn't see a way it was even possible that one of his escaped both the attack on the mansion and Lach taking his life back. It would have to be a young one to be so completely without understanding...

Adrian shook his head. Akito was right. It didn't make sense.

"Let's go sniff around over there." Akito nodded toward the drainage area.

The others hadn't come back out yet, but Adrian was sure there was no one left in the building. And what could it hurt as long as they stayed in the sun?

As they walked over, Akito kept glancing at him out of the side of his eye.

The Dark Hours 219

"Don't trust me?" Adrian asked.

"Don't know you."

"At least you're not a total fucking idiot then. I know it's supposed to be different among the Therians, but I wouldn't be alive if I trusted easily."

"Then how the hell did you ever trust a Therian in the first place?"

Adrian could still feel the wild flavor of Perry in his blood. "Long story, but you've heard the saying, 'the enemy of my enemy is my friend?'"

Akito nodded.

"It was easier to trust someone else who hated vampires. The better question is: how the hell did Perry ever trust me?"

The question sat like a heavy stone in his gut. He wanted to be the selfless kind of person who could wish they'd never met. Perry's trust in a vampire had led to his death. But Adrian wouldn't take it back, even if he could.

Akito was staring at him openly now. It was unnerving, especially from an immortal, but Adrian held his gaze. Then, as if seeing what he was looking for, Akito nodded and said, "From one person who hates vampires to another, I don't trust Jonathan."

"Pretty sure the whole tribe knows that."

Akito reached out and grabbed his arm. It was an impulsive movement, and the pup drew his own hand back quickly but still said, "At least you aren't pretending to be something you're not. He's hiding something."

His hands were open, and his face was etched with raw sincerity. Didn't mean he was right, but he definitely thought he was. And saying as much to Adrian couldn't come easy.

Santa Maria. He was actually going to try and be diplomatic. He'd just have to blame the Therian blood and trauma on his recent uptick in caring.

"I'll keep it in mind. And I believe you, that you're picking up on something, but remember Jonathan's in a lot of pain. He could've betrayed us all so many times already and secured his family. He's earned some trust."

Akito's lips flattened into a line, but he didn't say anything more.

Together they slid down into the drainage area. It was a concrete ravine with plants breaking through here and there at the seams. A stream several feet across ran shallowly along with the typical flotsam and jetsam snagging on branches and floating serenely by. Based on the direction, it would eventually join the James River.

Adrian headed downstream, and Akito went the opposite. Over the slight sound of running water, Akito's active sniffing could be heard. Ambitious, but pointless. If this rogue was smart enough to use water to move, they weren't going to be sniffing him out just the two of them.

Rounding a slight bend, Adrian was met with more of the same. The drainage area wound among the old buildings until he lost sight of it. They'd need a bigger team to search it.

Akito shouted, and Adrian was running back through the water before he could even process that they were in the sun and nothing should be able to hurt the boy. In the distance, his colorful hair caught in the light and then disappeared into the concrete.

Merda! It was a drain pipe. A large one, and Akito was putting his body into the darkness inside it.

Alerting their quarry be damned.

"Get your fucking head out of there!"

Akito jerked up, but then rolled his eyes as Adrian skidded to a stop next to him.

"I wasn't going all the way in. I'm not stupid."

"I don't know you well enough to trust you either. For all I know, you're the most ignorant *figlio di puttana* ever to grace the fucking new world—sticking your fucking body in a possible fucking vampire lair! —and if I get you killed, your uncle is not going to just let it slide."

Akito snorted, but said, "Put your head in and sniff, ass face."

Adrian pushed between him and the pipe. The more space between the boy and the dark, the better.

A slight trickle of water was coming from the pipe even without

The Dark Hours

rain. With annoyance pricking his gums where his fangs hid, Adrian pushed his head in slightly and took a breath. The air was cool, and there was a faint odor of old blood combined with the smell of wet, rusting metal.

Cazzo di merda.

The fucker was in the drainage system. Maybe even in the sewers. A lone vampire could execute successful guerrilla warfare from the underground. Some covens grew from individuals surviving out of old subways and sewers for just that reason. Their prey may have more sense than he'd given it credit for. And that was never good.

Adrian stormed up the ravine with Akito following quickly behind him.

"So what's the plan of attack? Do we have Brad go in with the light and—"

Adrian cut him off. "Absolutely, if you feel like dying today. You have no idea what a maze it is down there. There's a million places a vampire could use as a bug-out hole, and if he's been living there, his smell will be everywhere."

Adrian snarled and shook his head.

"No. We have to gather up the team and get back to Meg. This has the potential to be very bad."

31

COMMUNITY

Clare's Notes:

My mother was a light-bearer and likely a vampire hunter. She might have died because of it.

Tear stains crinkle the paper and run the ink here

...alone.

It was warm for a fall day, and Miriam took advantage of it, sitting at the long outdoor table to eat the venison that had been hunted by one of the resident Therians.

If her dad ever saw this place, there would be no convincing him it wasn't a cult.

The inhabitants seemed to have a tendency toward loose, flowing clothes. Granted, those might be practical for the Therian members considering loose clothes might survive a transformation. Of course, mentioning shape-shifting to her dad as the reason for said fashion

The Dark Hours

wouldn't go over well either. He'd probably stop worrying about cults and start worrying about her sanity. No, him coming here was not a good idea; however, the leadership had agreed that Miriam going to visit her parents shouldn't be a risk as long as she kept said visits infrequent, like once or twice a month. The leadership also advised she wait a few days and get a feel for "the community" before making a decision about staying herself.

It had been nice to know she really had a say in the matter.

The place wasn't run by the Therians like Miriam had been expecting. The people themselves seemed cautiously friendly and diverse. There were a couple families with Therian members among the whole, and to her surprise, the survivors welcomed the extra protection.

The main section was full of controlled chaos. Children ran about the long central building with its play yard and eating area, shouting and playing like children anywhere would. While most were barefoot, they didn't look ill-kept. The buildings were rustic, but well-placed solar panels supplied electricity. All the while, people worked together at community tasks like making food, tending the garden, and keeping an eye on the little ones.

This was not the fear-filled environment she'd been expecting. There was safety here, and if not for the need for seclusion, this would seem beyond ideal. She would do whatever she had to, but it was shit that these two extremes were her only options. There had to be a middle ground between being in a Therian battle against the world and being completely isolated from it.

Longing for Perry rose up and ruined any appetite she still had. He'd isolated himself too, and even more so than the people here. He'd literally found a cave in the woods and had been content to stay there. And oh, she understood that, but so far, separation hadn't helped or solved anything other than giving her time to think.

Miriam glanced around at the community of people milling about, eating and chatting. Maybe they weren't as isolated as they seemed, and for certain, this was the best option she'd found yet. The stakes were so much higher now. She wasn't just living her life, taking risks where she wanted to. Her choices would affect not only her baby but also her family and friends. Being here allowed her to at least still have some contact with the outside world.

Phoenix kicked and rolled as dinner finally made its way down, and Miriam pushed back with her hand on her belly. The ethereal kick-kick that landed under her palm in response made her chuckle.

"Hi there. You like that better than traveling food, huh?"

"May I sit here?"

Miriam started at the soft voice that accompanied, what she was certain, was a Therian. Its source was a round woman, a little shorter than herself, with brown hair swept in a braid around her head and green eyes accentuated by the plum color of her simple shirt.

Miriam patted the empty stretch of bench next to her, and the woman sat.

"I'm Becca."

Okay. "Miriam."

"When you're done, I'll show you to our cabin."

"Our what?"

"Thomas said it was time you had a proper place to sleep instead of the main lodge."

It had been noisy.

"That is, so long as you plan on staying."

Miriam sighed. Yes. Yes, she did plan on staying.

The green, spicy smell of the log cabin greeted Miriam before she could fully see the bundles of herbs and flowers that hung from much of the rafter space. Despite her overactive olfactory senses, the smell was enjoyable, calming even. The main room had wood floors and a table that had to be handmade to one side and a kitchen-ish area with a sink that drained into a bucket and a small cast iron stove to the other. Toward the back were the rooms. Hers was rustic and tight, hardly fitting a small bed and chest for clothes, but Miriam preferred it that way. Like with her tent, it would be a quiet place to rest but not where she'd spend her day.

Becca didn't seem to have a Meg-sent agenda. Or any agenda at all. It made for a nice change.

The Dark Hours

After Miriam had gotten herself settled, Becca made tea from a blend of herbs she purported were good for pregnancy and nausea. Trying not to sound too suspicious, because *she* sure as hell didn't know what plants to avoid during pregnancy, Miriam asked where Becca learned her herbs.

Everything about the woman became animated as she talked about the plants around them and their properties. She'd begun learning in the 1600's and continued to learn as information became more widely available. But, she insisted for all the advances, some of the early knowledge was still the best.

"It's what got me killed though. They executed me as a witch."

Miriam choked on her drink of tea. "Excuse me?"

Becca looked mortified. "Oh. I'm sorry. All of us Therians have a story like that, you know, some wild thing that led to them being here. I didn't think how that would sound to you."

"Oh, I'm sure they do," Miriam said dryly. "It's not the turning part that got me so much as the being executed as a witch."

Becca shrugged as though that still wasn't a big deal. "Everyone has to die someway, and I had an unusual interest in plants. And no interest in men. I scorned one man too many, and suddenly I must be a witch. What I really am is on the autism spectrum, and back then, you didn't have to be far off neurotypical to be blamed for the blight at the neighbor's farm."

Like her friend Aiden from high school. His need to sit at a certain angle to the teacher and arrange his workspace just so had made him a target for bullying despite his great sense of humor. He was just far enough from "normal" to be a target. It probably wouldn't be too much a reach for today's bullies to be yesterday's witch hunters.

"My village used stoning. You don't have to look horrified. Had they hung me or drowned me, Thomas probably wouldn't have been able to help. Lucky for me, they dumped my body in the woods so it wouldn't offend the sacred ground of their cemetery, and there was just enough life left for him to turn me."

The woman took another sip of her tea, and Miriam forced her mouth closed.

"I know that sounds bad, but it was centuries ago, and I'm happy now. Here my knowledge of plants is wanted, and no one expects me to be anything other than who I am."

The woman's story, so casually delivered, was horrific. But in it was a different narrative of what it meant to be Therian. Perry and his gran had a story of questing for answers and revenge. Other's had stories of maulings and accidental turning. Through it all was the withdrawal and isolation she'd seen. Yet here was a story of thriving, not despite the immortal world but because of it. Becca wasn't holding herself above or apart but was being fulfilled in who she was.

Miriam had judged what it meant to live with Therians based on her own experience with them, and here was Becca with a wholly other narrative of what it could look like. It gave her a new scope of possibilities for the life growing inside her and just enough hope to look into what she'd been avoiding.

"Do you know much about the differences between a human and Therian pregnancy?"

32

GROWING

Clare's Notes:

There's a vampire out there drawing attention to itself. So now, all the local immortals are trying to find it before the scary international immortals step in and all hell breaks loose. Great.

The spider felt bigger than he had been.

Each night he'd fed until his body would hold no more, and the next night when he woke, he'd grown. But it was like a shadow grows. His body held the same, looked the same, but *he* was more.

Now when he hunted, he could hunt with more than his eyes. He truly was a spider with a web stretched out beneath him. Little meals passing by pricked the strands he stretched out. He hadn't learned to make his prey stick in the web yet, but it would come. He was still growing.

Maybe when he was done growing, his here-body would conform to his true form. The whole world would contain his web and all the little ants would know their place, as he did. They were there for him: for his pleasure, amusement, and nourishment. Horrid, base creatures that they were in life, they were actually delightful in death.

And he'd found a great mass of them close to the river. They were young and full of life and hope, while also being loud and blind to their surroundings. There was a lot of light there, but so many of these young ones sought out the shadows. They shared drinks and substances that made them laugh and stumble.

And they stayed out very late.

That there were so many made it harder to hunt. The spider waited for ants to fall into his web. Falling into an anthill would be a grave mistake. No matter the size of the spider, enough ants could bring it down. Mustn't do that.

But they smelled so very alluring under the stench of soaps and chemicals. So, he watched and listened before hunting.

There was a concept in his mind, an ant-mimic. Maybe, until he was full grown, he could look like them, act like them, and hide under their very lights.

He was soon convinced it would be harder than it looked. His own clothing was stained delicious, but the little fun bags would hardly see their dried juices that way. That would be easy enough to remedy though. Just had to be careful with dinner tonight.

He listened to a group near the trees he perched in. The words they used caused images to rise up in his mind, but how they even came up with such inconsequential things to be concerned about was baffling. Still, he recognized enough to be able to pick out the strong from the vulnerable. There were those that held a gaze and those that dropped their eyes. Those that smiled sharply and those that pressed their lips tight. Those that watched with a straight back and those who made themselves small.

Once he looked the part, he would start with those small ones. If they were stumbling or didn't look too closely, it should be easy. He could practice his mimicry until they smelled heavy of fear, and then he'd take them. His experience thus far told him they would be the least likely to scream or fight. As much as he loved the

The Dark Hours

screaming and fighting, screams here might bring too many other pests.

A pair branched off from the group he'd been watching, walking into a cluster of trees near the water and under him. Excellent.

They were close enough to the group that a shout would alert the others, but if he took care of the male quickly, the female might go still and silent long enough that he could kill her too. He could glut on one and have the other's clothing still bright and clean for new, bigger games.

But while he waited for the ideal moment, the female pushed the male to the ground and crouched on top of him. She brought her lips to his neck, and a hot jealousy clenched his hands into the branch he perched on. She didn't feed though, just played with nibbles and false bites while inconveniently blocking a quick kill.

He needed her to *move!*

She sat up and looked around. Had she felt that, felt the command of his spider-self?

Pleasure tingled through him at the force of his growing power. He'd been having fun so far, but clearly he was capable of so much more. What if he could control the little pests? He needn't live in the shadows and travel the damp sewers when he could be set up and worshiped as the god he clearly was.

Step one was still the same though. He would try to blend in while strengthening his abilities. And that required fresh clothes.

He focused intently on the female until he could feel her even as he saw her. It used strength in a way he wasn't used to, but that was fine. He'd fill up again soon. Then, with all his anger and intent, he willed her to move again. He could hear the surge in the rhythm of her heart. This time, she scrambled up and looked around. Perfect.

He dropped, grabbed the male's head with both hands, and gave it a quick twist. The male had barely flopped, and true to his intuition, the female hadn't moved.

"Could you bring me others like this?" He hadn't spoken since he woke, and the sound was strange, somehow not what he'd been expecting.

Her breath had been coming in quick little pants since he'd jumped down, but now she took a lungful of air. She was going to scream.

Oh well. It was worth trying.

He flew at her, letting her body cushion their fall, and crushed her jugular with his teeth. At the first deep pull of blood, her body came to life and thrashed against him, but the fight left her all too quick. He let the world fade against the hot, gushing pleasure.

There was the flavor, so good, but then there was the life itself. Each one different. This one, he could tell now, would've never brought him morsels for dinner. The life was light and playful and hopeful.

And how he wanted to play now, to grab the limp flesh and parade it about for all the lovely screams. But he had a new thing to hope for. He was a growing god, and gods had better plans. He finished off his meal and carried her to the river.

The water ran deep and fast in this area. He was going to just let her float away, but no. This was a good place for hunts. Mustn't alert the ants they were in danger. So, he dragged her into the cold, dark flood. Through the deepening waters, the city lights offered just enough to see the bubbles and blood swirl up from the gap in her neck. The further he went, the more his vision was reduced to shadows. Shadow was enough though. He found a rock about half as large as he was and pushed it with his back until it rolled from its hollowed place. He wedged her body down between his and the rock, then let it roll back with a deadened thud.

He broke the surface slowly, keeping watch on the banks. They were silent. All the noise was closer to the buildings, and even that was lessening as the night grew cold.

The male was right where he'd left him, still bright with warm blood. Even with a full stomach, it was tempting. Maybe after he had the clothes off, he'd have a little fun. In the meantime, however, he'd have to get his new toy back to the tunnels.

Hoisting the body up, he threw an arm over its shoulder, and wrapped his other around its waist. The feet would drag a little, but it was his first mimic. He'd seen them do this. Of course, not when the other was dead. They were usually just stupid with chemicals that made their blood run thin and bodies smell strong, but the pose was similar enough that he should be able to make it back even if someone glanced his way.

"So, what do you want to do tonight?" he said, practicing the sort of thing he'd heard from the ants as he carried his prize.

But again his voice came out strange. At the first word, they'd know he was a predator. No good. They had to be convinced he was a god first, and then they might choose to sacrifice themselves on the altar of his thirst.

Those thoughts brought such lovely images. Stone and metal tables overflowing with blood and pieces of flesh. Yes. This was what he was meant for. He tried again.

"I could do with a drink. You?"

That one made him laugh, but the sound was still wrong. He must hide his power, like what happened when the sun shut off the flow of his strength. The thought made him angry, bite-y. But that was the wrong way. That was more his true form. He must be less. Less, like in the morning with its painful light.

A shiver ran through him and pulled his spider self deep inside. He was blinking and blind in the night. Panic burst through him. He couldn't see, couldn't smell, couldn't *feel*...

He was like them...but the power was still there, sitting in silent wait.

"It's cold tonight." The voice that came out of him was higher and smoother than before. It didn't ring of danger.

It was perfect.

Picking his way back was harder now, but he should practice. If he was going to play mimic with the ants, he needed to be able to walk in the night with them. Walk with them and talk with them.

A giggle escaped him.

33

BAIT

Clare's Notes:

Akito said Marylin Monroe was a Therian and had to fake her death so people wouldn't notice she wasn't aging. Not sure I believe him. He seems the type to joke about something like that, but also...it's possible.

Adrian was pissed.

They didn't have a plan. They had the barest idea of a fucking plan. And it was a horrible idea, worse than attacking Nidhi Manor to save his ass. That at least had a chance at being successful. Sending Therians out in this mess at night was suicide. It didn't matter that they'd be patrolling in groups in semi-public places.

What mattered was they were going to get killed.

The meeting had passed in a blur once they'd started hashing it out.

"Stay a moment," Meg said as the others filed out of her office. "When was the last time you've eaten?"

"This is what you want to talk to me about? Vampires world-wide

The Dark Hours 233

have their eyes on Richmond, your people are heading out now to act like bait for a psychopath, and you want to know when I've eaten last?"

"Put your teeth away, and yes. That's what I want to talk to you about."

Adrian closed his lips and could feel the sharp points in his mouth. He hadn't even noticed when they'd emerged.

Meg grunted. "I couldn't believe it at first, but...you're right. This isn't a blood boon. Whatever was done has permanently altered you. There isn't time now to figure out what all that means, but I can tell you've put off eating too long."

"I'm not hungry."

"That's bullshit, young man. I can smell it on you. Whatever other Therian gifts you now have, you must know, we never die of hunger. The beast rises and feeds if we don't feed it first. Even your flash of teeth just now may be a sign of it coming on."

He looked away. The appetite for blood was still there, though it lacked the parching thirst.

But if he drank, would it undo everything? He'd been to the cafeteria, but he could have been smelling wood for all it appealed to him. He didn't long for the rare slabs of meat and their scant accompaniment of limp vegetation.

More than ever, he felt the drive to hunt.

And the fear that caused him only made him angrier. He'd tangoed with the beast in Perry, but feeling it try to burst from his own skin was another matter. He was losing control and—

"Put your teeth away! My God, you're acting just like a pup, and I really don't have time for this. Come now, let's get you some food. What do you want?"

"I don't want to eat."

Meg's eyes were sharp, but surprisingly, her tone wasn't. "Despite all that's happened, you fear yourself as much as ever." She placed her hand at his elbow and guided him toward the door. "There won't be death this time, I promise." But her voice caught a little on the words.

Adrian's mind flooded with images, the broken bodies of his feedings. Ending with Perry.

And his mind couldn't hold it.

He wasn't aware he was running down the hall or that Meg's growling shout was following him until bright light stepped into his path and stopped him.

He wanted it—reached out and took hold of it. Heat was under his hands, under his lips. The flavor was intoxicating, promising. It fed a different kind of hunger.

Strong hands pulled him back, even as blue eyes fluttered open and went wide.

"Adrian, stop struggling!"

His mind cleared, but the fog was still threatening to close in. He looked behind him to see Meg, eyes yellow, gripping him so tightly there were tears in his shirt. Clare stood in front of him, breath coming fast from her slightly parted lips. He could still taste the velvet and salt of them, and the thought brought the fog closer.

No...not fog.

The Therian animal. He could feel the shape of it. The fucking feral beast that now moved under his skin. The beast that would take what it wanted if he didn't feed it.

"I'm sorry," he said to no one. To both of them.

He turned to go to his room, but Meg's grip hadn't lessened.

"Send something. I don't care what. I'll eat."

He shook his arm loose, stalked down the hall, and slammed his door.

"Are you okay, Ms. Zetler?"

Clare blinked and looked back at Meg. Strength and command rippled from her even as her own eyes dimmed back to blue.

"I..." She shook her head, but she could still feel the pressure of his lips on hers. "He didn't hurt me."

The Dark Hours

Meg nodded, gaze drifting past Clare to the closed door several rooms down.

"He hasn't fed since his change," was all she said, like it was a perfect explanation for what had just happened.

"I wasn't aware that immortal hunger led to kisses at random." Clare was trying to joke, but she didn't seem to have caught her breath yet.

"Therians continue to be created because if we don't stay well fed, we can lose our human reasoning. Our animal instincts take over...and hunger isn't our only instinct." Meg leveled her with a look that was full of warning and implication. "I trust that, even with your level of reckless endangerment, you have enough sense to avoid him until he's fed."

Meg didn't wait for an answer. She turned and yelled orders for food. Akito, who'd come from the Control Room at the commotion, was the first to move.

And Clare stood there knowing she wouldn't follow after Adrian but unable to deny the desire to feel his fingers digging into her shoulders again. Then she realized David was staring from the same doorway Akito had come from.

Right. Because they would've been working when that little scene took place. Heat crept up her neck and through her cheeks. Well, if there was any doubt or chance of denying it, that was gone now. David turned and said something into the room, then came down the hall toward her.

She looked away and ran a hand over her eyes, but he didn't take the hint since cheap, scuffed sneakers appeared on the dated tile flooring at her feet.

"It's fine. You can go back to work," she said.

"Shut up and come on." David lightly pushed her toward her own open door.

"Ugh!"

She stomped a little—great, now she was throwing tantrums like a two-year-old. Something else to thank the bastard for—but she went. Once she heard the door click, she turned.

"Half the time I think I hate him and the other half all I can think about is..." The clean, woodsy smell of him when he was close to her. The way his closeness made her heart beat... "What's wrong with me?"

He shrugged. "Same thing that's wrong with me apparently."

Oh, he was good. He did like someone, and he was using the information as bait to help her feel better.

And it was definitely going to work.

"You do like someone here!"

His beleaguered sigh as he plopped down on her bed may have been him questioning his choice in tactics, but as she sat next to him, he nodded.

"I just hope it's not as obvious to him as it is to you."

"What? Why?"

He rolled his eyes. "Really, Clare? Even if he was interested in humans and in men, he'd still have to be interested in me specifically. And, attraction aside, I don't even know if *I* want to be with a Therian."

Well, he was still here, but that didn't seem like it would be helpful to point out during this rare foray into sharing actual feelings.

"I never thought that I would find..." He paused and shifted toward her. "Did you know that's why I applied at *You Know It*? I hate dating apps, and I thought a fashion magazine sounded like a ripe environment for low hanging fruit."

Considering the way he dressed at work, that was a shocking revelation. But then nothing about him had ever been conventional.

"I didn't know."

He waved the response away. "Of course not. How would you know? And what's ironic is, *you* didn't even know, and you're the closest relationship I developed there." He gave a weak chuckle. "I get it though. I'm not everyone's cup of tea, and they're not mine either. So imagine my shock when my life is thrown into utter mayhem, and I'm here, and I find someone I can't stop thinking about."

He looked at her then, and it held a considerable amount of "I know you know exactly what I'm talking about."

She nodded. "And you want someone to snap you out of it because there couldn't possibly be something worse to want." She drew in a deep breath. "But it doesn't matter because you already want it."

He closed his eyes and swallowed. Clare didn't have to ask to know he was picturing someone, and as amazing as it was to hold the feeling in common, she was dying to know *who* he was picturing.

Patience wasn't her strong suit. Her whole career was structured around digging information from people. That's what she did, and she loved it. But she loved David more; fashionless, asocial, and all.

If it killed her, this one time, she wouldn't ask the question.

He opened his eyes and offered her a small smile. "It's Sune."

"Oh, thank God. I was trying so hard not to ask."

"I know. And you deserve all the torment of not knowing, but I'm a good friend."

"You are." They both smiled for a moment, and then her brain seized the information. "Sune! Oh, that makes sense. He's quiet and techy, and—"

"Gorgeous."

"Well, I was going to say easy to be around but whatever."

"I could drown myself in those dark eyes," he said, staring off to nowhere in particular.

"Okay. Closeted romantic much?"

"I've picked my closets wisely over the years. The last thing I needed was for people to know this impenetrable cynic has a gooey center. I'd get roped into all kinds of things. You know, like world-ending favors."

"That's a little close to home," Clare teased.

"Damn, then I missed. That should've been a bullseye. Maybe you need to adjust your glasses?"

"Maybe you can just leave and go back to your love nest—I mean work."

He raised a single finger. "Guilty, but it doesn't leave this room. And I mean that, Clare. I don't need or want your help. I'm not even sure what it is that I do want."

She lifted her hands in surrender. "I only ask one thing for my lack of services on your behalf."

"The history of granting you favors has gone very badly for me."

Clare tsk'ed at him but then leaned her head over on his shoulder. He didn't move for a breath, as if unsure, but then leaned back.

"I know social interaction isn't your thing, but I'd love if you came by every now and then to vent all your mushy romantic notions. I miss you and need something to distract me from my own ridiculous feelings."

She felt his huff of breath, but he didn't say no.

"What a pair we make," he said after a moment. "Dead set on not connecting with people, so we connect with each other. Avoiding life so hard we end up falling for mythological death bringers."

"Makes perfect sense to me," she said.

"I'm just going to blame it all on you."

"Fair enough." Clare took a deep breath. The tenseness in her body from the interaction with Adrian was easing under their familiar banter. "So, wanna tell me what else you like about Sune?"

Before he could answer, there was a knock at her door.

They both sat up and looked at each other. David shrugged, and Clare went to the door.

Akito stood there with a steak of dubious doneness, half a barely cooked bird, and a heap of floppy bacon. Despite appearances, it smelled amazing. He peered behind her.

"Adrian's not here?"

Clare glanced back at David, then at Akito. "No. Last I saw him, he went to his room."

He handed her the plate without any explanation as he sprinted to the Control Room.

Right then...

Clare took the plate down the hall to Adrian's quarters. After only a moment of hesitation, she entered. Like hers, it felt like a hotel room. The bed was neatly made, and a leather coat hung on a hook near the door. Setting the plate down on a little desk, she peered into the bathroom. Toiletries were arranged on the sink and in the shower, but like the room, it was empty. She grabbed his coat, turning it over like there was a clue there, while her mind continued to grind.

He wasn't in the cafeteria or Akito would have seen him there. He could be with Jonathan. Clare's heart began to drum in her chest. Coat still in hand, she jogged to Jonathan's. Three knocks and silence.

No, not now. Surely Jonathan knew now was not the time to do whatever he wanted Adrian to help him with. She could hear footsteps in the hall behind her as she grabbed the handle and pushed the door open.

There was no one there.

She turned to see Akito with a question on his face and shook her head.

"Bastard son of a fuck! Jonathan did this on purpose!" Akito was already beginning to phase as he growled out. "Go to your room. Adrian's not on the screen leaving, so they might still be here. Last thing we need is your smell in the way. Don't just stand there. Go!"

Then David was there, pulling her toward her room.

"Come on," he said, voice lowered. "You don't want to be anywhere near if he and Jonathan go at it again."

There were other faces in the hall now, but Clare's mind was stuck on the image of Akito's, his purple hair beginning to be swallowed up in orange red. It was beautiful, even while the shifting of his other features felt grotesque in transition. David hadn't even paused. He pushed her in her room, shut the door, and slumped his back against it.

His eyes were wide, but his voice was steady as he said, "How do you think Kitsune would feel about a long-distance relationship?"

34

HIJACKED

Clare's Notes:

Oh God. What have I gotten myself into?

Jonathan had heard enough from his room to know Adrian was compromised somehow. How, he didn't know. Then again, he wasn't sure if anyone really knew what was happening with the former vampire.

His door had been slightly ajar, so Jonathan just walked in. Adrian was dressed in black cargo pants and a tight black shirt. He sat, head in hands at the end of his bed, but looked up when Jonathan entered. Those normally cunning eyes were distant and yellow ringed.

In the end, he hadn't even had to lie.

"Siri has my son, and I know where she is."

The struggle wasn't convincing Adrian to come. No, the struggle was holding him back.

"Show me," Adrian snarled.

Jonathan had spent long hours in the control room. The window

The Dark Hours 241

of opportunity to get out of the warehouse unnoticed was small but possible, so long as they weren't careless. All the doors were well monitored but the roof was not. A cargo trailer sat on the east side of the building, he assumed for appearance's sake, though anything could be in there. If he could get them to the roof unnoticed, the jump to the far side of the trailer probably wouldn't be picked up by the cameras. From there, the trailer blocked the view.

Finding the maintenance hatch to the roof had been relatively easy. It was in the janitorial closet across from the lounge area, but he hadn't tried it at the time. Now he prayed to a deity he no longer believed in that it was unlocked. For once, his prayer was heard.

Other than a loud metal groan, the hatch gave them no difficulties. Adrian pulled himself up into the dark hole with a lithe surety that was exceptional even among immortals. Jonathan hurried after him. There was no telling where his current lack of inhibitions would lead him if left alone.

The night wind was cold, and even though the warehouse was in an industrial area of Richmond, there was still a scent of trees mingled on the concrete-tinged air. How long had it been since he'd been outside? Adrian stood beside him, breathing heavily.

"Which way?"

Everything about Adrian felt primal and barely contained. That could work to Jonathan's advantage or get everyone killed.

"We have to get out of the camera range first. They won't let us go otherwise." Jonathan jogged to the building's edge, and Adrian followed. "See that trailer. We have to jump past it. Once we're clear, we'll have to run. They'll be looking for us."

A soft growl came from Adrian. While it didn't cut into his instincts like a Therian growl, his vision shimmered anyway. He didn't fight it. This night belonged to the vampire.

Adrian took a running leap and soared over the trailer. Jonathan landed next to him a moment later. Then he was up and running. He knew the way like a compass needle knows north but still had no idea how to get there. Going on foot, they'd be overtaken eventually. They needed a vehicle.

Which meant they were going to have to find a human.

Images flashed in his mind. He had to block those out, couldn't think about it. This was the only chance his son had. Nothing else mattered, not what Adrian might do to a human in his current state, nor the images that Jonathan would never be able to erase after.

He wasn't even Jonathan anymore, was he? Jonathan had been a human with a job and a family. Jonathan hurt when others hurt.

But not this thing that wore his face and his name.

When he and Adrian found this random human and tore it from its vehicle, he was going to feel a deep, hungry thrill. He was going to want to cut into its supple skin and make it scream. God, just thinking about it made his own throat ache, but his heart ached too. And he couldn't let it anymore. He had one thing to do, and there was no place in his plan for soft, human feeling.

They weaved and ran between buildings toward the main road. There was something beautiful in the pumping rhythm of his body that gave seemingly without end. So long as he fed it. Feet pounded without exertion, cold bit without injury. He was a thing, alive and with a purpose—a purpose he could now smell.

He veered toward a parking lot outside what must be a machine shop and slowed in order to stay in the shadows. A small group of people stood vaping outside the building. Their bodies radiated with the red heat of their blood in the night.

Adrian stopped next to him, nose wrinkling.

"We need a car. Let me handle this," Jonathan said.

Adrian flashed his teeth in response. And Jonathan wasn't going to die that way tonight, not at the hands of a barely contained *creature*, not when he was this close to holding his son again.

"No!"

The force of the word didn't come from fear or hate but from the deep fierceness of a parent protecting their child. Adrian growled but looked away.

For one moment, Jonathan froze.

It was unthinkable. Adrian had deferred to him. This was the state Siri had wanted him in: controllable, if only just. And he might

The Dark Hours

243

not stay this way. It could be some trick the Therian blood was playing on his brain, a respect for shows of authority. It might only be the need to feed. So, no matter what else happened, feeding had to be avoided.

As the group of men began to trail back in, Jonathan crept forward between cars. The last man in the line was huge, tall and muscled. His back was to Jonathan as he called out, "Excuse me. Can you help me? I think I took a wrong turn somewhere."

The man turned. He was close enough now Jonathan could smell the testosterone in his AB blood. At 5'11", Jonathan wasn't short, but the man was almost a head taller and clearly unthreatened by a stranger accosting him in the night. He let the door shut and stepped out of the ring cast by the building light.

"Where ya heading?"

Try to do it without blood. Better if Adrian doesn't have the smell...

A howl sounded in the distance. The Therians were coming, and he could hear Adrian shuffling.

Out of time.

After having to contend with vampires for the past year, the beast of a man posed about as much threat as a child. He likely didn't even see Jonathan move before his feet had been swept out from under him. He fell with an echoing thud, and Jonathan had a knee on his chest. There were four heart beats of time that Jonathan hurt for him, but then the man swung out in retaliation. Jonathan grabbed the fist mid-swing and squeezed. The crack of bones mingled with the man's throaty scream, and the pleasure of it hit like a drug.

Sweet and sickening.

"Keys and car, unless you'd like the other one broken," he said as he released the mangled hand.

The man's eyes flicked between his hand and Jonathan, and he didn't move. The scent of blood was blossoming from the back of his head.

"Keys and car!"

He jolted, and his good hand reached across for the other pocket.

Jonathan shifted off, and the man held the jangling keys in a shaking hand. The man flinched back as Jonathan grabbed them, a motion that pulled at his vampiric instincts to hunt and play.

"Which car," he asked through gritted teeth.

"Oh God. Another one!"

Jonathan whipped around.

Adrian regarded the scene panting through parted lips with fangs showing. Who knew what was going through his head, but then he held his hand out for the keys. Not what Jonathan had been expecting, but he handed them over.

With a push of a button, a car a few lanes back beeped. Good. Now there was only one more thing to take care of.

The man lay cradling his hand, eyes wide and flicking over the scene. When Jonathan turned back, he brought his arm up over his head instinctively. Not that human instincts would do anything. Jonathan brought his fist to bear right under an exposed ear. The body beneath him jerked with the force of the blow then lay still.

He didn't, couldn't, wait to see if there was still breathing. Adrian tossed him the keys, and they jogged to the car.

"You okay?" It was asked with suspicion, not care.

"You're one to talk," Jonathan said as he whipped the car out of the parking lot. "You seemed barely lucid a moment ago."

"Listen, fucker, I know I'm messed up right now. It's like my mind is coming and going out of focus. So, while it's here, I'm going to ask you again: Are you okay?"

"I'm fine. Just going to save my human son from a psychopathic immortal." Jonathan found the main road and pointed them toward downtown while ignoring the desire to claw out of his own skin.

"Going after Siri is as stupid an idea as I'm capable of." Adrian shook his head. "But there's no way I can know where that *troia* is and just sit by. Especially not when she has your son. I promised I'd help you, but when we get there, you don't have to come. You don't have to do this."

Didn't have to do this??

Jonathan screamed and hit the steering wheel.

The Dark Hours 245

"I hate you!" He screamed again and felt the edges of himself cracking. "Of course I'm going!"

Words began to flow, and he couldn't stop them.

"Do you think I'm going to trust you with the one thing that still matters to me? That's why my wife's dead. You failed me. The Therians failed me. Not this time. I'm in it. I'm saving my son." He pounded his chest with the words. "I'm. Doing. This."

The determined pain of his path came out in something between a sob and a yell, and he pressed down on the accelerator.

35

DIRECTION

Clare's Notes:

Therians smell game-y. Vampires smell like a raw steak. Neither win. Humans are superior. We have soap.

Clare and David had been making small talk trying to ignore the fading sounds from the hallway. Absent-mindedly, she put on Adrian's coat. It was heavy and smelled more like some spice she couldn't name than it did of leather. Didn't fit too badly though.

"Not sure if he'd be more angry that you're wearing his coat or that you look better than he does in it."

Despite David's joking, his arms remained tight around himself. Clare felt vulnerable and useless too, and she had her very own attack Watcher she could tap into if she needed. She couldn't imagine how defenseless David felt.

"You know what I miss? Online gaming. Do you think the survivor colonies have internet," he asked.

Clare fingered the quality, inner lining. "I don't know, but I could ask Miriam. It'd give me something to do." Something other than

The Dark Hours 247

wonder where Adrian was or if his kiss was anything more than runaway animal urges.

David went still. "That thing, like how you talked to me when I was—when they had me?"

"Yeah..."

"Can you use it to talk to Jonathan or Adrian?" he asked.

"I'm such an idiot! Why didn't I think of that?"

"Who cares. Just do it, and then everyone can come back and stop acting stupid."

"Right. Umm. Okay."

Clare shut her eyes where she sat on her bed. She'd closed herself off from the liminal space when she finished talking with Miriam, in hopes of a peaceful evening. Should've known better than to expect that here. All it took was the slightest reach, and she had access to the new, dizzying sensations of that place. Before she could even choose who to focus on, she was swept up in the connection.

Drowning. Choking down pain until it turned into numb acceptance. Everything forfeit, everything except one thing. The last remnant of anything worth existing for. The one thing that could still lay claim to whatever soul he had.

Then, she was there, in a bubble, deep down under the icy maelstrom. Nothing touched here but fierce love. She could just make out the shape of it. The shape was laughter and mess and promise. It was the shape of life. No, not of life. Of *a* life. And the core of everything in Jonathan was orbiting around its beauty.

In a blink, she was out of the light-filled center and in the whipping frenzy of murderous anger. It revolved with desperate need around that tiny light. Even the suffocating pain evaporated under its fierce protective movement. Only one thing mattered.

Not much longer now.

Clare came to with a gasp, her chest tight and burning with a resolution not her own. She couldn't bear to hold on to him any longer but knew when she came away that she had something important. Somewhere in all that, whatever *that* was, she'd intercepted what she needed to know.

248   J.E. KRAFT

David looked at her expectantly, but she shook a hand at him. Not yet. She needed a moment. It was right there, like a word on the tip of the tongue. So close. All of it was adding up to something: the pain, love, anger, the resolve...

"I'm missing something," she said, rubbing her eyes like that would help it magically pop into focus.

"Well, I'm missing everything, so why don't you clue me in on what's happening."

She stood. "I got caught up in Jonathan's...being? Soul? I don't know. I could feel him, and he's angry but resolved. I feel like I should be able to see what it means. It's like all the parts make up a picture, but it's one of those pictures you have to cross your eyes to get it to pop into focus."

"Could you tell if Adrian's with him?"

"I didn't touch him, but I'm sure they're together." She knew the angry determination connected somehow to Adrian. His mark was there on Jonathan's soul.

"Voluntarily?"

"I'd have to touch Adrian to be sure, but I can't see Jonathan overpowering him in any scenario. Why? What are you thinking?"

"There's only been one thing he's had resolve about since he got here, and that's his son," David said. "If he knew where his son was, why not tell the Therians? Yeah, things are crazy around here, but Meg has resources to help get his son from any human agency he might be found in. Even if vampires had him, a lot of these Therians would love an excuse to clean off stragglers. Why sneak off? Why take Adrian when he's compromised?"

And the picture snapped into focus. She hadn't seen it before because she couldn't believe it of him. Jonathan was wounded but sweet. He had an engram like Adrian, so he could still value life. And he did: his son's life.

And he was going to trade Adrian's for it.

David must've read it all on her face. He grabbed her hand, and they were running toward the control room. Sune was in his favorite spot and a smattering of other Therians filled the room doing God-

The Dark Hours 249

only-knew-what tasks. Meg paced, a knuckle to her upper lip. Her cursory glance toward Clare landed and then bored into her.

"What do you know?"

Every eye turned toward her.

She didn't know where or why yet, but that was secondary.

"Jonathan's using Adrian to get his son back."

Meg's upper lip curled.

"And I'm sure I can track them."

Meg turned to the room. "Sune, buzz Kenyon. Tell him to bring burners to my car. Summon everyone still here. We'll meet the returning team." She snapped her fingers as she walked past Clare. "Come."

THE GARAGE BAY filled quickly and crackled with Therians half phased. The door opened as the other group of Therians were returning from their search. Some loped on oversized paws. Others jogged on two legs, but with a strange, powerful gait. The group didn't look human even from afar and less so the closer they got. She knew they could hear the beating of her heart, but that didn't stop it from racing in the crush of them. New abilities or no, her human instincts were begging her to run.

Clare reached for David's hand. He grabbed hold and squeezed as the group filled around them. The bay nearly vibrated with the power of their collective presence, and as intimidating as it was to be among all the teeth and claws, it was amazing too. Akito, at least, had been easy to spot. He was the only fox there, and even fully changed, he moved with the same energy and attitude.

Aberdeen looking canine and for once, powerful, came up to Meg.

"We lost their trail. They attacked a human. Took his car."

In the moment she'd been focused on Aberdeen, Akito had changed. He pressed himself forward and, his voice still thick, said, "There's no 'they' to that shit. I've been telling you fuckheads something's wrong with Jonathan!"

The wrinkle of Meg's nose was quick and subtle. Clare barely saw it, but it wasn't lost on Akito. He backed up a step and lowered his eyes. The group silenced, looking at their leader.

And she was.

Authority and potency radiated from Meg in a way Clare hadn't felt before, despite all their encounters. It was no wonder some cultures made gods of them. How could any human feel equal to this? She glanced at David. He met her gaze, but strangely, it wasn't with fear.

Meg's words broke the silence and stole her attention.

"Clare's going to track for us." This was met with a low susurrus. "We can't risk a convoy, so we'll split into four vehicles."

She grabbed a burner phone from Kenyon and tossed it to Aberdeen, then another went to a dark Latino man who hadn't talked to Clare the entire time she'd been there. She couldn't make out who the third was tossed to in the crowd, but Kenyon kept the fourth.

"This is very likely a trap."

Murmurs of agreement this time and anxious shifting bodies.

"But we can't risk the information about our location and operations here falling into *their* hands."

The agreement was punctuated with yips and other inhuman sounds.

"Those who stay will prepare the warehouse for an emergency evac. Those who go need to be battle-tested and ready. Kitsune will coordinate from here. Should communications go dark, make sure you're not followed. Take days if you have to, then regroup at the caves."

As if they'd practiced this before—and who knew maybe they had—those with the phones called out to who they wanted with them. Without asking questions, others began streaming back into the building. Even David gave her hand a parting squeeze and went in. Meg directed each of the assembled teams to a bay and vehicle. Akito was the only exception to the organized tumult. He'd paced among the groups, and when he remained ignored, he came up to Meg.

The Dark Hours   251

"I can do this! Let me do this."

"Listen, welp, this isn't the moment for you to cut your teeth on meat for the first time. Fall into your place, or I'll put you in it."

His hand curled into a fist, but he walked away, slamming the door as he went back into the building.

Meg turned her attention to Clare. "You'll go with Kenyon. And this time, Ms. Zetler, stay in the vehicle. If I lose more people because of you..." She flashed her teeth with each of the last words and then turned to go, leaving the threat to speak for itself.

It could have been the new perception she had or even just from staying with them for so long, but Clare felt the weight of that threat. Of Meg. She hadn't realized she'd lowered her eyes until she startled when Kenyon touched her arm to lead her to the oversized Ford SUV in the center of the bay.

"If things go badly this time," he said as he opened the passenger door for her, "no one's coming."

He waited, giving her a chance to process that and back out.

No one's coming.

That wasn't quite right because they were the ones coming, and it was a hell of a lot better a plan than when she single-handedly took on a vampire stronghold with squirt guns. As far as her recent temptings of fate went, this one was only moderately stupid.

She got in and shouldn't have been surprised by the faint musty smell of animal. Only then did it even occur to her to wonder if she smelled bad to them. It was definitely too late to ask if sensitive werewolf noses had a scent preference for body wash. Though, it would make a hilarious article for *You Know It*.

All the teenagers have been asking, and You Know It *has the answers! God-like Therians prefer their human cattle in spicy and earthy scents. Strong floral smells and three-times-too-heavy male fragrances are discouraged.*

Kenyon brought the old combustion engine to life with a roar. Therians trusted electronics in their cars like they trusted vampires, and Clare couldn't help but be a little happy for it. The rumble was comforting. He pulled the Ford out of the bay, and the other bay doors opened with more vehicles joining the caravan. Right. She had a different job now. This time, as she began to open her senses, Clare reached for Adrian. Getting swept up in Jonathan's swirl of emotion was not an experience she wished to repeat if she didn't have to.

And Adrian was there. He felt very...animal: raw and powerful. Clare swallowed, took in a breath, and focused on the space between them. She could orient herself toward him like a compass needle knowing true North.

"They're going that way." She pointed toward the driver side window.

Kenyon nodded. "They're heading into the city."

36

FOCUS

Clare's Notes:

My Watcher seems to be involved in something when not around me. What do they do, and where do they come from? Are they born or made? No one seems to know.

The Therians took the same highway into the city that she had —was that only a few weeks ago?—when she went on her suicide run to save David. Night-time traffic was sparse, and the strobing of the streetlights made her think of her own halo.

It had been described like that, like a light that came from her and illuminated what it touched. A light that attracted vampires like a moth to flame—which was super great since they were driving right into a city besieged with vampires and specifically into a vampire nest.

Déjà vu at its finest. Well, here's to hoping that it ended better than last time.

Sun flares were being passed out from an under-seat bin when Clare felt the connection inside her shift.

"That way! It's moved that way."

"That's east. Just stay with it. I need to know if they took 64 or got off at an exit before that," Kenyon said, his lyrical Irish accent getting stronger with his excitement.

"It's not 64. I feel the distance slowing."

"Good! That's good. Crazy Mule, call it in to Sune. We're getting off across the river. We'll take the 74B southbound. Team Two take 74A. Teams Three and Four take 74C. We'll go eastward and converge toward the directions as we get them. Everyone keep your eyes out in the meantime. Maybe we'll get lucky."

The clock in the vehicle read 12:11. They weren't far, about five minutes from the exit.

With the next direction planned, Clare inhaled and let herself sink further into the liminal space. She'd been following Adrian's connection, but now she had a moment, she could *stretch* and communicate. Adrian's life wasn't the cold ice of vampire life. It moved like the ocean, fierce in some places and steady in others. She spoke soundlessly into its depths.

"Adrian."

All of him shifted and focused on her like the unnerving stare of a predator watching prey. So, he definitely heard her then.

"Do you know where Jonathan's taking you? Can you get away? He's just using you to get his son back."

There was no ripple of surprise in his life, no alarm.

"Adrian, where are you going?"

Nothing other than his hungry stare, and suddenly she was reminded of the Watchers. Far away in her body, her mouth went dry.

"The Therians are with me. We're coming to help you."

Anger exploded out of him like a blast and flung Clare back into herself. There were ghosts of pain in places that didn't exist on her physical body.

"He's unwilling, then," Kenyon said.

Clare turned to him. "What? Like, were you able to listen in on that?"

The Dark Hours 255

"No, but any slightly phased immortal could've felt you when you came flailing back. It wasn't graceful."

Her cheeks were burning by the time he finished. There really was no privacy with the Therians.

"What did you tell him?" Kenyon asked.

"I told him that Jonathan was using him, and when I said we were coming to help, he pushed back at me."

"Why would you tell him that?"

"Why wouldn't I? I was trying to get him to tell me where they were going. Or, I don't know, jump out of the car rather than be taken to a secondary location. What was I supposed to tell him?"

Kenyon was shaking his head.

"He must have some motivation for going with Jonathan. Last time we came for him, he lost his best friend. He doesn't mind gambling his own life, but he won't want to gamble any of ours. Shite, girl, it was probably the worst thing you could've communicated to him. See if you can still find him. We're coming up on the exits."

Of course. How could she have been so dense? Clare pushed her embarrassment away. There wasn't time to wallow in mistakes.

She *stretched*. Before she could reach out for her connection to Adrian, she sensed heat. Her Watcher didn't interfere, but it was definitely paying attention after whatever Adrian had just done. Her connection to him was still there, but his life was spiking wildly with rage. She didn't dare draw close to it. Instead, she fell back and dimmed her senses until she was holding only to the connection.

"I can find him."

JONATHAN TRIED to focus on driving even though Adrian had started gripping the car door and growling with low pants. His eyes were a liquid gold, and a short black-brown fur dappled patches of his skin. Jonathan had taken off with a legendary vampire killer while said creature was in a wildly unstable state of being. If he had the ability to feel anything at that moment, he'd probably have been terrified.

But he didn't feel anything. There was only a cold stream of thoughts. Either he would make it to the place Siri had imprinted in his soul, or he wouldn't. Either Adrian would kill him now—or later, it didn't matter—or he wouldn't. Either he would get his son back, or he would die in the effort.

That was it.

There was nothing beyond that. There couldn't be. If he didn't save his son, nothing else existed. If he did save his son, whatever existence there was, he'd accept it.

Feelings couldn't factor into it. Anytime they surfaced, they only weakened his resolve. Fuck feelings, fuck Adrian, and fuck the Therians.

Only. One. Thing. Mattered.

And then, finally, he felt himself falling into place. He'd been resisting for so long. There'd been two pieces of himself: the human and the vampire. It'd made him weak. He could feel that now as he let the human go and fell fully into the vampire for the first time. There was a strength here he'd refused to accept.

No longer.

He glanced at the still growling beast next to him. Adrian had never seemed weak, but he could see it now. So much strength was wasted in resisting himself. That was good at the moment. It might go badly for Siri when Adrian unleashed, but the chaos created could only bode well for Jonathan.

He navigated the maze of roads downtown without thinking. The map of them was etched on his brain, making it easy to pick his way toward the pull in his soul. As they neared, he found a spot to park.

Adrian didn't speak but got out of the car and followed. They were lucky no one was walking on the sidewalk at that particular moment. Neither of them was making any effort to hide the spectacle of what they were.

The smell hit them at the same time, and Adrian let loose a snarl: vampires. Without tracking it, Jonathan knew it would be the stone building two ahead of them with an opening for an underground parking garage. He glanced at Adrian. The blackish fur was spread-

The Dark Hours

ing, as were the amount of sharp teeth in his more pointed face. The molten eyes looked through Jonathan and narrowed. With a single head nod, he motioned Jonathan forward and took up the rear with the sound of seams popping.

Adrian knew.

He knew Jonathan was walking them into a trap. And he was taking up a position behind him. Not even that made him afraid.

Either he would live through tonight, or he would die trying.

CLARE WATCHED the roads off the exit pass, trying to hold on to the information coming in from both realms. It was giving her a headache. She had enough adrenaline and endorphins flowing through her veins that she was surprised she could feel anything, let alone be distracted by it. It could be worse though. Her body could choose this moment to rebel against the birth control shot she'd been given and start her period. That would make an amazing headline: *Woman on Way to Death Battle with Vampires is Betrayed by Uterus.*

She stifled a chuckle, and when Kenyon looked her way, she just waved him off. Clare wasn't about to explain her feminist gallows humor, especially when she was using it as a distraction from actually facing what was going on. There was no reason to be heading to her possible death completely immersed in reality.

Until she felt her compass needle tug.

"It's that way."

Clare closed her eyes and pulled her focus more tightly to Adrian. She was vaguely aware of Crazy Mule giving directions in the background.

"Yes. Ahead and a little to our left."

Then suddenly, "You've passed him!"

Clare opened her eyes and pointed out Kenyon's window. "He's close. That way."

Kenyon whipped the car into a parking spot on the side of the road. As the group streamed out, he turned a slightly shifting face on Clare.

"We can sniff them out from here. You aren't officially part of this tribe." He gripped the steering wheel, and his lips pressed into a tight line before he said, "But I won't make you stay in the car. You've seen battle, you've proven yourself, and *I* won't turn away an ally."

She hadn't been planning on staying in the car. Not that she'd made a conscious decision, she just knew herself better now. Clare opened her mouth to speak, but Kenyon held up a finger.

"Not everyone would agree with me, and now is not the time for distraction. So, wait to follow until all the groups pass. You can guard our flank. If we're separated, get out of the city anyway you can. It's not safe for you here." There was no apology in his look. He wasn't speaking down to her, and she couldn't be sure, but perhaps there was a hint of pride in his tone. "I'm sure you'll manage to find us again if you want to."

Kenyon reached across her, tapped the glove box open, and handed her a bottle.

"What's this?"

"Chlorophyll eye drops. It'll help with your night vision. Put two drops in each eye. They'll sting."

As he got out of the car to join the others waiting on the sidewalk, an older gray truck joined them. Aberdeen was out and up to the group before the next Therian could exit. Aside from the glow of strange eyes and the tenseness in their stances, it could have been a group of friends meeting for a Thursday of fun downtown. The group was already moving away when the last person hopped out of the truck.

It was Akito.

Clare darted a look back. Kenyon and the group were walking away. As he neared, she reached over, cracked the driver-side door, and hissed at him. "What are you doing here?"

He froze, looked both ways, then slipped into the car. "Shh."

Clare checked again; Kenyon and the others were still walking.

"Meg told you not to come."

The Dark Hours 259

"The team I came with didn't hear that. Besides, you're one to talk when it comes to listening to Meg."

True, but she...yeah no, she had no room to talk. But there was just something about Akito that made her feel protective. He seemed young and vibrant, and the Therians had lost enough in the last battle.

"What are you planning on doing?" she asked.

He looked at her, and his gaze was strangely penetrating. "Probably the same thing you plan on doing. Hanging back a little, and then joining the fray."

She sighed. "Yeah, I was afraid of that. I don't suppose there's any way I can convince you not to?"

A toothy grin spread across his face. "I'll stay if you stay."

Normally, she enjoyed wit and banter, but keeping Akito safe drained her supply of gallows humor. "What about your uncle?"

"You know I just call him that as like a term of familiar respect, right?"

"Sune's not your uncle?"

"Well, kinda, actually. He goes way back with my family but..." Akito looked after where the group had been, but wasn't actually seeing anything. "He saved my life. He's more like a father."

"So please don't go. Don't throw away the life that Sune gave you."

"There's no way you can understand what he gave me." His teeth flashed as he spoke. "I'm not throwing that away. I'm fighting for it."

"By going into a vampire den instead of helping the tribe evacuate?" It was a sad day, or rather night, when she was the voice of reason in a conversation.

"By not running away anymore!"

With the heat in his words, Clare knew there was more to the conversation than what Akito was saying. For a fraction of a second, she could see past the exterior he presented. He burned bright and beautiful, full of fear and passion and motion. As quick as it came, it was gone.

Clare blinked.

Whether she'd stretched, or bonded, or slipped into the liminal realm, she had no idea what was happening anymore. It didn't really matter though. With a flick of her hand, she clicked open the bottle. The drops prickled like a dry wind in her right eye, and then burned like hot pepper juice. She sucked in a quick breath with the pain.

"What are you doing?"

Clare hurried and did the left eye before she could chicken out.

"Battle prep, I hope," she said with eyes squinched shut. "Just do me a favor and please don't die. I'm trying not to die myself, and I think it would be really bad for my morale." Guess there was still a little bit of humor left in her supply.

He snorted, and she opened her eyes as the pain subsided. Everything was much clearer. It was still in the blue tones of night, but she could easily make out the features in the car and the eager tightness of Akito's face. Oh God, what was she doing? She should stay in the car and make sure he did too.

Clare covered her face with her hands and breathed. A touch on her shoulder startled her.

"I hear you're kind of a badass." There was admiration in his eyes.

"Thanks." She gave a half-hearted laugh. "Pretty sure I'm just missing the good sense most people are born with." Her throat tightened, and she couldn't help but wonder if either of them would make it out of this.

All right. No more stalling. She knew what she was about.

"Let's go."

37

DOORS

Clare's Notes:

There's no way my dad knew about my mom.

The parking garage's lights were off. Yellow caution tape crossed the barrier and a sign read "closed for renovations." The metallic-and-grime smell of the place blended well with the coppery hint of blood on the air.

Jonathan was several feet in when he realized he only heard his own footfalls. Adrian hadn't followed him, but it didn't matter now. What he needed was to know which way to go. Ahead and deeper in the blackness of the garage? To the elevator at his right? Or to the thick metal door on his left?

Closing his eyes, Jonathan reached out. He hadn't purposely *stretched* to Siri before, but he didn't know how else to let her know they were there. Groping with his senses, he found her. The moment she registered his presence, it was like a silent scream ripped through her being.

Jonathan snapped his attention back to the garage.

Something was wrong.

But it didn't matter. They still had his son. He turned to find Adrian, but at that moment, a door clanked open.

He turned back to see a handful of vampires. He remembered the one at the head of the group as being security at Nidhi. The vampire lifted his chin in recognition as well. Despite the nod, the group fanned out in defensive positions.

A thought surfaced that he should do something to signal that Adrian was with him.

Ha.

He hoped they all died.

The door they came through was a little over ten parking spots away, and that was where he needed to be. He had to survive that long. Once inside, he could come up with a new target. This one was hard enough for the moment.

Jonathan started walking.

The group responded without talking. Two of the five angled toward him. The others sped toward his flank. They'd be after Adrian. Only two between him and the door then: security vamp and a smaller male he'd seen around the mansion but never interacted with.

He picked up his pace. When he was within jumping distance, he lunged at the smaller of the two, using surprise and body weight to take him to the ground. Surprise only helped for a moment. Before fang or fist could land, he was launched off and across the garage. He turned his body, and he landed on his feet, skidding backwards even as he crouched down to steady himself.

Security was closer to him now. From the crouch, he threw himself at his middle. He never made contact, never even saw the dodge before his body was flipped and slammed down. A foot crushed down heavy on his chest. Jonathan grabbed it and tried to move the weight from over his heart.

The man laughed. "What are you even trying to do?"

He pressed harder until Jonathan both felt and heard a rib snap. The sharp pain made him want to gasp, but his chest wouldn't move.

The Dark Hours

There were sounds coming from outside the garage now, but the smaller vampire stalked over and leered down at him, black eyes crinkling in enjoyment.

"I'll break the arms off while your foot holds him," he said in a breathy, higher voice. "We'll have him taken care of before the other problem is sorted."

He bent to grab Jonathan's arm. The angle was perfect. Jonathan rammed his fingers into the rubbery flesh of those black eyes until they gave out with twin bursts of fluid. Then he turned the motion, slamming the vampire's head against the leg pressing on his chest and crushing the bone of the sockets into the fleshy brain behind them.

The man on top of him was falling. Jonathan rolled, taking head and body with him and driving them into the cement for good measure. It took less pressure than he was expecting. Gore covered his hand and chest. He scrambled up and turned to see Security in a recovering crouch. His eyes were wide with surprise for a heartbeat, and then with a hiss, he was coming.

This time, Jonathan let the fight come to him and used the intervening seconds to send life to the ribs that were still radiating pain. He stepped to the side just before impact. A hand caught him in the shoulder, but it was better than elsewhere. Jonathan twisted away with the hit, letting momentum carry the bigger body past him. He threw himself on the exposed back of the vampire and sank his teeth into either side of the spinal column. Rank, dead blood filled his mouth.

Before he could rip the thing out, he was pulled over Security and slammed back down. Jonathan was no match for his strength, and the fury-contorted face coming at him promised death.

And death came, but it came in a blur of black and blood.

Security's head had been separated from his body before Jonathan could even make sense of what he'd seen.

Adrian wasn't resisting any more. He was fully in himself and a terror of teeth and fur. Yellow eyes rested in a black ocean. Long, pointed ears accentuated a face somewhere between fox and canine.

His clothing hung ripped about his muscled form. A pointed tongue flicked between pointed teeth as he turned his gaze on Jonathan.

There was an invitation there even as the skin on Adrian's snout wrinkled in a soundless snarl.

Through the door then.

Jonathan went first, aware of the beast at his back. Survive through the door, and...

The door swung inward, revealing a posh apartment. Deval's hand could be seen in the rich accents of gold on white and black. A group of at least a dozen vampires were frozen in defensive poses for a single breath. Then, everyone moved at once.

Jonathan spun to the left, toward a blonde female in the kitchen area. He didn't see Adrian enter, but he felt the wind of his passing as he threw himself into the fray with a roar. The woman had grabbed a long knife from a set hanging over the island countertop and was coming at him at a run.

Jonathan was still weak. But he wasn't afraid. Fear was for people with options.

Using both hands, and all his strength, he ripped the knife arm off his attacker.

He would either die or he wouldn't.

She fell, thrown off balance by his savagery, but two other vampires had already replaced her.

No.

He wouldn't die. Not now. Not when he was so close.

They were on him. He couldn't dodge them both. Fangs missed his neck but tore into his shoulder. Jonathan brought his hand up to rip at the offender, but it was blocked. The second vamp, tawny and willowy though he was, held his arm in one hand and gripped Jonathan's neck with the other.

An impact brought the whole group down in a tangle of limbs.

Jonathan shoved and tore at arms and legs until he could spring free. The source of the impact was a head-less body still trapping one of his attackers and spurting dark blood on the white kitchen tiles.

The Dark Hours 265

There was no time to look at Adrian. The sounds of screams and snarls were enough to know he was still there.

The woman who'd attacked him first was nowhere to be seen, but her knife was still clutched in the detached arm that now rested in easy reach. Jonathan wrenched it free just in time to meet the charge of the tawny vampire.

The vampire faltered, eyes flicking over Jonathan for a just moment as a scream sounded. His last moment.

Jonathan thrust into the sacred spot in his left breast and twisted it. With a sputtering hiss the thing sank to the floor. Just as the smothered vampire clawed himself free and back to his feet.

Jonathan would not die.

He tightened his grip on his blade as a cacophony of yipping, howling, and keening echoed in from the garage.

Therians.

The numbness fell away as the sound drew on instincts he'd finally let free.

Hate vibrated in his bones. Everything in him wanted to whirl around to face the incoming attack. It took all his will to remain facing the vampire nearest him. His attacker however, was trying to watch three fronts: Jonathan, Adrian, and the advancing Therians.

One blink of distraction, and Jonathan leapt.

His hands came down on either side of the vamp's head and twisted. The sound of its neck cracking flashed unbidden the memory of Jonathan dangling in Adrian's grip. The memory of the pain was there, but alongside the pain had been a desperate hope that it would all be worth it if Adrian could help him.

His wife had still been alive then.

Emotion escaped its prison and coursed through him. The crush of loss was blinding, and he cried out as he sank to his knees with the temporarily limp body still in his grip. It was as if every part of him was being squeezed with grief.

Not this. Not now.

He needed the numbness, needed it for Zephyr. But his limbs

refused to move as completely as if he was the one with the broken neck.

Hands were lifting him, and his body came back to life. He thrashed out against whatever had him in its grip, but found himself on his feet staring into eyes that were like a solar eclipse, a ring of gold in a sea of black.

Adrian reached a blood covered paw down and ripped the heart from the now twitching vampire below them. Then the Therians were flooding the room with fiery lights blazing, and with his defenses broken like a stained-glass window, hot fury was coming through. He wanted blood. Not to drink for once, but to watch it flow like a river that could drown everything under its smell and heat.

He felt the rumble in his throat more than heard it. But then the dark beast in front of him was roaring in his face and pushed him back against the stainless steel refrigerator.

He could not die. Not tonight.

Jonathan screamed back at the darkness, at the fangs and the blood. He lunged.

The pain was instant. Bones cracked under the grip on his shoulder, pushing him to the ground. He sank his fangs into the wrist, and a taste like old ground beef filled his mouth. The claws released their grip. Then pain splintered through his jaw.

Jonathan fell back from the blow, good hand raised to hold the dislocated jaw while pushing life to heal.

"Stop." The command was ground out in a voice like stone rubbing on stone.

Adrian was heaving, froth now spilling between his sharp, clenched teeth. His eyes were wide, and the black fingers that ended in cruel daggers shook. Amid the shrieks of fighting, the thickening odor of blood, and Jonathan's betrayal, Adrian was holding on to a piece of himself.

Barely.

But he was doing it.

That was a war Jonathan had already lost, and Adrian was a fool not to see that. Whatever cracks had appeared in the void of his

The Dark Hours 267

soul sealed shut as quickly. It was just as well Adrian didn't see. Jonathan didn't have his son yet, and it was clear to him now that if he had to fight either Adrian or Siri, he wouldn't live to hold him again.

Despite every survival instinct screaming against it, Jonathan closed his eyes and thought of the sun, thought of it streaming through flyaway toddler hair, gold on gold.

He hadn't gone deep enough into the memory to push the change back. That was impossible with the stench of Therian and blood heavy on the air, but when Jonathan opened his eyes, Adrian had turned back to the fight. He stayed down, letting the kitchen island shadow him from the burning lights.

The last vampire was being torn limb from limb under a murderous mass of fur, and more Therians were coming at the door.

"No!" Adrian managed to get out. "Leave!"

"He's betraying us all!"

The gray-red Lycan coming through the door spoke with Aberdeen's southern intonations as she thrust a claw in Jonathan's direction.

When Adrian didn't respond, she said to those around her, "He's too far gone in his phase. We have to get him home and fed."

"I'm. Still. Here." His gaze ended on Jonathan. "I'm choosing."

Adrian may have been trying to tell Jonathan something, but he was out of choices. His one choice was to live through the next room at whatever cost. He'd already paid so much. Under the surface were memories he'd never be able to wash away, memories carefully wrapped away from his mind so he could continue to exist for this one moment.

There was a small click, audible in the silence that had fallen, and then, a hiss.

"Out!" Adrian shouted as a fine smoke began to drift in the room.

Vampires were an every-creature-for-themselves type, and it was apparent even in their cut-throat organization. They would have climbed over each other to escape whatever fresh hell was about to ensue, but the Therians' training showed immediately as they fell in line and filed out with the practiced ease of circus animals leaving the big-top. Adrian watched them.

A half-phased tan Lycan stayed back.

"We can't leave him, and we won't leave you." Kenyon's lilt was unmistakable despite the grit in his voice. The bastard had never liked Jonathan anyway.

Adrian responded with a wordless snarl.

"That's what I thought you'd say, but like it or not, you're part of our tribe. We don't live alone, and we don't die alone. If it's worth your life, it's worth mine."

Smoke was hanging heavier in the room now, and their silhouettes were quickly becoming blurred, then obscured. The caustic smoke burned his throat, causing him to quit breathing. Not that he needed to breathe, but now he couldn't smell or see either. The heat in the smoke caused fog for even vampiric eyes. Simple and brilliant, the sort of solution Deval loved.

Jonathan crawled forward and pulled the knife from the chest of the vampire he'd felled earlier.

This wasn't the house of horrors that the mansion was, but they clearly had a plan in place for assault. As much of a curse as his eidetic memory could be, it came in handy at the moment. Jonathan cast back to the image of the room from when they'd first entered.

Three doors. All opened inward. Two were on either side of the living room. The other one was just ahead and to his left.

Through the next door then.

38

IMPACT

Clare's Notes:

Hybrids Exist. They don't take the form of their maker but something from "old world myth"???

Clare and Akito were nearly through an alleyway to the next block when a sound erupted, like the screaming of every animal in a nightmare forest.

Clare froze.

Akito passed her, ripping off his shirt as he sprinted under a harsh LED light, and then into the darkness beyond. Trying to navigate to Adrian, she must have opened more of her sense for the "other" because the pop of power when Akito changed was nearly tangible. Then an unnaturally large fox tore through the next circle of lamplight with a haunting caterwaul.

She swallowed at the thick nothing clogging her throat. What was she doing here? Did she really think *she* could help *them*? Akito had been so fast he was more like a blur. Meg was right. She was going to be in the way. Going to make things worse.

Pain seared through her then, as though her soul had been dipped in molten metal.

Jonathan.

There was no time to analyze whether it was physical or emotional. Clare wrenched the connection shut and ran.

There was no telling what the Therians were doing to him.

Coming out on the other side of the alley, Clare let the muffled sounds of chaos steer her toward the opening of a darkened parking deck. As she got closer, the yellow caution tape marking the entrance seemed mockingly ironic. Past it, sun flares swept erratically, shadowing the Therians behind them. As her eyes adjusted, she could make out the open door they were fanning out from. She stopped there on the edge of the garage, studying the writhing bodies and the darkness of the garage beyond.

Jonathan must still be in that room. And Adrian. But this was more than she could handle. At least when she went to rescue David, the vampires hadn't expected someone to march in through the front door.

They wouldn't make that mistake here. All this had been calculated.

The sound of feet coming too fast made her turn just in time to see reflective black eyes. A blow caused bright pain to radiate from her chest and sent her flying. She seemed to float for several minutes before smacking down hip first, then arm, then head.

A heavy metal clang echoed over the ringing in her ears. A door had been slammed down over the entrance.

"Son of a fuck!" It sounded like Akito.

"I'll pull the door up. Someone see if she's still alive."

Clare was in enough pain that she'd better be alive. But she couldn't see anything, couldn't open her eyes or move. Her mind was muddy and seemed to come in and out of focus.

Until something touched her. With a gasp, she clutched the hand on her shoulder and flailed out her senses for her Watcher. But when she opened her eyes, there was no nightmare facing her, only a human-looking Aberdeen. She stopped reaching with her senses.

The Dark Hours

"She's alive." And then, "Can you get up?"

From across the space, a yelp hammered into Clare's forming headache and then, "It's electrified."

"Clare."

She'd shut her eyes again. "I don't know."

The hand on her shoulder was pulling her into a seated position, and her hip was screaming out against it. The pain helped bring her back into the moment.

She reached out her other hand to hold on to Aberdeen but stopped mid-reach. Her hand was dripping blood across the palm where the skin had rubbed against the concrete and loose debris. She looked down. Adrian's jacket hadn't ripped, but it took the brunt of the skid. The only tear was in her jeans around the knee where bloodied flesh peeked through. All in all, it probably looked worse than it really was.

Aberdeen clasped her by the forearm and helped pull her up. A little cry escaped her as pain stabbed down her leg. Clare immediately shifted her weight off the injured leg again, but her vision had blurred, and the world seemed to tilt even though Aberdeen was holding her firmly.

Nope. This was bad.

"I'm fine. Go and help the others. I'll just lean against the wall until I get my bearings back."

Aberdeen took a deep breath, like she was about to argue. But then she looked at the group assessing the large, metal door that had descended over the garage entrance. Shaking her head, she led Clare to sit against the wall.

———

Jonathan crouched in the smoke and crept to the door.

Locked.

He reached out a hand and groped around the island, heading for the door on the far side.

"Jonathan," Kenyon called out. "Come on. Don't make this harder than it has to be. Adrian's already slipping. We lose our intellect in that state. He might not be able to recognize you from other vampires soon. I don't know what they promised you, but death is the only thing you can expect from them."

He walked while Kenyon talked. Didn't want to give them a sound to navigate by. The smoke could hide him in the carnage of the broken bodies, but it did nothing to hide the squelch his foot made in a spot of blood-soaked carpet.

He froze long enough to hear Kenyon move, then gave up all pretense of quiet, and ran for where the other door must be. It gave inward as he hit it. Jonathan tumbled into a room with less smoke as well as several monitors, cables running to computers, and other equipment. He turned to slam the door, but Kenyon was already there.

Neither moved for a moment.

"I'm not leaving without my son."

"He's not here. There's no one else here. Can't you see this was all a trap?"

"They have him. *She* has him!"

Kenyon stepped toward him. "And they'll kill him the moment they suspect you're no longer useful."

Jonathan lowered his head. "I know."

Kenyon took another step. Then another. A hand was on his shoulder. Jonathan put his hand on the one touching him.

Then, he brought up his other hand and drove the knife into Kenyon's heart. He looked back at the top right corner of the room where a small camera sat with a red light on.

"I know."

There was no going back.

Kenyon's body had barely fallen when Jonathan reached around to shut and lock the door.

It was stupid. There was no way out. He'd locked himself in a corner, but maybe it was a corner with a message. Something. If nothing else, it might buy enough time that he could survive whatever the vampires had planned next.

The Dark Hours

The main monitor flickered to life with a single tap of the keyboard and displayed nine video feeds and a small count-down widget with six minutes and thirty-nine seconds left. He could see Adrian in the main room picking his way toward where Jonathan hid. There was an empty bedroom suite. Several feeds covered the tumult of Therians in the garage. The locked kitchen door led to what looked to be a cold storage for blood.

There was nothing else, nothing to give him an idea what to do next.

The frame of the doorway shook as Adrian finally reached it. Jonathan slid the knife loose from its fleshy resting place. A small part of him knew he would replay all this over and over in his mind later. The surprise and pain that had been in Kenyon's eyes would be part of his special hell for all eternity.

But hell had to wait just a little longer.

The door shook again with the force of the body on the other side, and Jonathan glanced one more time at the monitors.

The knife dropped from his hands. There she was flowing in through a door behind the bags of blood.

Siri.

But no boy. Of course there wouldn't be. Why would she bring him here? As he watched, she opened a door and slipped into the smoke fogged kitchen. Her form became a wraith. The sounds at Jonathan's door stopped. With all the noise he was making, Adrian couldn't possibly have heard her, and yet, his new overpowered form sensed something.

"Adrian! It's going to explode! You have to come with me."

Jonathan could make out her words from his room.

So that's what the counter was for. Then he had five minutes to work his way to where she'd entered. One more door to survive.

Adrian only growled in answer, but Jonathan could see the shadow of his bulk moving toward hers on the screen.

"Please! I just want you to live!"

As quietly as possible, Jonathan opened the door, eased himself out, keeping low to the ground.

Clare couldn't focus on the roil of Therians around her. There was a high whine in her ears blanketing the frantic modulations of their conversation. Then, there was expansion. Her senses ballooned out, tugged by some peripheral stimulation.

Death. Death was coming, but she couldn't focus enough to get a clearer picture than Adrian, Jonathan, and death.

Clare pushed up from the wall. Her stomach pitched as she stood but didn't empty. She took a shaky step. The pain shooting down her hip was dizzying, but it held her weight. Setting her sight on the door with smoke pouring out, she hobbled forward. The garage may have been empty for all she noticed apart from the pain and her goal. It took no more than twenty steps and an eternity.

When she finally arrived, panting against the pain, Clare couldn't see past the smoke, but she could hear a familiar female voice.

"I can still fix you. You haven't fed. It's not permanent. You just have to come with me."

The smoke tickled her throat deeper and deeper until Clare began to cough.

Adrian hadn't quite gotten to Siri. Jonathan wasn't sure if her words were reaching him in that state, if he was finally tiring, or if something else had distracted him. Whatever the reason, Jonathan crept along at what seemed to be a safe distance.

A cough caused him to look in the other direction.

A light, obscured by smoke but still visible, shone in the doorway. Clare.

He couldn't tell if the hiss came from Adrian or Siri, but the light was blotted out as they both changed course.

Time seemed to stretch as he saw his options laid out in his mind. His fingers curled into blood slicked fists. There was only one choice, had only ever been one choice.

The Dark Hours 275

He continued through the final door.

———

THIS TIME the impact wasn't surprising.

Clare had felt her Watcher flare around her—felt it even in the physical plane—as Siri emerged, fangs bared, from the smoke. But the fiery being in the liminal realm did nothing to cushion her body from the fury that descended on her here. If she could just get her hands on Siri in either place...

But then she was hitting the ground again, air rushing out and hot pain rushing in.

"You!"

The weight crushing her body was vaulted off as a roar set her ears back to ringing. The ringing seemed even louder with the sudden silence as its backdrop.

"You'd choose that? I could save you, even save your *friends*," the last word was spat. "But she dies, and she dies now, or you all die!"

Clare managed to blink her eyes open.

In a black tank and athletic pants meant for movement, Siri stood with a wide defensive stance. Even her fingers were splayed as if each digit was ready to take on one of the flanking creatures.

Meg emerged, human and covered only with her own tumbling gray hair, from the throng of the phased and half phased.

"You're in no position to barter. Showing us the way out is now *your* only chance at surviving the night."

Then a blur of movement drew Clare's eyes. A dark mass lowered toward her, and her mind and body stilled.

Teeth and claws. Blood and fur. But even in that foreign face, she knew those eyes. And then she could see the soul behind them like some strange double vision. The sense of both realms colliding.

"Don't let him feed! I'd rather let us all die than lose him again."

She could feel the force of attention shift even as Adrian moved a hand to brush her neck, and the movement could have been hunger or affection. The lines between things seemed more and more imaginary these days.

"Save your people," Clare said to him.

A snort of breath was reply enough to let her know he understood.

He reached for her hand and gently slid the moonstone ring from her finger. The throw was quicker than she could follow, but Siri cried out as her hand fisted around it.

Clare's blood had covered the ring.

"When this is over, you *will* wear it again for me."

"This is fucking ridiculous. We don't have to listen to this rancid buttplug. We can find our own way out."

Clare didn't have to crane her head to know it was Akito. His less than tasteful quip was met with a chorus of affirmative sounds.

A beep sounded from somewhere in Siri's clothing. Her lips curled into a smile.

"In one minute, the explosives under this building will detonate. Adrian and I go first. You all can follow. The bitch stays."

"No." Meg drew the word out as if time were not a concern for her.

"No?" Siri said, incredulous. "You'd rather all die. Are you insane?"

"I don't know what else you've rigged up in your little house of horrors, but I'm certain your father's watching. He won't let the place come down with you in it."

Meg turned in a circle and addressed the space.

"Will you? Hello, Deval. You're a brilliant strategist, so I can only assume your daughter's being here was not part of your plan. It's tempting to kill her, to make you feel a fraction of the pain that your people have inflicted on me!" She paused, breathing ragged for a moment. Then Meg continued, voice quieter, "But my tribe has seen enough death. *I* have seen enough death. Let my people go, and your daughter will remain unharmed."

Siri looked murderous, and no one moved. A pop and a loud

The Dark Hours

screech caused several Therians to jump, but then the metal over the garage entrance began to roll up.

Adrian was over Clare. He grabbed her hand again, and she could feel his hunger. Eyes bright and never leaving hers, he brought her wounded hand to his mouth.

And bit.

Clare cried out. She couldn't help it, but she didn't tug her hand away. He'd asked, not in any way she could explain, but he'd asked and she'd agreed.

Which was probably the concussion talking.

The agreeing to it, that is, even with her strange new senses. But he *had* asked, and she trusted him enough, even in this state. That really had to be the concussion. Trust was never her strong suit.

Siri let out an enraged scream.

Adrian dropped her hand and bared blood covered teeth. But then he was shaking, the skin under his fur undulating. Pink foam collected in the dark corners of his lips as his breath seethed in and out. Finally, he let out a strangled cry as leathery skin burst from his sides unfurling into massive wings.

He crumpled to the ground beside her, heat radiating from his body.

Clare pushed herself closer to his heaving form.

"What have you done to him?" Siri's voice sounded small, and then she was shrieking, "What have you done?"

Fire seared Clare's scalp as Siri dragged her up by the hair. Clare grabbed at the hands holding her and was dropped as soon as contact was made, her blood returning fire for fire on Siri's skin.

She hit the ground with a scream that seemed to rouse Adrian from his torpor. He rose up, but Clare wasn't going to give Siri another opening. The vampire had made a careless attempt in her grief, but there was no doubt she meant to kill Clare.

Stretching, Clare latched onto the violent freeze of Siri's being and was washed under its malevolence. Siri grabbed back, and the pain of it sliced deep, filling Clare's being. It took everything to maintain her hold as the pain of Siri's attack ratcheted through her body in both realms.

Her Watcher, tensed and ready, sprang forward like a wildcat freed upon the life in Clare's desperate grasp. Whether it was her grip or Siri's age, Clare felt the cutting of Siri's anchor like the vibration of a huge bell from her palms all the way through her soul. It was like a soundless detonation.

Siri dropped.

"Run," Meg cried.

Adrian blinked slowly. And then he was moving.

He scooped Clare up in a single excruciating motion and was running before the sound of pain could escape her lips.

Clare registered the sight of the Therians fleeing. Then, there was an explosion of sound and blackness.

And nothing more.

39

FIRE

Clare's Notes:

Love might be a many-splendored thing, but unwanted attraction is a consuming cancer. No amount of logic can cut it out of me, and I'm afraid it'll kill me. Unless I kill Adrian first. That's a definite possibility.

Clare dreamt of fire.

It chased her through half a dozen dreams.

There was the booming that threw twisted car parts in the air, but when she looked at the flaming mountain where the vehicle should be, it was only her burning Watcher. In another dream, her Watcher danced through *You Know It* and Clare's house, setting fire to everything it touched. In another, she was flying through the air, and Adrian was carrying her on blazing wings. Yet another contained a percussive blast and heat melting her face, but she could see only blackness, hear only a dull ringing. Finally, there was Siri in the garage, alight with flame and screaming.

But she wasn't dying.

Instead, she stalked toward Clare, skin charring, and grabbed her. Clare thrashed against the clutching hands.

"Shhh. You're all right."

She opened her eyes to see Adrian's face, human and concerned, leaning over her. He was wearing baby blue scrubs and looked comically out of place...

Then the smell of antiseptic hit, and she couldn't breathe. Air got stuck in the squeeze of her throat as her gaze darted around.

Hospital bed. Curtain separators. IV stand and drip.

She was ripping at the IV in her arm before she'd registered what she was doing.

"Stop," Adrian said, taking hold of her hands. "Stop!" His voice was hushed and brow furrowed deeply.

"What am I doing here? Why am I here? What happened? Let me go! I don't want to be here." The words were tumbling out, and Clare couldn't stop them. "I want to go. Let me go. I want to go!"

Clare thrashed, and then the pain registered. Pain was everywhere. A gasp turned into a moan, and Adrian eased her back down on the bed. Surprisingly, the pain helped ground her and diminish the panic attack.

"It's okay. You're safe here."

Clare didn't even bother to shake her pounding head. There was no way she was going to explain that waking disoriented in a hospital had triggered as much of her childhood PTSD as was possible, short of taking her back to the crash site.

Clare took an aching, deep breath and then asked, "Where's here?"

"An urgent care facility outside of Richmond. Therian owned. Meg's people."

So not a hospital then. That knowledge helped loosen the knot in Clare's throat.

"What happened?"

Adrian stared off, then blinked several times like he was trying to clear away the vision. "The building came down."

"The others?"

The Dark Hours 281

Adrian shrugged and looked away.

"Meg, Akito, Aberdeen. Adrian, what happened?"

"I don't fucking know, okay? I don't remember much of what happened between the warehouse and the explosion." Adrian had his hands in his hair, but he brought them down and stared at them. "It's just flashes. All I know is that they're not here."

"You brought me here though."

He nodded. "There was rubble in my body. I was healing, walking with you in my arms. It was like I was coming back to my mind in steps. I would've never gone to one of the safe places first. I would've looked for the others. But I wasn't fucking thinking. By the time I realized, it'd been too long. Emergency crews would have already been dispatched, and I—"

Clare put a bandaged hand in his. "Okay. It's okay. So, we're here. We don't know about the others. What do we do now?"

Adrian stared at her, lips tight.

"What?"

"You killed Siri."

Yeah, she remembered that bit too.

"Deval will never stop hunting you," he said. "It would be nothing to him to spend 60 years searching for you, and once he's found you, he'll torture you daily for the rest of your life. You'll have to live completely off the grid. The caves are as good a place as any."

"Hard pass."

Adrian laughed, incredulous. "*Dio Santo*. You have a better idea? They monitor cameras, and he'll have the best facial recognition software looking for you on every continent. Nowhere is safe. And you can't kill him—"

"Why not?"

Adrian blinked at her, then said, "That's fucking insane! If it was that easy to kill Deval, don't you think Meg would have done it centuries ago!"

"You have no idea what I can do, what my Watcher can do," Clare said. "No one does. Like you said, *I* killed Siri."

"And almost got yourself killed in the process!" He gestured around at the medical surroundings.

"So you're saying, I'm better off living the rest of my days hiding in a cave?"

"*Porca Troia!*" He threw his hands up in the air. "At least you'd have days left to live."

A portly woman ripped the curtain to the side with a scowl.

"I'm glad you're conscious, but we open in 30 minutes, and not everyone who works here is Therian. They're going to have enough questions as it is without you two arguing about killing people. And *you* will not be doing that." She pointed at Clare. "Not for a while. You've sustained a concussion along with a lot of deep bruising. You'll be hobbling out of here and need rest for several days. At which time, you'll be lucky to so much as think about a long walk, let alone taking down a vampire high lord."

"Definitely Meg's people," Clare said.

Adrian nodded.

The woman ignored them. "Now that you're awake, I'll be back to assess you more thoroughly in a moment."

She left, but her words had brought Adrian and Clare down a little.

"The warehouse?" she asked quietly.

He shook his head. "The warehouse is compromised. We can't go back there."

Jonathan. Neither of them said the name, but Clare knew he was alive as much as she knew that she was. But she didn't follow that thread, suddenly feeling very tired and afraid of what she might find.

"I've no idea what you and Miriam found so repulsive about the caves, but at the very least, that's where the Therians will go to regroup and count our losses. Probably most have already made it there."

As much as she didn't want to admit it, that made sense as the next move. Clare sighed, immediately resenting the lash of pain that came with the motion.

"Once I'm better, I'm going after him."

The Dark Hours 283

Adrian huffed. "I'd expect nothing less."

Now that the immediate questions were settled, Clare's inner journalist had a pressing need for other answers. "Can we talk about what happened last night?"

He literally rolled his eyes up to heaven like he was beseeching God for help, then looked at her flatly.

"What do you want to talk about?"

"Everything."

"No."

"Okay, so you're a bat, for starters. Did you know? That has to be where the lore is from, which would mean you're not the first vampire to be turned by a Therian. You did look kinda beautiful, though." Clare could feel the heat rising to her cheeks even as that last bit slipped out.

"You're very concussed, and I don't want to talk about it."

Fair enough. But some things needed to be talked about.

Clare took a breath. "Do you remember kissing me?"

"I was out of my mind last night."

"So you do remember."

"Yes, Clare."

He looked away, and she couldn't read his expression. And it felt disgustingly needy to ask, but she had to know.

"Did you mean it?"

"What the fuck does that mean?" His words came out with a tired breath, but he didn't wait for her answer. "I kissed you because I wanted to kiss you. If you're asking if I meant anything more by it, I don't fucking know. Everything about you is infuriating, and it's likely we'll both be dead before the year is out—besides everything else that was going on. So, I didn't give it much thought."

"What about drinking my blood?"

He stood then but kept his voice lowered as he said, "*Madonna Santa*. What do you want? Do you want me to say it was more than just animal hunger when I was lost in the phase?"

His words stung her pride, but this time, she didn't take the bait. He hadn't made an actual denial.

"I don't know why you don't want to admit it, but I think we both know it was more."

He leaned over her then, and whispered, "Because everyone I care about dies."

"So it's easier to be an asshole and pretend you don't care about anyone," Clare whispered back.

He pushed off her bed and paced, fingers raking through his hair.

"This is who I am. I'm not going to change, not for you, or this new Therian form, and certainly not because we shared a moment that was..."

"At least have the balls to call it what it was. It was intimate, and vulnerable, and beautiful. And it terrifies you."

Adrian opened his mouth to respond, but the doctor chose that moment to bustle back in.

"All right. Let's see about getting you outta here and healing up. Then you can go about that vampire carnage away from my clinic."

Without a word, Adrian pushed past the doctor, snagged his coat from a chair, and left them alone.

EPILOGUE

They'd fought, literally, about who would give this news.

Deval had watched his daughter die that evening, and after giving the orders to demolish the building and kill all in it, he simply stood and went to his chambers.

Disturbing him seemed suicidal, but not delivering the message seemed as likely to result in death.

Kai, the loser of the fight, rapped softly. He was about to turn away when the door opened. Deval stood there, composure seeming to be held together by force of will. He said nothing, so Kai simply handed him the print out they'd received.

Deval,

Based on your last report, the Grand Council will grant you a little more time before we intervene.

We've remained patient thus far in acknowledgment of the centuries of adept, loyal service you've given us. It is possible, in the light of such service, that the egregious events of the past several weeks have not been from gross neglect but rather a Therian force of superior ability and strength.

Therefore, despite our deep disappointment, the Council are willing to be forgiving in exchange for these services:

• The Therian leader's capture. Never has a resistance done so much damage. They can't be allowed to continue, but your mention of their creating a hybrid gives value to capture over kill. We need to know how they did this.

• The hybrid. Regardless of whether you are able to bring it to us alive, we want the body.

• The light-bearer's death. As you know, they only grow stronger with age, and her abilities already seem extreme. Before you kill her, be sure she has no children. The trait passes.

• Restoration of peace in the Richmond area. This entails putting an end to the open slaughtering and quelling coven in-fighting. We will continue to help with media suppression as we understand your facilities are down.

If these services are outside your current ability, we will gladly find someone else who's able to provide them.

— MIKJALL

DEVAL CRUSHED the paper in his hands without looking up at the messenger who brought it. A good sign for survival, perhaps. Kai went ahead with the other, less likely to get him killed, news.

"There's one other thing, sir."

Their leader showed no signs of hearing.

"Per your request to utilize all human resources and all leads...We

The Dark Hours 287

had a weak lead on a suspected Therian activist that we'd never followed up on because it was outside of Richmond jurisdiction and—"

"Out with it!" Deval's words were rough and low.

Kai would have flinched had he not found himself held in the thrall of violent, black eyes. There was no intonation to the words that were suddenly pouring from him without his willing them.

"We believe we've found a Therian monitored survivor group in the northwest of the state. We're surveilling from a distance so as not to alert the inhabitants. Do you want them taken alive?"

Deval stepped fully from his room, pulling the door behind him. There was murder in his eyes, but his voice was quiet as he said, "Burn it. Kill the humans. Bring any Therian's here."

ENJOY THIS BOOK? LET THE WORLD KNOW!

Please rate it on Amazon, Goodreads, or wherever you get your books! As a dedicated keyboard goblin, venturing into the light of day and talking to people is a daunting task. But with just a few sentences or even a quick star rating, you can help me stay in my cozy writing cave and keep crafting more stories for you to enjoy! Your support means the world (and keeps this goblin typing away). Thank you!

ACKNOWLEDGMENTS

So much goes into finishing a book and then even more to get it to print. My dyslexic gratitude for the beta readers who catch what an editor and half a dozen passes of my own still manage to miss. Thanks to all those who not only accept my hermit-y writer nature but do the unthinkable and encourage me in it further. May the fruits of your endeavors entertain you.

ABOUT THE AUTHOR

J.E. Kraft wrote her first book, Kittens, when she was seven, and despite struggling with bullying, ADHD, and Dyslexia, she hasn't stopped writing since. She grew up into an awkward super geek, lover of animals, bugs, psychology, and science. She can be found in Tennessee with her husband, two kids, a cat, dog, lizard, frog, shrimp, and a variety of houseplants. When she's not busy writing, she advocates online for mental health awareness and crushes the hopes and dreams of her loved ones in board games.

For more visit www.jekraft.com

f **⊙**

Printed in the USA
CPSIA information can be obtained
at www.ICGtesting.com
CBHW031632150824
13252CB00014B/563